# FIFTEEN KEYS

# FIFTEEN KEYS

Written and Illustrated by

# PETER J BARBOUR

Bethlehem Writers Group, LLC
Center Valley, Pennsylvania, USA

# FIFTEEN KEYS

Published by the Bethlehem Writers Group, LLC
Center Valley, PA
https://bethlehemwritersgroup.com



Cover and text illustrations by Peter J Barbour
Author Photo by Barbara Barbour
Cover design by Marianne H. Donley and Carol L. Wright
Interior layout by Marianne H. Donley
Custom Ornamental Scene Image licensed by Depositphotos.com

Trade paperback ISBN: 978-1-954675-05-6
Ebook ISBN: 978-1-954675-06-3
Library of Congress Control Number: 2025906559

Printed in the United States of America.

*What comes from the heart goes to the heart.*
—Samuel Taylor Coleridge

*Dedicated to my family:*
*My wife Barbara*
*My sister Nancy*
*Sons and their wives:*
*Joshua and Melissa*
*Jonathan and Amy*
*Samuel and Sharlene*
*Grandsons and granddaughters:*
*Justin*
*Jacob*
*Elan*
*Etta*
*Quynh*
*Stuart*
*Oscar, the dog*
*In memory of my mother, Etta*

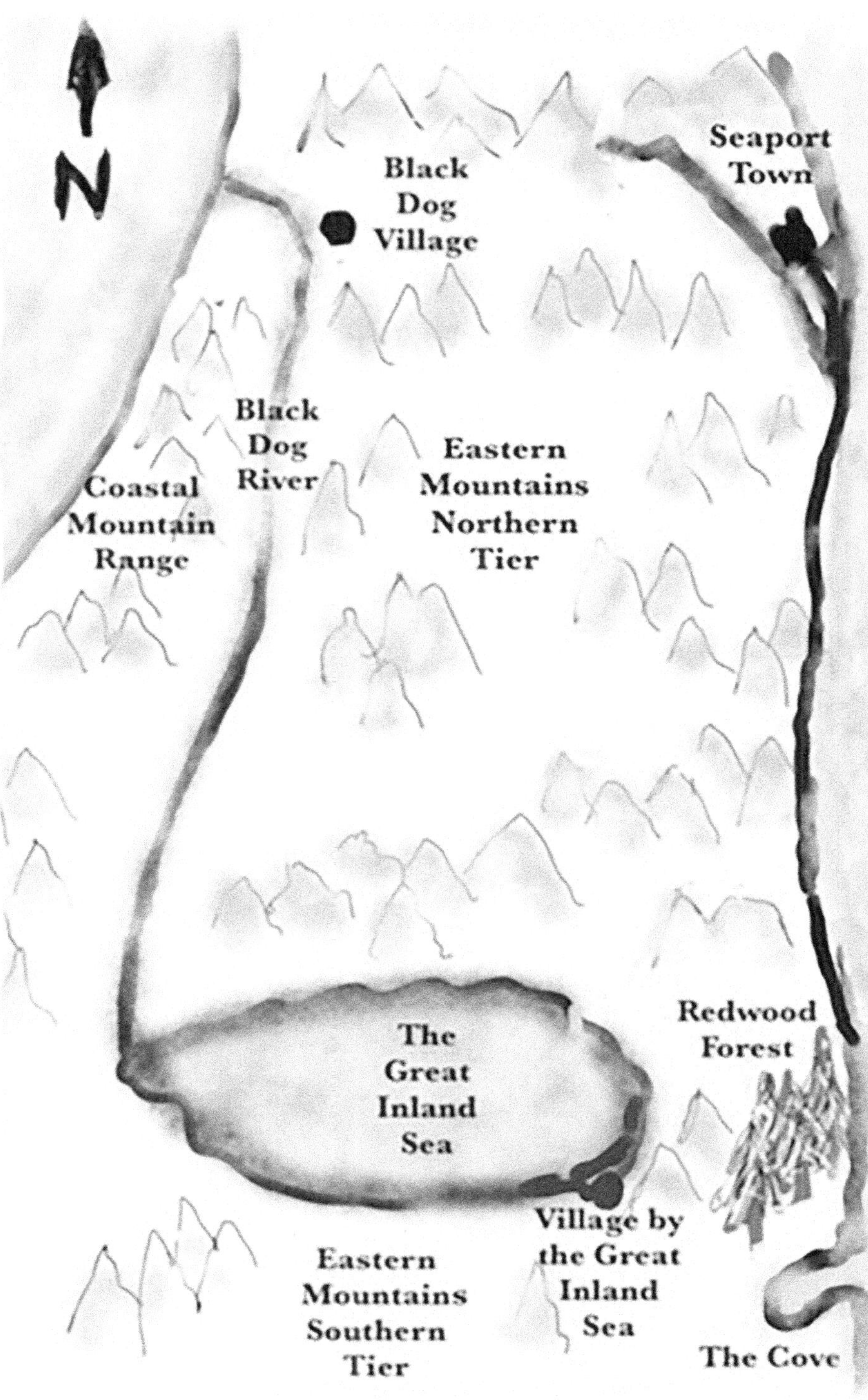

N
Seaport Town
Black Dog Village
Black Dog River
Eastern Mountains Northern Tier
Coastal Mountain Range
Redwood Forest
The Great Inland Sea
Village by the Great Inland Sea
Eastern Mountains Southern Tier
The Cove

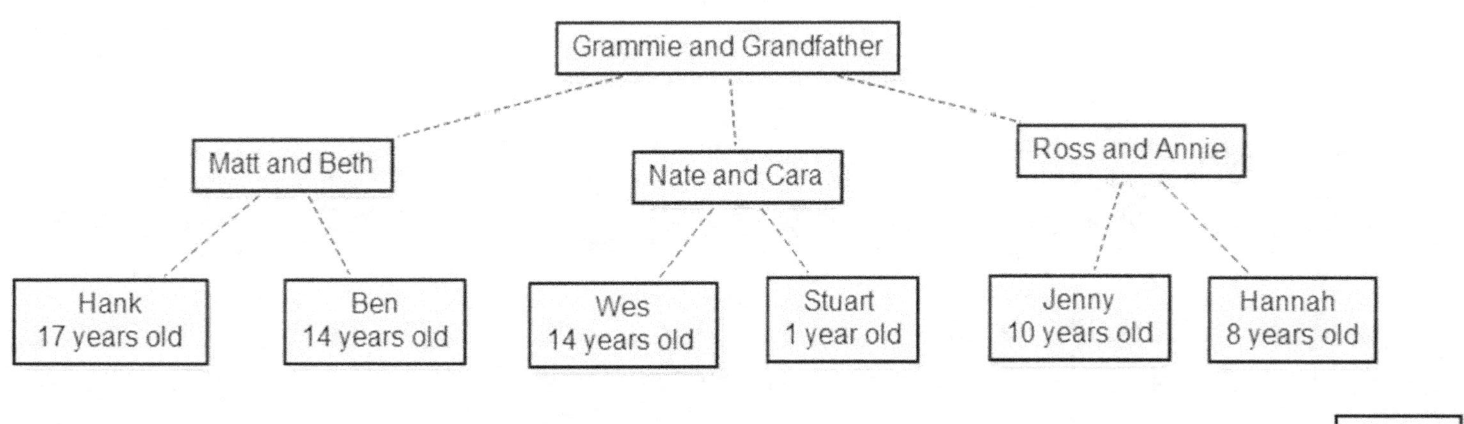

Falk Family Tree
Grammie and Grandfather
Matt and Beth
Nate and Cara
Ross and Annie
Hank
17 years old
Ben
14 years old
Wes
14 years old
Stuart
1 year old
Jenny
10 years old
Hannah
8 years old
Oscar
the dog

# Mother's Letter

*Fifteen keys in all and nothing new.*
*Have patience, be humble, grateful, and, most*
*important, true.*
*Have faith, honor all, and be generous too.*
*Show enthusiasm, establish order and strive for*
*simplicity. I have trust in you.*
*Practice silence, be happy, show compassion, and*
*maintain equanimity through and through.*

# Contents

# ONE

# The Beginning

HANK

*1890, early spring*
*A remote village somewhere in the Pacific Northwest*

I stood on a wooden stage in the meeting hall, an imposing building, the tallest structure in our village. My great-grandfather helped construct it with stone and logs, and it was still large enough to accommodate our whole community of forty families. Two friends suffered with me, or so I perceived; we had all just turned seventeen.

Sunlight streamed in through the windows above, rays visible as they probed the dust that seemed to forever hang in the air like a bunch of gnats. Sweat ran down my forehead. I wiped it with my sleeve. The people sitting on wooden benches in the audience gazed at me with eager anticipation. I didn't dare stare back, too afraid they'd see fear in my eyes. I stretched my neck, kept my eyes straight ahead, and hid my feelings. Two massive stone hearths, set to keep us warm, dried the stale smoky air that threatened to grip my throat and choke me.

Elder Jaq stood to our right in front of us as she explained the coming-of-age rite. "This vestige of our explorer heritage is a test for selected youth who will someday, themselves, become Elders of our village. Here they are." Elder Jaq made a sweeping hand gesture in our direction. "Joe Land, Frances Sing, and Hank Falk step up." I moved forward with Joe and Frances as commanded.

Taller than most women, Elder Jaq projected her booming voice at the crowd. She wore a long black robe and a tall, feathered, ceremonial hat that made me want to snicker, but I dared not laugh and show disrespect. I had agreed to participate in the ceremony, but I didn't want to be there. I wanted to jump from the stage and run away, but that was not an option.

What vestige of our heritage were we preserving? A past that most of us had forgotten, but somehow this ritual survived. As I waited to learn my fate, I shifted on my feet from right to left and back again, knees weak.

I stopped listening to Elder Jaq. *Why is my heart beating so fast, my hands shaking?* Mother and Father prepared me well for this day, but *am I confident enough to be able to go out on my own, to fend for myself, to meet life's challenges, alone?* I glanced in the direction of my brother, Ben. Our eyes met. Was Ben serious about his offer to join me? Could he convince Wes, our cousin, as well? Was that even allowed?

Father expected me to become an Elder, a respected gentleman, and a leader. He told me that this journey was a necessary step toward that end. Deep down, I questioned whether I'd be able to take on all that responsibility. Did I even want it?

*Grow up,* I told myself. *You can do it.* I continued to doubt my own readiness; I tilted my head back, lifted my chin, and squared my shoulders.

Town Hall Meeting

Could I survive the sea, the mountains, or wherever they sent me? I thought I could, but did I know for sure? Not everyone completed this rite of passage, and not because of weakness or ill-preparedness. Maybe they weren't lucky. Would I be lucky? I could only hope. Why was Father so willing to send me away?

We heard stories over the years about how Dimitri fell to his death traversing a steep wall in the western coastal mountains. Kathrine drowned, and they found Philip's body frozen in a cave in the north country. They said he looked like he'd turned to stone. Dying didn't scare me, not really, and some things, like shame, might be worse than death. Father said you must live with that. Was the fear of failure the thing that scared me? Was that a reason not to try?

"This time-honored rite has been carried out in our village for generations. You have the necessary tools to survive anywhere," Elder Jaq said and hesitated, a long dramatic pause, then turned to face us. "Now, we challenge each of you to go forth as children and learn about the world. Return as adults, strengthened by your journey, ready to become Elders, equipped to sit on the great council, mete out justice, and lead by example." She made eye contact with each of us in turn. "You must find keys that will open the doors to leadership and respect from your community. You begin by surviving in the wilderness as the original families survived before us. As you travel abroad, gain strength during your year away, and return with a heightened understanding of the world."

What did she mean? *Find keys that open doors?* Father had mentioned keys, but he gave little detail. His vagueness must be part of the ritual. *What do the keys look like, and where are the doors they open? If Joe, Frances, and I go in different directions, would we find keys to the same doors?* My mind continued to stray until Elder Jaq recaptured my attention.

"It is time to choose the way you will go. Savor the journey, learn as much as you can. Remember, your destination is not nearly as important as the road you follow. That path will determine whether you find the keys you seek. Now, it is time to choose your fate."

I stopped fidgeting and froze. Sweat ran down my back. The way traveled would be determined by the lot I chose from the deep, rough-worn wooden box that Elder Jaq held. Each of us would go our separate way, alone, to spend a year away from home. We all agreed that the way through the Eastern Mountains, wandering for a year before returning, was the hardest, most dangerous, and, worst of all, the loneliest selection. I tried to refocus on Elder Jaq's words, but my mind wouldn't let me. I closed my eyes and imagined I was somewhere else. I ignored the crowd that filled the room. Wes sat with Ben. I centered my attention on them. Our family, many friends, and neighbors from the village sat on the edge of their seats.

Eight Elders, each representing the eight original families, sat on the stage behind us. My grandfather was among them. I couldn't see them, but anger and resentment welled up in me as I felt the weight of their presence. They enforced this ritual. I swore if I got back here, my children would never participate in this. Time slowed. I felt the old wood and stone walls of the meeting hall crash in on me. My chest tightened, and darkness descended on me. I balled my hands into fists, my ears rang, my vision started to fade, but I willed myself to stay alert.

Joe, older than Frances and me by a few weeks, picked first. He showed no sign of concern as he thrust his hand confidently into the box and smiled as he revealed his selection. He drew the stick painted blue, signifying water. Joe beamed as he waved it for everyone to see. Traveling west from the village by sea as part of a crew, he'd be with other people while he looked for the keys. I envied him. The onlookers applauded. Someone shouted, "May good fortune shine on you!"

Frances chose next. Blood drained from her face. Her hand shook as she pulled her lot from the wooden box. As soon as she saw it, her hand shot up, and she waved the green and gray painted piece of wood back and forth. Her cheeks pinked. "I'm going west through the Coastal Range," she shouted. I smiled for her, destined to take a well-traveled trek to the coast and back. The audience cheered again.

I stepped forward and touched the red bandanna tucked neatly into my back pocket for luck. I closed my eyes and reached into the box. My movement was deliberate and cautious as I imagined a giant scorpion inside waiting to sting my hand. Three sticks remained, one in three chances to pick the journey through the Eastern Mountains. I tried to read each lot with my fingertips. I knew one was purple for the southern path along the Black Dog River. Another was white for the north country, and one was black and azure for the Eastern Mountains, but they all felt the same. I shuffled them, grabbed one at random and pulled it out. I opened my eyes and stared at it.

TWO

## Three Days Earlier

HANK

Before I left the house to take the sheep up to the pasture, on my way through the kitchen, I passed Father without saying hello. I held my head down and made no eye contact with him. My failure to acknowledge him must have caught his attention. He reached out and grabbed my arm before I got by, spun me around, and looked me in the eye.

"Hello, how are you?" Father said with an edge. "That's the way you start the day when you first meet someone."

"Hello. How are you?" I said in a flat tone.

"You are sulking again."

I started to react to his accusation but tried to control myself. "I'm not," I finally responded.

"Something is going on. What is it?"

I didn't want to talk to him about it, but I knew he wouldn't stop hounding me until I did.

"Tell me what's bothering you, now," Father demanded, his voice low, menacing.

I looked at him with narrowed eyes. What was on my

7

mind? We had been discussing it for months. At first, I hesitated. Why not remind him?

"I don't want to go on the journey," I barked back. "Simple, I don't want to go. I don't care if I'm turning seventeen. This ritual is senseless."

"What do you mean, you won't go?" He knit his brow and stared harder at me. "I didn't know that was a choice. I know you have concerns, but I thought you agreed to go. Our family is one of the original families." His face was red. "You want to become an Elder someday, correct?" He paused as if waiting for an answer. Before I could speak, he continued. "Our family has always produced Elders. This is the first and most important step toward that end." Father looked away. "There is no other path. I've explained that to you. By not going, you will tarnish our family's name." He took a breath, struggling to maintain composure, his face reddened further as he paced back and forth. "Your forefathers created a legacy, a chain of leaders, that remains unbroken." Sweat appeared on his brow. "No other family in the village can make that claim. Of course, you're going." Father stopped pacing. "Ben will go when he turns seventeen. How will that make you feel if your younger brother becomes an Elder and you do not?"

My head pounded. I thought my brain would explode out of my ears. How dare he use Ben to shame me. *I'm not continuing this conversation.* I ripped my arm free from his grasp and headed toward the back door, passing Mother on the way. I was sure she overheard Father and me arguing. She reached out and tried to hug me; I saw concern in her eyes. She had lectured me more than once about being disrespectful to Father. She looked deep into my eyes, pleading, as I moved past her.

Once outside I went to the woodpile, grabbed an ax,

and began splitting logs. I split half a cord before my anger abated, glad Father didn't follow and continue to harangue me.

Calmer, without saying goodbye to anyone, I headed to where we kept the sheep penned up at night. Our family, my father, and his brothers, Uncles Nate and Ross, farmed five hundred acres, passed down from generation to generation. We all shared in the work. It was my week to tend the sheep. Oscar, our herding dog, waited for me outside the pen. He wagged his tail and spun in place, eager to begin. I hugged him. "Hello, Oscar. How are you?"

Oscar and I led the flock to the foothills, where they fed on the lush, green grass, and I could be alone. The fresh smell of the meadow with a sprinkling of lavender settled me further, but, as the afternoon wore on, I realized the time to go home fast approached. I'd be facing off with Father again, with the reality of what was about to happen.

I sat on a rock overlooking the valley and took a deep breath. The sheep grazed on the hillside. In the distance, the Black Dog River meandered its way through the vale like a great snake. Willow trees and fields of grain waved in the breeze along its bank. Clouds poured over the Coastal Range, filled the gap where the river emptied into the sea, and formed a dense evening fog that threatened to invade and swallow our village, Black Dog, named for the river.

I turned to look at the towering, jagged rocks of the Eastern Mountains behind me. Light from the setting sun reflected off the crags, causing them to glow a bright vermilion. A tear formed at the corner of my eye. This was my home. Why should I leave? But, if I stayed, I feared I would shame myself, as Father predicted, and tarnish our name. I sighed and tried to redirect my attention to tending the flock.

The afternoon shadows lengthened as the sun disappeared below the horizon, and the mountain air cooled. I pulled my jacket closed and took the red bandanna from my back pants pocket and tied it around my neck. My younger brother, Ben, and my cousin, Wes, appeared in the distance, running toward me.

"Oscar, get sheep," I commanded, and he took off in a large arc to gather the sheep. For the moment, marshaling the flock and directing Oscar were all that filled my thoughts. I stopped dwelling on the ceremony and on having to go away.

Ben raced ahead of Wes who fell farther behind with each of Ben's strides. Ben's long red hair trailed behind him as his thin body cut the air with grace. He approached the foot of the hill where the sheep grazed and never slowed until he reached the top. Wes would arrive some moments later, having given up on running. He held his jacket in one hand and his cap in the other as he sauntered up the rise.

"So, Hank, are you ready?" Ben said, as soon as he crested the hill. He had a big smile on his face as he looked up at me.

"Of course I'm ready. Let's take the sheep home."

"Not the sheep. Actually, I was referring to the big day. Your journey. It's almost here." Ben was so animated he could hardly stand still. "I heard Mother and Father arguing. You set them on fire, didn't you?" He twirled in place. "Father raised his voice and stomped around. I stayed out of his sight." He paused. "Don't you want to go on your journey?"

"Why are you wearing short pants?" I asked, hoping to change the subject. "It's cold up here. I'm surprised Mother let you out of the house."

Hank and Oscar waiting for Ben and Wes

Ben glanced down at his bare legs. "They're knee pants, and it's not that cold."

Wes crested the hill. I didn't want to continue the discussion about Father with Ben, so I ran to Wes and gave him a light punch on the arm.

"You're late," I said.

"Okay, but I'm here now. Ready to go." Wes put on his jacket and smoothed down his hair before placing his flat cap on his head.

I alerted Oscar with a long whistle and shouted, "Away to me."

With Ben in front, Oscar patrolling the flank, and Wes and me in the rear, we headed home.

"Are you set for your journey?" Wes asked as we walked.

"Of course," I said. "Why? Don't you think I'm ready?" *Am I ready?*

"I can't imagine going," Wes went on. "Just because you turn seventeen doesn't mean you are set to leave the village and go out on your own. What if you lose your way? What if a bear attacks you? What if you don't want to go?"

"I must go. Everyone in our family goes when they turn seventeen. According to Father, you need to go if you want to be an Elder." My heart sped up. I couldn't seem to breathe, but I tried to appear calm and held my head up as we marched with the flock.

"The Elders are special, important people in our community. Don't you want to be like them?" Wes said.

"Why must I leave to become like them? Can't I discover how to be important staying here? What am I supposed to learn on this journey?"

We reached the barn, secured the sheep in their pens, and filled the troughs with water. Wes waved to us as he left to head home where his father, Uncle Nate, and mother, Aunt Cara, waited for him. Ben and I dropped Oscar off with Uncle Ross and Aunt Annie. He was the family's dog primarily trained by Uncle Ross and generally stayed there. We told Uncle Ross that we'd finished our chores and were headed home. Our cousins, Jenny and Hannah, ran to the door to greet Oscar and waved goodbye to us.

"Aren't you excited about the ceremony? It's your time," Ben said as we continued down the path. Ben waved his arms, jumped up and down, and danced around me.

"You're ready. Father's been preparing you for your journey for years. You've practiced living in the woods, eating off the land, building shelters. I know you can do it. Also, when you go, can I have your room?"

"Ben, it's nice to see you're excited for me, but you don't have to go right now."

"I'd go right now if I could." Ben gestured with his arms.

I waved Ben off. "You expect me to believe that?" Maybe he did believe that. He frequently accompanied Father and me as I trained.

"I would," Ben said, stamping his feet.

I shrugged. "Maybe. But what if someone doesn't want to go? That someone likes it here, feels good here. They like being around family, even like being around you. . . . What if I feel that way?" I pushed Ben away. "And I'm not giving you my room because I'm not leaving." I kicked a stone into the air. "I don't see why I should follow this ritual. Father says I need to bring back keys. What if I can't find them? I'll never be able to come home."

"What will you do?" Ben asked. "By the way, I heard they provide clues."

"You heard," I said. "Right." *Should I believe him?* "You know, Ben, I think I must go. As I see it now, I never really had a choice. I couldn't bear Father's disappointment in me." I lowered my head. "I'm happy here and can't imagine a greater place to be." I looked Ben in the eyes. "If I don't go, Father will never forgive me. He'll be ashamed of me. He and I can't even discuss it anymore." I paused and exhaled slowly. "I don't want to be alone for a whole year. If I don't find the keys, will the Elders let me return? Is there anything to be grateful for in any of this?"

"Actually, remember what Grammie says. 'When you

must deal with something that isn't pleasant, you'll feel better about it if you can see any good in it." He lowered his voice as if I'd pay greater attention if he used a stage whisper. "Are you sure I can't have your room?"

My brow furrowed as I recalled Grammie's words. "She always said to make a list of pros and cons. What's the good in it? I'd be free, no one giving me directions, and responsible only to me. I will meet new people, experience new things, and probably make Father happy. I'm not sure those things outweigh the things I'll miss, like the rest of my family and friends. What am I to achieve by being away for a year? I don't get it. And, yes, I'm sure, you can't have my room."

"Okay. If you leave, you must deal with change, with new and different things, and that sounds exciting to me. Actually, if you are concerned about being alone, why can't I come with you? I bet Wes would join us, too."

"You'd come with me? No way." My heart sped up; my senses heightened. *Is this a possibility?*

"I heard Father say to Mother that you will get enlightened and be enriched by the journey. We can get enlightened together; and if that enriches us, we'll come back wealthy men. I'll even clean my room before we go. That will make my leaving easier for Mother. She's always after me about cleaning up my mess." Ben turned and jumped in the air. "I'll leave a note. They'll know I'm with you. That should make everything all right. And when we come home with the keys, we'll open the doors together, ready to be Elders."

"How can we go together?" I asked.

"The rules of the rite say you can't travel with Joe or Frances. The rules don't say you can't go with me and Wes. There's a story about two brothers who did it before. Why can't we? Wes and I must do it in a couple of years. We can go early."

I shook my head trying to follow Ben's logic. *Is there a book of ritual rules?* I squinted at him. "Two brothers? I bet you're making this up so that I'd agree to let Wes and you join me. And Father never said anything about enrichment leading to wealth." When I considered it further, I found the idea intriguing, even comforting. "I wouldn't be alone. I'd be with you and Wes." *How will Father feel when all three of us are gone?*

"If you're coming with me, I hope you will have more than just short pants to wear," I said.

# THREE

# Town Hall, My Lot

### HANK

I held the lot in my hand and pressed it into my palm until it hurt. Quiet pervaded the great assembly hall as everyone waited for me to reveal my fate. I placed the painted piece of wood in front of me, released my grip, one finger at a time, and examined its colors. No matter how I positioned it, the hues remained the same: black and azure; blue for the sky, and black for the Eastern Mountains.

"I'm going over the Eastern Mountains," I said in a soft breathless voice, so soft I didn't think anyone could hear me. I took a short, shallow breath. My stomach flipped. Ben popped out of his seat and ran to the stage. He danced in place, waving his arms. The crowd stood cheering and clapping loudly.

"We're going over the Eastern Mountains," Ben whispered. "Actually, I love heights." His head bobbed, and his crazy red hair bounced. He spoke into my ear, "It's time to tell Wes." Ben caught our parents' eyes and shouted across the room to them, "Mother, Father, Hank is going over the Eastern Mountains."

Mother closed her eyes. She pressed her lips together and grimaced. Father jumped out of his chair and stood tall, beaming. Each family member stepped up to me, shook my hand, and wished me luck. Now that I knew my fate, the thought of Ben and Wes joining me was reassuring. I smiled for the first time in a long time and didn't care if their coming with me violated any rules.

THE NEXT DAY I started to gather supplies for the journey. Father tried to talk to me, but I avoided him. It appeared that he believed things between us were all right. Of course, if I proceeded according to my lot, he'd be happy. That was enough to cheer him and leave me alone while Ben and I made our plans. As I arranged things to pack, Ben filled me in on Wes.

"After we had a lengthy talk about his coming with you and me," Ben said, "I asked Wes, 'Are you in or out?' Instead of answering me, he takes four eggs, cracks the shells, and pours the eggs into a bowl. That's how he responded to me, Hank. Then, he came up with another what if . . . 'What if we get mauled by a bear?' I stared at him and shook my head. I said, 'You're not going to be mauled by a bear. Just say you're in. Actually, I think it will be fun. We must go when we are seventeen, anyway. That's not that far from now.' He says, 'I must ask my father for permission.' I told him, 'Uncle Nate can't find out.' I said, 'You'll be with us. Uncle Nate will be okay with that.' Then, Wes beat the eggs, added milk, a little salt, pepper, chopped garlic, and cheese. He said, 'I don't think so. Not without permission.' Hank, he always says he can't, always. So, Wes pours the egg mixture from the bowl into a skillet and puts it on a flat stone in the hearth. I told him, 'I like my eggs well done.' Then, I said, 'Got any bread for toast?'"

"Please get to the point," I said as my patience wore thin.

Ben gave me a puzzled look, before continuing. "'I know you are coming with us.' I say to him. 'Come on, say yes.' Wes came up with a few more 'what ifs,' but in the end, he agreed to go with us. Actually, he makes delicious eggs and toast."

"Good," I said and rolled my eyes. "I don't remember if anyone ever drew the Eastern Mountains lot before. We'll meet secretly, the three of us, to work out a plan and make sure we have everything we need. No one can suspect what we're doing. By the time they figure it out, we'll be too far ahead, and they won't be able to follow us. Imagine, three brave young boys set out to climb the great Eastern Mountains. We'll go down in history."

"Actually," Ben said, "I think John Patrick drew the Eastern Mountains when he went on his journey. I'm sure others have done it."

"If others have gone and done it before, that just means it is possible to do. John Patrick came back, didn't he?"

"I don't know, maybe." Ben turned down his mouth. "Apparently, not everyone does."

WE MET THE NEXT DAY, secretly, as I planned.

"Who will do our chores when we are gone?" Wes asked, his speech rushed and urgent.

"Are you feeling guilty?" Ben asked and shook his head. "You always worry."

"I really don't care who does mine," I said. "Father wants me away, and my jobs become his problem." *He hasn't considered my feelings about having to go. Why should I worry about his?* "Who did the work before there was us?" I asked Ben. "Besides, Jenny and Hannah are almost old enough to work in the garden and tend the sheep with Oscar. They'll get by."

My sadness and fear left me. I flexed my muscles. I wanted us to be on our way, and our parents couldn't know our plan. Anger and a sense of righteous rebellion replaced my anxiety. I took solace in my defiance, pleased to have companions, albeit my little brother and cousin. I anticipated the challenge with courage. *Father expects I'm going to go by way of the Eastern Mountains, alone. Well, he's half right. That is the way we'll go, three invincible explorers.* I trusted Ben would keep the secret, but I worried about Wes.

Eastern Mountains

FOUR

# Runaways

HANK

The week before our departure, Father cornered me. Mother stood behind him, her eyes pleading again, shoulders sagging, her hands thrust deep into her apron pockets. I knew she didn't want me to go without reconciling with Father. She wouldn't interfere, not with Father so committed to having me go through with the ordeal.

"The way over the Eastern Mountains is not well known. It's even dangerous," Father warned with appropriate concern. "Make sure you bring a good length of rope and prepare for cold. It can snow at those altitudes even in summer."

Mother nodded in agreement, but as she stared at me, her eyes said she longed to speak, yet she remained silent.

"Promise to travel only during the day," Mother said at last, her voice soft, full of apprehension. "It's too dangerous to travel at night. Also, promise, you'll come home safe and sound."

"Of course, I will," I responded, looking into her eyes,

while at the same time refusing to acknowledge Father's attempt to offer me advice.

I'm sure Father wanted to say more, but I was no longer listening. He didn't listen to me, and it's not much of a conversation if neither party listens to the other.

"I need to pack," I informed them and stomped off to my room to review the list of equipment I planned to take. Basics included an oilcloth blanket; clothes, some warm and some light; flint and an iron rock in case the matches got wet or ran out; a leather pouch for water; a knife; a small hatchet; a pocket compass; a short spade, and rope, taking care not to take too much or too little. I threw in a small journal and a pencil to keep a record of our travels and slipped a gold dollar into a pouch on the side of the pack for luck. After two full days of sorting through everything, I judged that my backpack held a manageable amount of gear. I hoped Ben and Wes packed similar stuff.

Father walked into my room as I unpacked and repacked. He looked over my shoulder and fidgeted. I'm sure he wanted to assist me. I ignored him. As he oversaw me in silence, neither of us talking, guilt threatened to overtake me. I wanted to let him participate in the preparations, but I couldn't. I continued to treat him like he was invisible.

"I guess you don't need my help," Father said. He looked sad.

I didn't respond. He turned and left. As he walked away, I looked up, started to call him back, but couldn't find my voice, and let him go.

TWO DAYS BEFORE OUR DEPARTURE, Ben and Wes met me in a shed near the paddocks. No one else knew we were there.

"Show me what each of you brought." I laid out my provisions, expecting them to do the same.

"I'm going to bring a bag of seeds for growing vegetables and berries," Ben said. He tipped his chin up and looked at me. I think he wanted a reaction. He continued, "We can plant them if we have to settle somewhere, in the event we don't find the keys and can't return home."

"Settle somewhere? We'll find the keys," I assured him. "Leave the bag of seeds behind."

Ben slipped the bag of seeds into his sack anyway. "You never know," he mumbled, but I didn't bother to object further. *Will we find the keys?* I didn't want Ben or Wes to know my true feelings. It was my belief that the location of the keys was a closely guarded secret.

"I got salt, pepper, spices, and lamb and yogurt jerky," I said. "I'm also packing beans, but mostly we'll live off the land."

Ben held up knives, forks, spoons, and a cup. He smiled. "And these two cords are for making snares, and the soft pouch like yours is for water. I have tin plates and a pot."

Wes pointed at his stash. "See here, I'm bringing fishing gear, line, and hooks."

They each showed me their clothes and a piece of oilcloth on which to sleep and to keep dry in the rain. Knapsacks repacked, ready to go, Wes and Ben hid theirs on a shelf in the back of the shed.

"One more thing," Wes asked. "How do we know which way to go?"

"East over the mountains," Ben said. "That's obvious."

I tried to reassure them. "Father has told me enough so that I have a good understanding once we cross the mountains. I wrote some things down. We'll use the sun, stars, and my compass to help guide us." I only wished I was reassured.

"Does Uncle Nate know about our plans?" I asked Wes as we left the shed, fearing that he may have let on to his father.

"No, I didn't tell anyone. I took care getting all my stuff together. I don't think anyone caught on to what we're up to, but what if they do know? Cousin Jenny saw me gathering things. What if she asks me what I'm doing?"

I took Ben's and Wes's hands in mine and held them with a firm grip. "Repeat after me," I said and looked straight into Wes's eyes. "I will not reveal our plan to anyone. Do we agree?"

"Yes!" we all said together. Then in solemn tones, we repeated the phrase.

"There is one more thing. Do you remember that book about Tom Sawyer? I got to read it at school."

"I remember the book. Haven't read it myself yet," Ben said.

"Me neither," said Wes.

"Well, Tom made his gang members swear an oath with blood," I said in a whisper.

Wes stepped back and touched his parted lips. Ben looked at me, eyes wide. I paused, hoping to create more drama. "Instead of blood, let's seal the deal by spitting into our hands and shaking on it."

Wes and Ben approached me. We spat into our palms, put our hands together, and shook.

AT THE END of that week, I said goodbye to my friends, parents, aunts, uncles, and cousins. For my last meal, Mother served my favorite dish: mutton stew with potatoes and carrots. The next morning as the sun rose, I said my final goodbyes to my parents and Ben.

"Bye, big brother," Ben said and hugged me. He sobbed in a convincing way. "I don't know when I'll see you again. I'll miss you, Hank."

I patted him on the back. "I'll miss you too."

Ben continued to pretend to cry. Mother looked at him, wrinkled her brow, and cocked her head, but didn't say anything further.

Before I set out, Mother snuck a small, thin wooden box into my hand. "Look at this box later when you stop to rest," she whispered. Without examining it, I slipped the package into my pocket, finished my goodbyes, and waved one last time before starting to walk.

I took the path that led me into the pasture where the sheep grazed under my uncle's watchful eye. "Bye, Uncle Ross," I shouted to him as I passed.

"Good luck, and Godspeed," Uncle Ross called back. Oscar popped up and looked in my direction, left the flock, and ran to join me. Uncle Ross didn't call him back.

Oscar marched with me up into the hills until that path ended. I stopped, put my pack down, and squatted next to Oscar. He licked my face, and I wrapped my arms around him and gave him a squeeze. "Go home, boy," I commanded. He looked at me, turned, and took off running.

Once out of sight, well into the hills, I found a suitable rock on which to sit at the crossroads where Ben and Wes agreed to meet me. The warmth of the sun and the dry air, laden with the fresh scent of grass and late spring flowers, soothed me. The box Mother gave me stuck out of my pocket when I sat, so I placed it in a safe place in my sack. Soon, Ben and Wes approached. Ben wore knee pants. Wes donned his cap and tied his jacket around his waist.

"I hope you brought long pants," I said to my little brother.

"Actually, I invented pants legs with buttons. I can attach them to my knee pants if need be."

"Did you cover your tracks as I suggested?"

"Yes," Ben answered. He started to giggle, appearing pleased with his deception. "We won't be missed for a while. The parents think we are in school, and the school thinks we're home. Father is working on the river. I last saw Mother busy in the garden. We took the trail that takes you south before turning east. We avoided Uncle Ross and Oscar in the meadow with the sheep. The trees hid us just like you said. Nobody saw us." He crossed his arms in front of him.

Wes looked pale; he started to sob and choked back a tear. "I'm not sure I want to go. What if . . ."

I didn't let him finish; instead, I stood and started to walk. Ben followed. We said nothing further. Before we turned a corner and were lost from sight, Wes picked up his pack and ran to catch up to us. When Wes reached us, I gave Ben a bag of minced beef jerky and Wes a bag of pepper. We tossed the jerky and pepper around to cover our trail in case someone tried to track us with dogs. We headed to the high country, where it would be hard to track us over the rocky ground. We had the advantage of a head start and our pursuers' uncertainty over what path we took.

We kept a fast pace through the foothills, maintaining our speed as we climbed higher and higher into the mountains. The trails made by the mountain goats and deer provided us with a path as we scrambled over boulders, crossed little streams, and traversed ledges. Up and up, we climbed. After the first day, we no longer saw our village in the valley with its peaceful river running through it and smoke rising from the chimneys off in the distance. We dared not light a fire lest someone see us. We woke at dawn and walked until dusk without a break as we tried to keep ahead of anyone who might pursue us. Ben turned over a host of rocks. He said, "I'm looking for keys." I told him to stop. He was leaving a trail.

After several days, well into the mountains, we camped without fear. We searched for flat ground on which to sleep, gathered wood, and sat around a fire wrapped in our canvas blankets, too excited to sleep even though we were exhausted.

"Actually, if we find a place we like, we can always settle there," Ben said.

"You keep acting as if we won't be going home," Wes responded, his voice hesitant.

"I want to live on the top of the world, with a view of everything around me in all directions," Ben said.

"I miss my mother and father," Wes said. "I agreed to go along because I thought we'd be going home one day." Wes wiped his nose on his sleeve and started to fidget. His voice wavering.

"We'll go home," I said with more conviction than I felt. Wes never let us see him cry after that first day, although I could sense at times, he was close to tears.

Wes and Ben called themselves the twin cousins because they almost shared the same birthday. Ben was just a few weeks older than Wes, and I was almost three years older than they were. Our parents expected me to keep an eye on them even while I played with my friends. It seemed to me that I had looked after them forever. Now, as we lay under the stars, waiting for sleep, the weight of that responsibility made me shudder. *Should I have agreed to let them come along?*

Tiredness overcame me, and I fell asleep. Dreams of mountains, rocky crags, bottomless canyons, and walking filled my head. The sun woke us at dawn, and we prepared to leave. Before we broke camp, I took the box that Mother gave me out of my pack and showed it to Ben and Wes. I shook it. Something inside rattled. I worked the clasp but couldn't budge it. The edges felt smooth without seams that might define a lid, side panels, or bottom.

"How do we find out what's inside?" I said to myself aloud.

Ben took the box and rubbed it as he looked for the secret to opening it. He tried to pry the clasp, then squeezed it, and pushed on each side of the box, all without success. He passed the box to Wes.

Wes smiled. "I know how these secret boxes work." He waved his hand over the box and tossed it in the air. The box hit the ground but remained closed.

I picked up a rock, held the box against another rock, and prepared to smash it. The latch clicked, and the lid popped open.

The opened box

FIVE

# At Home in the Valley

JENNY

I was almost ten years old the day the boys took off on their journey. When I learned they'd gone, I took off my shoes and threw them. I kicked, bared my teeth, and growled like an angry dog. Then I started to wail. Was I angry or sad? I think mostly angry.

"Not fair," I shouted, because all I ever wanted to do was whatever they did, and I could do it better. "Why didn't they take me with them? Besides, without them, who will I walk to school with?" I banged the walls with my fists, slammed doors, and emptied all my dresser drawers onto the floor of my room. Hannah, my younger sister, reacted to my distress. Her brow knitted, lips held tight and quivering, as she squatted next to me and pulled at my sleeve. Tears ran down her cheeks.

"Jenny, they'll be safe," Hannah said as she tried to calm me. She cried along with me, but I'm not sure she understood why I cried. My little sister was too young to join them, but I could have gone. I sat on the floor surrounded by my clothes and sobbed out of control.

30

"Jenny, dear," Mother said as she pulled me close to her, tears streaming down her face. "We'll bring the boys back. They'll be okay." I pushed her away, the same way I pushed Hannah away.

"Their secret would have been safe with me," I said. "Why didn't they, at least, let me in on their plan before they took off?" Unable to stifle my sniffles between sobs and gasps for breath, I struggled to make my speech clear. "I understand why they didn't tell Hannah. She couldn't be trusted to stay quiet and would have blurted something that would have given them away. Why didn't they tell me?"

Mother pulled me close to her once again. I fought her. My cheeks burned, but she persisted, and my fists began to relax; my arms fell to my sides. I breathed in the clean smell of Mother's hair and felt the warmth of her body against mine. I put my arms around her and hugged. My sobbing slowed.

Wes and Ben scurried around for days before Hank departed. After moping and complaining for months before the ceremony, Hank smiled. His eyes sparkled, and he acted ready to go. I bet he knew that Wes and Ben planned to join him.

"You better never run away like those boys," Mother whispered in my ear as she held me. She released her grip and waved a finger at me. "Promise."

Mother led me into the living area of our home where Aunt Cara, Wes's mother, paced the floor and wrung her hands. She shook, eyes wet with crying, and her voice trembled as she demanded, "Go after them, now, Nate. You're his father. Drag Wes back by his ears if you must. He's not ready for this journey." Aunt Cara looked pale, her voice shrill.

I tried to read Uncle Matt, Hank's father. At first, his

face turned red. He held his breath, then punched a wall, shattering the plaster and leaving a hole. "That Hank," he said and started to pick up a glass to hurl it but stopped. He must have realized he wasn't winning points with his anger.

"How dare Hank take off with Ben and Wes," Uncle Matt snarled.

Aunt Cara bawled away, waving her arms, Aunt Beth paced, and Mother tried to console everyone. Uncle Matt stood, hooked his thumbs into his belt, and took a deep breath. "Hank can handle himself, and so can Ben and Wes," he declared. "The two younger ones are in good hands. They'll be fine, but I'll need to make things square with the Elders."

Aunt Beth's nostrils flared, and her lips curled. She turned to Uncle Matt and stepped into his space. "Go find them and don't come back without Ben and Wes. Their journeys will come soon enough."

Frightened by Aunt Beth's behavior, having never seen her so angry, I reached up and touched my mother's face to attract her attention. "I won't run away. I promise," I assured her, although I knew that someday, I would go on a journey like Hank. *Maybe taking someone along is a good idea?*

I was with Aunt Beth when she discovered Ben's note. As she walked into Ben's room, she gasped. His room was clean and neat. She searched the area as if a crime had been committed there. He had pinned a note to the pillow on his smooth bed with care, leaving not a wrinkle on the covers. He explained that he and Wes were joining Hank, not to worry, he'd return, but didn't know when. He signed it, "Love, Ben." Aunt Beth froze, a hint of a smile appeared on her face, and then she screamed before running to Uncle Matt.

Wes had also left a note for Aunt Cara saying that he

would miss her and Father, but he planned to join his cousins even though he wasn't sure about which way they were going. He reassured her he'd be careful. They said Aunt Cara immediately lost all the color in her face and collapsed on Wes's bed before the wailing started. Her cries reached all the way to the river.

Ben's sneaking off did not surprise me. On the other hand, Wes's departure left me with my jaw slack and mouth wide open. Wes preferred to play checkers quietly with his friends rather than take risks like Ben, who delighted in sitting at the tops of trees.

Uncle Matt stomped around apparently unconvinced by his own claim that the younger boys would be in good hands. Aunt Beth demanded he recruit Uncle Nate and Father to head after the boys immediately. Our whole family followed the men to the foothills, where we all scoured the area, returning without Ben or Wes. Aunt Beth suggested asking the village Elders for help.

"We'll form teams to hunt for the boys," the Elders said. "Let's assume they headed east according to Hank's lot. We'll go into the hills in different directions and take dogs to track them. The Elders will meet to discuss repercussions for their actions, if any, later."

Father took Oscar. I promised not to slow him down, and he allowed me to go along. Oscar picked up a scent and led us to a spot where the boys spread pepper and jerky on the ground to throw off the dogs. Father said that trick only works in stories. Oscar sneezed and snorted but liked eating the spicy beef. We signaled to the other trackers who joined us. After a few minutes of rooting around this spot, the dogs were on the boys' trail again. The dogs kept their noses down, barking and pulling on the leashes, until we came to a field of rocks. Oscar stopped, sniffed the ground, circled back and forth, lost. All the dogs were as confused as ours. We split up again but couldn't find any tracks or clues and gave up as the sun began to set.

"Any luck?" I called to each party as they returned. "No," was everyone's response.

With too many places to look and a big head start, the runaways eluded the band of neighbors and friends pursuing them. Everyone came back empty-handed. My cousins just up and disappeared like smoke rising into thin air.

WITH WES, Ben, and Hank gone, my life changed. I learned a bunch of new chores. Because I was too young to do them myself, Father took me with him and showed me how until I could perform them on my own. He said it was time to grow up. Father still did most of the work. Tending the sheep was best. That's because we did that with Oscar.

Weeks passed before the dust settled, and we established new routines in our village, but I didn't think it would ever be routine for Aunt Cara, who couldn't seem to stop worrying about Wes. Aunt Beth appeared more confident than Aunt Cara. I saw her put her arms around Aunt Cara more than once. "The boys will return safe and sound," she said as she touched Aunt Cara's chin, lifted her head, and looked her in the eye. "I'm sure of it."

Each morning as the sun's first light appeared over the Eastern Mountains, Father woke me. We ate breakfast and called Oscar. He came running to us, his big bushy tail cutting the air behind him like a giant dolphin fin like the ones we sometimes saw in the river. His long, floppy, black ears moved from side to side, and his fluffy, black coat and full, lion-like mane shimmered in the morning light.

After we all ate, Father would announce, "Time to wake the sheep, move them out of their pens and up to the foothills."

Father taught me how to make Oscar do what I wanted him to do. I held a big stick with a curve at the top called a crook. When I pointed left, Oscar went left around the flock. When I pointed right, he went right. Oscar obeyed me, and the sheep obeyed Oscar. Of course, Father could get me out of any trouble I got into when I somehow managed to make Oscar scatter sheep all over the field.

Some days, I helped Mother in the vegetable garden. Hannah often tagged along. Everyone said we looked a lot alike, Hannah and me, except I was taller. We both had straight, dark hair tied into a ponytail. I had two, one on each side of my head. She had only one, on the top of hers. We wore denim overalls. Mine were once Wes's, and Hannah's were once mine.

"Now that you are ten, you're old enough to tend the sheep with Oscar by yourself," Father said. He started by leaving Oscar and me alone in the pasture some afternoons. He'd return just before sunset to help me bring in the sheep, just like Hank, Wes, and Ben used to do.

I took off my coat and sat on the hillside once the sun melted the morning chill. With Oscar by my side, I inhaled, closed my eyes for a second, and listened to the sheep bleat and chew. They have an odor about them, not terrible; some say it is a mixture of lanolin in their skin and dirt. As I breathed, the smell of the grass came through, dry and earthy from baking in the sun. I let my mind wander until it drifted to my cousins. My cheeks no longer burned when I thought about how they left without telling me their plan. Instead, I lowered my head and sighed, hoping they were safe, straining my brain until it hurt to picture what each looked like, to never forget, and tried to imagine what they were doing now.

Jenny and Oscar tending the sheep

# SIX

# The Mountains

HANK

The opened box

I put the rock down and picked up the opened box. The lid started to close again. Ben grabbed it from me. He shook it until a small, folded square of paper fluttered to the ground. The top snapped shut and the clasp closed. I reached down, retrieved the paper, and unfolded it.

"Mother sent us a message," I announced.

"Us?" Ben and Wes said together and stepped closer to me.

"She figured out our plan and said nothing?" Ben said.

They looked over my shoulder as we read the note.

*Dearest Hank and, I suspect, Ben and Wes,*

*You think you're clever, but I knew you were up to something by the way you three snuck around for days after the ceremony. I'll keep your secret and act my part. I'm not sure how Father will react when he learns what you've done. I'm pretty sure he'll be furious. I can only imagine. He will push the whole town to come after you.*

*Hank, I'm not happy with your decision to take Ben and Wes with you, and if they get caught and are brought home, so be it. I believe that if the trackers don't bring Ben and Wes back, knowing that you are traveling together will give me peace. You'll be safer. Even if Father is furious, his anger will pass. The Elders will meet and discuss what you did.*

*Be careful. I want you to return, so here are clues to the location of the keys. These are the same clues Grammie provided me when I went on my trek.*

> *The keys are in plain sight, so always be looking.*
> *Balance is a helpful clue.*
> *Fifteen keys in all and nothing new.*
> *Have patience, be humble, grateful, and, most*
> *     important, true.*
> *Have faith, honor all, and be generous too.*
> *Show enthusiasm, establish order and strive for*
> *     simplicity. I have trust in you.*
> *Practice silence, be happy, show compassion, and*
> *     maintain equanimity through and through.*

*Be safe, and always remember that I love you.*

*Mother*

*p.s. Find fifteen keys, but there may be more.*
*That's what's fun. Stay alert, you are never done.*

"What's equanimity?" Ben asked as he pinched the bridge of his nose, then let go, and shook his head.

"I don't know," Wes said and rubbed his chin.

"Mother and Father never talk about their treks. I guess that's part of the mystery and secretness," I said. "She couldn't just tell us. She had to make it some kind of riddle."

Wes took the wooden case, pressed down on the top, and slid the bottom forward. The clasp fell open, and the lid popped up. "Look what I did," he said and handed it to me. I refolded the paper and put it back in, hoping Mother's clues would be helpful but not sure how to interpret them. *Equanimity—what* is *that?*

The peaks seemed endless as we climbed, avoiding the sheer rock walls and swinging from ropes to traverse narrow cliff trails and boulders. Some days, we measured our progress in only hundreds of feet as we stopped, surveyed an area, and mapped our next move with care. In the long alpine meadows, the scent of flowers enveloped us. We stopped to lie in the grass, gaze at the clouds passing overhead, listened to the birds, and kept an eye out for mountain goats tracking, almost vertically, up the sides of rocks above us.

ONE BRIGHT CLEAR summer's day, we entered a narrow pass. As I scanned the rock walls, I caught a glimpse of something moving along a stone shelf above us. I stopped, tried to focus on it, and decided to alert Ben, who was just ahead of me, scanning the bushes for keys.

"I think we have company. Something moved near the bushes over there." I pointed in that direction. "Cougars live in these mountains, but Father said you rarely encounter them." I touched Ben's arm. "We crossed fresh scat earlier in the day. That is a sign one is nearby. Father warned, if you see one of those big cats, it's probably stalking you." I appreciated that shared wisdom now, and what he taught me to do.

"Where?" Ben said and raised his pointed stick. We each carried one for balance and protection.

"Wes," I called. "Be alert: mountain lion."

Wes, as usual, fifty steps behind us, looked up when I called to him. His eyes grew big, and he took off running down the path toward me.

"Don't run!" I screamed, but not soon enough.

The mountain lion entered the path behind Wes and, in two graceful, powerful strides, leaped on Wes's back and took him down. Ben and I ran to him. I threw my stick at the cougar and hit it in the back. The spear bounced off, but the animal let go of Wes and glared at me. My heart pounded as I looked into the big cat's cold, yellow eyes. The beast stared back, bared its teeth, and snarled, emitting a low, blood-chilling growl. Wes rolled to the side of the path, lay on his belly, and tried to control his breathing as he covered his face. I locked eyes with the cougar's and reached down for a loose rock to throw.

"Stay close to me," I said to Ben. My muscles tightened, and my heart raced. "Shout and wave your stick."

The mountain lion stood still and continued to menace me with its threatening stare, fangs glistening with saliva. I grasped my red bandanna with my left hand, pulled it out of my back pocket, and waved. At the same time, I threw the stone hard. Ben and I bellowed and jumped up and down. Ben shook his stick, while Wes lay still in the dirt just feet from the cat and played dead. The rock missed its mark, but it made the animal move aside and lose interest in us. The big cat backed off, slinked into the brush, and out of sight. Ben cheered and began a victory dance. Wes remained still, unmoving, scratched, cut, and too frightened to speak. I ran to him, sat him up and inspected and cleaned his wounds. Luckily, none were deep.

With the crisis past, I settled down, and my heartbeat and breathing slowed.

"We need to move on," I said, hoping Wes was ready.

Ben and I coaxed Wes up. He rocked in place and rubbed his hands but allowed us to resume our journey. Wes continued to look in the direction the animal was last seen and carried his stick pointed at the ready to defend himself. He walked backward for the rest of the day.

"I was happier when I knew where that big cat was," Wes muttered as we trekked on.

We settled in for the evening as the sun set. While I still had light, I made notes in my journal. Each morning, I made a tick on the inside cover so I could keep track of the days. When I finished writing, I placed the little book back in its pouch for safekeeping.

The mountain lion

# SEVEN

# Winter in the Mountains

## HANK

One step at a time, weeks became months, and still, the mountains lay before us with no keys in sight.

"Are you concerned that we haven't found a single key?" Wes asked me. Ben found a stone shaped like a key, but I didn't imagine it would open any doors. Besides, it didn't fit with Mother's letter.

"Not really," I answered, but I lied. Mother's letter said the keys were in plain sight. *Are they?*

Without a map, we followed the stars, my compass, and the sun to guide us. I wondered if we headed in the right direction or just walked in circles. No longer was the warmth of summer with us, days shortened, and the air, cool and fresh, bit at our hands and faces, forcing us to pull gloves from our packs. I had my red bandanna to cover my face. Ben and Wes had scarves. Snow accumulated in the higher elevations as early as late summer. Now, the flakes fell on us. When I looked at Ben and Wes, they were as white as the surroundings.

"I think we should settle in for the winter. We don't want to be caught in a blizzard unprepared," I said.

"We can camp, resupply, and wait out the worst of the cold weather," Ben said, and I knew he was right. Up high, summer is short, and winter can come early.

Ben found a suitable spot, at a lower elevation where trees and bushes grew on a broad ledge facing east, overlooking a broad meadow, protected from the wind.

"This way, the sun will greet us each morning," Ben said.

We sat together high above our new home and looked out on a vista that extended across valleys from one peak to the next. Stunned by the grandeur and scale of the scene, the three of us paused, in silence, watching the play of the ever-changing clouds drift toward the horizon.

We gathered branches and used them to construct a lean-to against the rock wall. I filled in the gaps between the sticks with mud, twigs, and dead grass. I appreciated how well Father instructed me on our many trips into the wilderness as part of my survival training. Wes fashioned a hearth with stones, and Ben collected a large pile of dry wood and stashed it under a rock outcrop.

To catch small game, I set out several snares—simple primitive contraptions, easy to improvise. I twisted a wire into a loop, the noose: the trigger: two hooks linked together set to separate when disturbed. A bent sapling acted as a spring that released when the hook triggers disengaged. Father taught me how to hunt this way to survive. Signs of animal activity, including trails, burrows, and scat, helped me place the traps in high-trafficked areas where I might bag a rabbit or a squirrel.

We combed the area around us for edibles. Once we were well stocked with food and fuel, there wasn't much to do but wait for winter. We consumed fresh what we caught in our traps, having limited means of preserving the meat. We stored nuts, acorns for roasting, and seeds in a sack that we hung from a tree branch outside the hut. On the edge of the ledge away from our shelter, Wes created an outhouse of sorts with a grand panorama of the heights that surrounded us. In the valley, where we grew up, the winters were mild and wet, but with little snowfall, and the cold was never severe. When Ben buttoned his pants legs on his shorts, I knew winter had arrived.

Almost every day, I took out Mother's message and read it, committing the letter to memory. I didn't know where to look for the keys and maintained a healthy dose of self-doubt about my ability to lead us. So far, however, as I reflected on our progress, we had met each trial with success. *Was that just luck?* Challenges met made me appreciate even more what Father did to prepare me, and I wished we had parted on a happier note.

SNOW FELL IN THICK SHEETS, forming banks that threatened to bury cur dwelling. The winds howled like angry dogs and tore at our shelter, threatening to rip the structure apart. As the white powder accumulated and froze, the lean-to became an igloo, an improved defense against the wind and ice. We cleared the drifts at the entrance daily. Days stretched into weeks, and our food supplies began to dwindle. The traps yielded fewer animals.

We had plenty of wood, but the fire in the hearth never seemed hot enough. We heated stones and kept them close for warmth. I made a single entry in my journal: *Running out of food.*

"I'm hungry," Ben said as he clenched his jaw and folded his arms across his chest.

"We're all hungry," I said and tried not to show my annoyance at Ben's complaining, but my words still came out with an edge.

Wes stood; his head struck the ceiling of the hut. He grabbed a shoe and threw it. The missile hit Ben, who jumped up and took a swing at Wes. I stepped between them as fists flew.

"Enough," I shouted. "Our food is almost gone. We need to go out and look for more, or we will starve. I'm tired of sharing with the mice. Don't waste your energy fighting. The days are short, and the nights are bitter. That doesn't give us much time to search."

"Is anything left to eat out there?" Wes asked and started to say, "What if . . ."

"Pine nuts and acorns, maybe blackberries, if the birds and little varmints haven't eaten everything," I said. "Look for watercress around springs. You can find some even now, and there may be milkweed still. The seeds are edible. Tomorrow, we'll check the rest of the snares and look for food."

That night, I'm not sure anyone slept. Once the sun rose high enough in the sky, we ventured out wrapped in oilcloth blankets and layers of clothes. Each of us took off in a different direction. I made my way down the mountain along narrow places between boulders and trees where snow didn't accumulate to great depth. Squinting against the bright, yet cool, sunlight, I moved with caution. I still slipped and fell into drifts and dug myself out more than once using my pointed stick.

A spring, protected by a ledge, yielded a cache of watercress. I filled my water bag and pockets with as much as they could hold and headed back to our camp. In the lean-to, Ben sat by the fire removing pine nuts from a pile of pine cones.

"Have you seen Wes?" I asked while unpacking the food I found.

"No, he hasn't returned," Ben said.

"It's getting late. The sun is beginning to set. I better go look for him."

"It shouldn't be hard to track him in the snow."

Ben had worked his way up the mountain. Wes tracked along the ridge and left a clear trail of footprints.

"Wes," I called over and over, but he didn't respond, and any echo was swallowed by the snow.

Wes's tracks led me to a cliff. I walked to the edge, leaned forward, and looked down. The height made me dizzy. I stepped back. My feet slid on ice hidden beneath the snow, and my legs shot out from under me. The small of my back struck the ground first; the back of my head followed.

Dazed, I lay still, oriented myself, and rolled over onto my belly with care. Half of me hung over the lip of the ledge. I dug my fingers into the snow and tried to ease my body back onto the sill. Each move caused me to slip backward. Spreading my arms and lying still didn't help. Gravity, aided by ice, made falling into the chasm below inevitable.

Despite the cold, sweat ran into my eyes and obscured my vision. My muscles tensed. Clawing the ice-covered rock in a desperate attempt to grab anything to hold proved hopeless. Then, I was airborne, falling. Bracing for the worst, I fell feet first, into a snowbank just fifteen feet below the cliff.

I sank into the soft powder up to my neck, still alive, grateful not to be splattered all over the rocks below or impaled by the trees. My heart raced, nostrils flared, arms flailed, and legs kicked, trying to swim my way out of the drift. *Did Wes suffer a similar fate or worse?*

"Wes, Ben!" I called and called, but the snow muffled the sound, like shouting into a pillow. I folded my bandanna, tied it around my head to keep my ears warm, and pulled the oilcloth blanket around me and over my head. Chills overtook my body. My teeth chattered.

The sun dipped below the mountains, the moon rose, and the stars shone. Light reflected off the snow, giving everything a cool, blue hue. The temperature continued to fall, and I feared neither Wes nor Ben would find me. I let out a long low sigh and felt a lump form in my throat. Fatigue overcame me. I fought against a desire to sleep, no longer certain how long I could battle the cold.

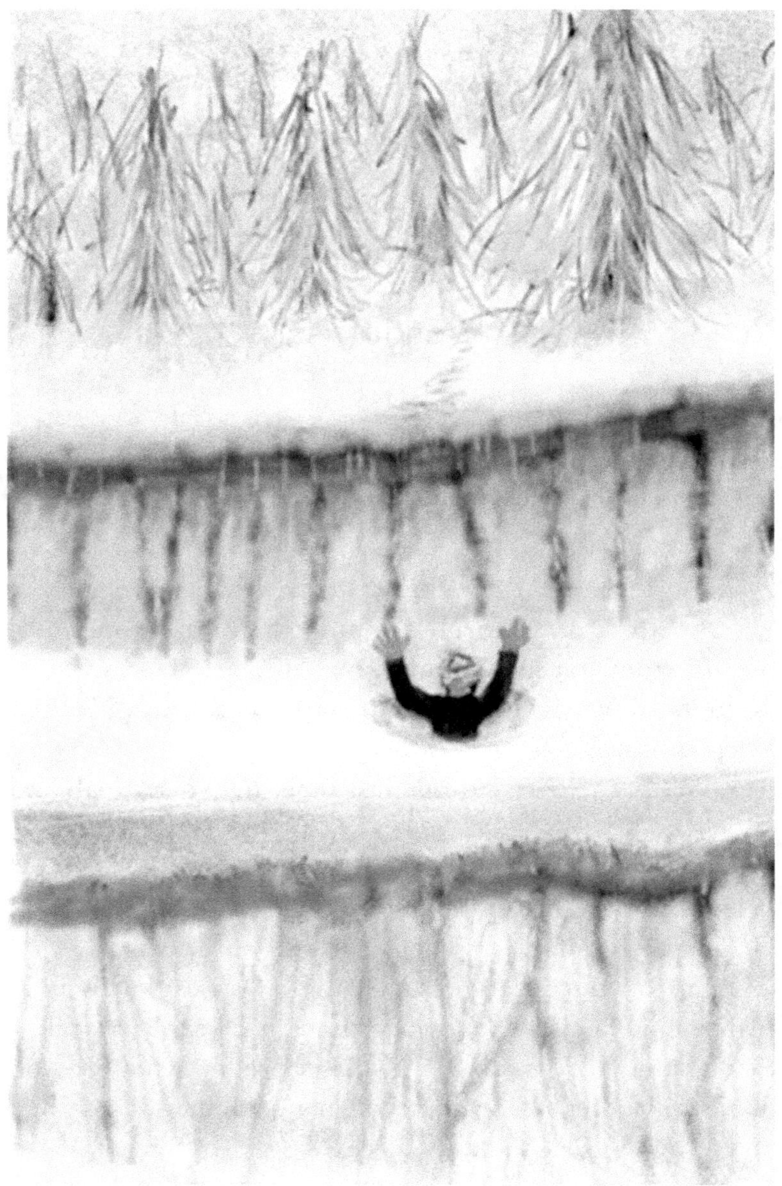

Falling off the ledge

# EIGHT

# Cold and Hungry

## HANK

*Don't give in to the cold. Fight to stay awake.* I struggled to get out of the drift, not sure where that would take me. In front, blackness threatened me, an abyss with no bottom. To my right and left was snow. *I must have fallen onto a ledge. How wide? Up is the only way out.*

"Wes, Ben," I called one last time, my voice weak and hopeless.

"Hank?" Wes looked down at me from the ledge I'd fallen from. He had a puzzled, disturbed look on his face. He knit his brow and frowned.

"I'm on my way back to camp," Wes said. "I didn't realize how far I'd wandered. I thought I heard you call. I found some acorns, and . . ." He paused. "What are you doing down there? Do you need a hand? Should I fetch Ben and a rope?"

"Yes, good plan." My speech was slurred. I took a deep breath, tried to smile, but my face had stiffened from the cold. "Be careful. The edge is covered with ice under the snow."

Wes moved back slowly to avoid slipping and disappeared. He quickly returned with Ben. They dropped a rope to me. I grabbed the line, took off my gloves, and worked the rope around my chest, fumbling with my stiff, cold hands, and managed to tie a knot.

"Okay," I called. "Start to pull me up."

The rope tightened, and their voices carried into the valley, "One, two, three, pull." I began to move up inches at a time. Out of the snow, and hopeful. The line gave way. I slipped backward toward the chasm. I gasped, tensed all my muscles, and prepared for a long free-fall into the darkness when I jerked to a stop. Ben's head appeared above me.

"Sorry, I slipped. There's a lot of ice here. Hold on, and we'll try again."

Ice and snow rained down on me.

"Try tying the end to a tree or run it around something, so I don't fall again."

"We cleared ice from the edge," Ben shouted.

The rope tightened again, and I began to rise. They pulled me up in small steps as they grunted and strained against my weight.

"This is killing my hands," Ben complained, but he held on.

"Put your mittens on. The leather palms will help your grip," Wes shouted at Ben. "I won't let it slip."

Up two pulls, then stop, and like a ratchet, I rose until I reached up and grabbed the ledge. I struggled to pull myself up, only to slip back one more time.

"Don't wriggle," Ben called. "Wes, wrap the rope around the tree another loop, tie it, and come help me."

Once the rope was secure, four hands appeared above me. Wes and Ben grabbed my hands, and together, they pulled me back onto the ledge. I shivered violently as they each took an arm and guided me back to camp.

Ben added more wood to the fire; and as the temperature in the hut rose, my shaking stopped, and sensation returned to my hands and feet. Wes placed his berries and acorns with the cache of food Ben and I accumulated while Ben dressed the one scrawny rabbit we managed to snare.

"A feast for kings," I said, thankful for what we had.

AS THE DAYS PASSED, our situation remained dire. The snares yielded only an occasional rabbit or squirrel, and we gleaned all the edibles from our surroundings. We considered eating the mice.

"Do you think we'd fare better at a lower elevation in a different location?" Ben asked. "Winter may last well into spring. I don't think this place can support us any longer."

We fashioned snowshoes from branches and spruce boughs and tied them to our boots. To avoid the high country, impassable due to ice and snow, we traveled along the valley floors. That led us south, not our intended direction, which was east. Ben's suggestion proved right. Deer and occasional bighorn sheep crossed our path in the distance. Ben found a fresh carcass of a deer, picked clean.

"These tracks were made by wolves," I said. "We've heard them howling at night. I didn't realize how close they were." *I hope they don't discover us.* I scanned the surrounding woods.

We walked south for days, refurbishing the makeshift

snowshoes as they fell apart, camping in simple shelters surrounded by a brush perimeter to keep away the wolves and coyotes. We set snares at night and looked for edibles under the snow.

"The snares were empty again," Ben reported almost every morning.

"No doubt robbed by some predator cleverer than us," I said with despair.

The three of us spoke little. As we walked, our shoulders drooped, our stomachs growled, our stride shortened, and the pace slowed. At night, one of us sat awake by the fire, sharp stick ready, on guard, while the others slept. Some nights, during my watch, eyes reflected light from our fire as they stared at me from the surrounding forest. Wolves with their cold, calculating eyes, no doubt as hungry as we were, no doubt sizing us up for supper. I kept my pointed stick ready at my side and stoked the fire or stood and waved my arms, threw snowballs or stones at them, and shooed them away.

Our spirits brightened when Wes spotted a hunting lodge tucked away behind a big stone outcrop. Wes ran to it and opened the door.

"Nobody's here," he shouted and hurried inside. Wes opened the shuttered windows and let in light. The layer of dust covering everything suggested it had been unoccupied for some time. We cleaned up the place, chased out the mice that had taken up residence, and stuffed every nook and cranny with sticks and stones to keep them out. In one corner, Ben discovered a large metal box that contained provisions, including a sack of flour, jars of corn relish and other vegetables, and pickles.

"I say we eat," Ben said.

"It's not ours," Wes said. "What if . . ."

"We're starving," I said. "I think we will be forgiven if we help ourselves to some. We can trade for the food and give something of value in exchange when we leave. We won't eat everything."

"What do you want to eat first?" Ben asked but didn't wait for Wes and me to answer. "I'm opening the relish."

"Make sure the top pops when you open it and it smells okay," I said.

Ben started a fire in the hearth. I paced off the cabin's dimensions, ten by twelve feet. With only one small bed. Ben and Wes slept on the floor that first night. I slept on the bed. We would take turns sleeping on the bed after that. The hearth fire kept the cabin warm and cozy. As I lay awake, I felt grateful for our good fortune.

Something rattled in my backpack. Fearing it might be a mouse, I got out of bed to explore what caused the disturbance. Mother's box shook. Once out of the pack, the lid popped open. I removed her letter and reread it. On line three the word *grateful* appeared. I stared at the paper for a long minute, then scratched my head still uncertain what it all meant. I refolded the letter, placed it back in the box, and returned the box to my pack. I got out my journal and started the entry with *Grateful?*

During the day, we tended our snares and scavenged for food, supplementing what we found from the stores available, careful not to exhaust them. Less than a mile from the lodge we found a pond, set hooks with corn from the relish for bait, lowered the lines through holes we cut into the ice, and caught fish. Life improved, and winter, at long last, began to wane as the days grew longer.

"There are bears in the area," Wes reported. "Out of their winter dens, probably looking for food."

"Did you see one?" Ben asked, jumping from one foot to another.

"Saw some fresh scat and tracks," Wes said. "I don't want to see one, not up close."

"I do. They're like big, fuzzy dogs," Ben said.

I just shook my head, favoring Wes's attitude. Ben and Wes looked like skeletons. I'm sure I looked no better, but the cabin had restored our hope. If a bear got hold of one of us, they wouldn't have much of a meal. I bit my lower lip; we'd been lucky and that's better than good.

"Hank," Wes said, "We've been out here for months already."

"Ten months, according to my journal when I last added up the days," I said.

"We haven't found a single key." Wes said. He had that anxious look about him. "It's been more about survival than discovering keys."

"I found a stick that kind of looked like a key," Ben said.

"Maybe we're not looking in the right places," I said. "Mother said they are in plain sight. In any case, we're not going to find any keys sitting here. I think it's time to move on."

"We can't just go without leaving something in exchange for the use of the cabin and the supplies we consumed," Wes said.

That night, we were startled awake by a loud pounding on the door. I grabbed my pointed stick. Ben and Wes ran to the door and started to open it.

"Stop," I said. "Keep the door closed." I held my pointed stick at the ready. "Who's there!" I shouted.

No response from the other side.

"Go away!" Wes called, then joined Ben at the door to hold it shut.

I tried to look out the window. It must have been very early morning. The only light in the cabin was from the dying embers in the hearth, the moon and stars obscured by clouds and mist. The banging continued and grew louder. Ben and Wes strained against the door to keep it closed. The thump, thump, thump continued and then abruptly stopped.

Peering out the window, I thought I saw movement by the door. Then, the greased paper covering the window burst apart, and two eyes met mine. I stepped back, tripping over my own feet to get away as quickly as I could; my stick fell out of my hand.

"What is it?" Wes shouted, his voice high-pitched and urgent. Ben continued to hold the door. There, in the window opening was the biggest bear's head I'd ever imagined. Teeth bared, it snarled and growled, reaching inside with one paw, its sharp claws swiping at us.

The bear reaches through the cabin window

# NINE

## Messyman

### HANK

"Get out," I shouted over and over, fearing the bear would pull the cabin down on us. The walls shook. I picked up my stick and swatted the paw. Ben and Wes joined in shouting, banging, and poking the bear. The bear must have decided we weren't worth the trouble. It pulled out of the window and headed back into the woods.

None of us slept the rest of the night. When the sun came up, I suggested we leave, concerned that there might be more bears in the area. I didn't relish the idea of another visit in the middle of the night. We found a roll of oiled paper under the cot and were able to repair the window that was torn apart by the bear.

As I stuffed my possessions into my pack, I considered what we might use as payment for our stay in the cabin. Ben and Wes looked through their things as well. We were careful not to over pack. Everything we brought, we needed. Even though the monetary worth of what we could leave might not be great, its practical value would be considerable to us.

"We have fire stones. We can leave matches. They are dispensable," I said.

Wes put some hooks and lines for fishing on the table. Ben threw in a snare. I retrieved the gold dollar that I placed in a pouch on the inside of my pack for good fortune and left it with the other offerings. *Who knows where or when I would spend that coin anyway?* It warmed my heart to share the luck. We didn't have to leave these things, and we weren't asked. I heard Mother's box rattle in my backpack again. *What's that all about?*

I tore a page from the journal I'd brought, and we composed a note for our hosts.

*Dear friends,*

*Thank you. We three travelers are so very grateful to have found your hunting lodge. We were starving, so we helped ourselves to some of your food. In exchange, we want you to have these things we leave under this note. I doubt this will cover the cost of lodging here in the cabin and for what we ate. If we can get back home to the Valley of the Black Dog, that is where you will find us. We would be happy to meet you there and pay what you think we owe you above what we left.*

*Sincerely,*
*Hank Falk, Ben Falk, and Wes Falk*

WEEKS PASSED. The trees and bushes wore new growth as reds and greens replaced the white that adorned the branches through the winter. We quickened our pace and marveled as the land around us came back to life. Plants poked up through the remaining patches of snow, small game became plentiful, and small streams from the retreating ice ran down the mountain.

"Put the sun in front of you in the morning and behind you in the evening. That will take us east," I said and waved my hand in the direction I thought we should go. Some days, we continued our trek into the night with only the stars to guide us and a full moon to light our way.

"It seems we are always going up," Ben said as we crossed yet another high ledge above the valley floor. As we gained altitude, our heads brushed the dense vapors that hid the mountain peaks. We bent at the waist to keep from getting lost in the clouds.

I led us down a rock-strewn trail that we navigated with ease until a massive piece of granite blocked our way.

"Any suggestions on how we go around this rock?" I asked.

"Walk around it," Ben suggested, shook his head, and raised his arms. "What else?" He started to jog clockwise along the obstruction, gauging its width.

Wes walked beside the monolith in the opposite direction. He didn't go far.

"Come here," he called. "There's a stairway carved into the rock. It leads up—right into the cloud."

We both ran to Wes. I tilted my head back, hoping to gain a better perspective. A slow smile spread across my face. *Where do the steps lead?* I put my foot on the first tread and looked up, trying to locate the top of the staircase.

Where do the steps lead?

In the cloud-dimmed light, I strained my eyes, but the end remained out of sight. The sound of dripping water echoed from above. I stepped on the second tread, then took one step at a time as I climbed up. Ben and Wes followed.

At the top, a misty haze enveloped us and diffused the sunlight into a warm, comforting glow. Bright rainbows floated in the mist on soft breezes and wavered with the grace of dancers all around us. We reached out with cupped hands, trying to capture a rainbow, but as soon as we touched them, they dissipated in a shimmer. Our voices, like the softened light, sounded muffled. I inhaled the cool, moist vapors the scent of which reminded me of the air after a summer rain.

I spotted a path that seemed to float on water, an illusion created by soft dew that covered everything. As I tentatively tested the surface of the path, my feet sank into its spongy surface, but the way supported me well. We trekked on and soon came to a cottage with a barn and outhouse behind, all shrouded in the foggy haze. A walkway led through an opening in a fence that surrounded an ample yard. Rails lay on the ground in places. Everything appeared in disrepair.

"Someone must live here," Ben said. "I saw chickens running free on the lawn, and a cow is peeking out of the barn."

Wes studied the enclosure. "What a mess. Look, they left rocks, broken chairs, a table standing on its side, sticks, bits of pottery, boxes, barrels, wheels, and other things scattered everywhere. What looks like a garden is overgrown and wild."

"Maybe we can scavenge some food," Ben said. "I think I see vegetables hidden in the weeds."

"Let's take a closer look. Maybe if someone lives here, they can tell us where we are," I said.

Ben walked up to the door, took the door knocker in his hand, and rapped three times. The knocker fell off the door and clattered to the ground. We listened for footsteps and heard a strange rustling of paper and banging of falling objects.

"Who's there?" A nervous voice was muffled by the door. "No one ever comes this way. Who are you, and what do you want?"

"I'm Ben, here with Hank, my brother, and Wes, my cousin," Ben shouted at the closed door.

"We would like to know where we are," I said.

"Oh, that's easy. You are here. Isn't that obvious?"

"Okay, that's accurate but unhelpful," Wes said and started to walk away.

The door opened. Papers, boxes, rags, and a cloud of dust spilled out. In the doorway, a man stood waist-deep in paper, broken boxes, books, pieces of wood, and toys.

"Sorry, I would clean up the house, if I found the broom," he said. "Come in, if you like, but be careful where you step. My name is Ansel, but everyone calls me Messyman."

Ben and I walked in, my lips drawn tight. Wes followed. As we entered, what could have been the parlor was in chaos. I passed by the backs of chairs poking up through the confusion. The path twisted and turned around piles of more paper; containers overflowing with more books, clothes, and broken objects surrounded us. Dirty dishes, pots, and pans rose in tall stacks to the kitchen ceiling. The smell of dust and garbage assaulted my nose.

I looked from the disarray surrounding me to our host. He patted down his long, salt-and-pepper-colored hair that spread across his scalp in every direction, then he smoothed out the stained shirt that hung askew on his sloping shoulders. All at once, he must have become aware of how disheveled he looked. He furrowed his brow, and a flush of pink enhanced his pale cheeks. He stroked his long, bushy, gray beard, which held crumbs, dried egg yolk, and some unidentifiable morsel of meat. Visible beneath his long, full, wild eyebrows, his tired, old eyes appeared unfocused and moist. He swallowed before he spoke.

"Welcome to my home, such as it is. With great sadness, I live in this disorder, as you can see, and regret I accomplish nothing. I can't find my garden tools, lost in the yard, I think. I can't find the dish soap; the dishes remain uncleaned. I misplaced my mop. Oh, don't go into the washroom. I doubt you will be able to find the tub, and the towels are dirty, piled in a mess on the floor."

Ben, Wes, and I looked around as we stood waist-deep in clutter. I thought about looking for keys since after traveling for months, we hadn't found even one. After all, Mother's note indicated that they were in plain sight. I frowned at the disorder around me. *Would we find anything here?*

Wes nudged Ben. "Kind of looks like your room on a good day," he whispered and laughed. Ben shoved Wes, causing him to stagger and trip over a hidden obstacle. I reached for Wes, but not in time. He disappeared beneath the piles of trash. The debris rippled as Wes thrashed below its surface, fighting to stand, emerging from under the mess, eyes wide, mouth agape.

Ben laughed. "Enjoy your dip into the unknown?"

"Not funny," Wes shot back as he scanned the room, looking for something that might be lurking beneath the litter.

"Nothing to be afraid of," Messyman reassured. "Rhonda, my cat, keeps the mice and rats at bay."

I cleared my throat. Aghast at the condition of Messyman's home, I placed my hand over my mouth, *Oh my. This much disorder would not work at home. How does one keep track of their things, complete anything, or even dress in the morning?*

"How can you survive this way?" Wes asked, his voice an octave above its usual level.

"How do your neighbors feel living next to you?" I asked.

"No one resides nearby, as I'm sure you noticed when you arrived. Empty cottages are all that surrounds me now. People lived near me once, but they told me I disrespected them by not keeping my place more orderly. They offered to help me clean up, but I didn't feel worthy of their assistance. So, they chose to move but left things behind, so many treasures. I brought them all here."

"Do you need this?" I asked as I held up a mug I pulled at random from the jumble. It had no handle and a large chip from the rim marred it.

"Ooh, I looked all over for that. Do you realize what a treasure that is? There was a time when I traveled and acquired that piece of porcelain when I vacationed at the beach many years ago, long before I found the rock staircase that led to this haven in the clouds. That cup is magic. With it, you can hear the ocean. Thank you for finding it."

He took the mug from me and held it to his ear. His pupils dilated, and he appeared transported to another place. As he listened, his forehead creases unwrinkled, and his eyelids dropped. "That's so nice," he said and felt around by the wall until he found a shelf under a mountain of crumpled papers and placed the vessel there. It vanished into the general disorder in a flash.

"Have you always lived this way?" Ben asked.

Messyman looked away. He appeared to be gathering his thoughts, narrowed his eyes again, and refocused.

"I believe a time existed when I knew where I kept the gardening tools. The flower and vegetable beds were neat, and flowers came up in rows. There was one section for tomatoes, and one for zucchini, and one for green beans. I cleaned the halls in my home, and I walked without tripping over a broken table, or a misplaced barrel covered by old clothes, papers, and empty boxes.

"It must have been nice," I said. "What happened?"

"It all began when I found that I couldn't be sure if something old might come in handy, or became scarce, or valuable, or hold some special meaning." Messyman crinkled his nose and took a breath before continuing. "First, I filled my basement with my treasures. I ran out of room there and started storing things in the living room, and then the dining room. Things got out of hand in the kitchen, and I couldn't get to the sink, reach the cupboards, or use the table. You know. It takes a long time to accumulate this much stuff. Where do you put it all?"

He paused, and a tear appeared in the corner of his eye. "That's not the whole story." Messyman shook his head. "No, I'm afraid my road to disorder started long before I moved here. When I was a child, I left my room a mess. I threw my clothes, toys, school papers, books, everything, everywhere."

"Who could sleep in that turmoil?" Wes whispered in Ben's ear, but not nearly softly enough.

"No one could, that's who," Messyman responded as he looked at Wes. "I began to nap in the hall outside my room.

I found no peace in that mess. No two things went together. I didn't finish my schoolwork because I couldn't find my books or pencils, or rulers, or anything." A tear ran down Messyman's cheek.

"Didn't your mother and father tell you to clean your mess?" Ben asked.

"Yes, of course, they did. My mother came into my room to help me pick things up, but things didn't stay neat, and eventually, she refused to go into my room. She said it was my responsibility to maintain order, but I never got the room cleaned—things were so messy that I didn't know where to start. Looking at the wasteland my room became, I turned and walked away. I spent time in my brother's room but messed up his toys, just like I messed up mine. 'Leave,' he demanded. Nothing, not my homework, not my chores, not anything, was done. That's when they stopped calling me Ansel and started calling me Messyman."

"That's very sad," I said. As we talked, Wes made himself busy clearing a circle around his legs to be able to see his feet. I looked around for any keys that might be in view.

"When I turned eighteen, old enough to leave home, my parents sent me off with a sack of essentials. It didn't take long before that bag overflowed with things that I picked up along the way, a hat here, a broken jug there, the end of a broom, an old newspaper. When I stopped for the evening to rest, I unpacked the sacks; they somehow multiplied from one to two to four to eight. I needed a cart to carry my possessions, then two carts, then a big wagon. I wore out my welcome everywhere I went. Then, I found the rock stairs that led into the cloud. I just followed them, and here I am, a messy man who lives with his head in the clouds. I made a lot of trips up and down those steps to bring everything I owned here." He took a deep breath and exhaled in a low, steady whistle. "Thank you for letting me share all this with you. I don't have many opportunities to unburden myself this way."

I thought about Mother's note.

*Have patience, be humble, grateful, and most important, true. Have faith, honor all, and be generous too. Show enthusiasm, establish order, and strive for simplicity. I have trust in you. Practice silence, be happy, show compassion, and maintain equanimity through and through.*

*Establish order, it said. Perhaps we are meant to clean up this place and find a key that is hiding in the mess.* I turned to Messyman.

"This much disorder isn't good," I said.

"I agree, not good. Yes. I will dedicate myself to being neater." He looked around. "Well then, I'll start by putting this home in order. Let me see, where can I start?" Messyman walked into the kitchen.

I took Ben and Wes aside.

"*Establishing order* is a clue," I said.

Wes headed to the door. I held him back.

"I believe we need to take this opportunity to look for keys," I said, then called to Messyman. "Can we help you clean this place?"

"Absolutely not. My mess, my job to fix this," he responded, but we refused to take no for an answer.

We cleaned for days, placed all the trash that littered the house and yard in boxes, organized things, stacked the cartons in straight rows and alphabetical order, according to the content, and moved them behind the house. I tried to throw out some containers, but Messyman would have none of that. He insisted all the boxes held treasures. For all our effort, Ben found two keys and Wes found one. Messyman identified and kept all three. Wes expressed relief that nothing evil was lurking in the hodgepodge of junk. Rhonda, we observed, did a very good job of keeping the mice and rats away.

We bid Ansel, no longer a messy man for our collective effort, farewell and left as soon as we could. I wondered how long it would take him to undo our work. We took the path back to the rock stairway and climbed down. The route past the rock wall proved easy and not as much out of our way as I thought.

"Do you really think Ansel will keep his house in order?" Ben asked.

"I don't think so, and living in total disorder cannot be good," Wes said. He took his cap from his backpack and placed it on his head. "What if my room looked that way? Mother would make me sleep on the floor in the hall?"

"Not getting things done as a result isn't good either," I added, moving my hand to my back pocket and feeling for my lucky bandanna, hoping I didn't leave it behind.

"You know what, *order* might be a key we're looking for," Wes said.

"I think of all those times Mother and Father told me to put my things in order," Ben said. "I listened, didn't I? Actually, I cleaned my room before we left."

"You did, I remember," I assured him.

I thought about what Wes just said. Sufficient order is good. Mother indicated that balance was a clue. *Was Wes right? Maybe order, in just the right amount . . . Did we find a key?* I felt the box rattle in my pack and knew that I was right. I recorded *Order* in my journal.

"Wes," I shouted, "I think you are right. *Order* is a key! I need to read Mother's note again, but it all seems to make sense." *So, Gratitude must also be a key.*

We never discovered where we were or what might lie ahead. As we walked just beneath the clouds, my thoughts started to drift to Jenny and Hannah.

TEN

## Choices

JENNY

Doing chores with Father always made me smile. However, running errands for Mother made me dance. It got me out of the house and off the farm, sometimes for hours, with a possibility that I might even happen upon an adventure.

"Jenny, go into the village to the general store and pick up a round of cheese," Mother called to me, and I hopped right to it. She sent me to fetch things she ordered or to drop off things she wanted to give to her friends. If I bumped into Mrs. Jones, she sometimes invited me in for a piece of pie. Thinking about the possibilities made my tongue happy. I might even have time to visit my friends.

Just as I was about to depart, Mother caught me. "Take Hannah with you." Hannah, my little sister was two years younger, a tag-along, whose company I didn't always enjoy.

Things to buy—cheese, Hub wafers, and a cake in a cup

"WHEN WE GET TO TOWN, can you guess what I'm going to buy?" I said to Hannah as we walked along the road to the village on that cool, early spring day. We stayed warm in our long, woolen sweaters, hand-me-downs from our cousins, like all our clothes. Mine hung below my waist. Hannah's reached to her knees. I chuckled to myself, as she strolled along in that old jersey dress. I missed Hank, Wes, and Ben, but I still got a knot in my stomach when I thought about their sneaking off without letting me know beforehand.

"Easy question, we're going to buy a round of cheese, just like Mother told us to," Hannah responded.

I turned and faced her. "Yes, but as long as we are in the general store, we can buy Hub Wafers, or, if Mrs. Johnston is selling her cupcakes, let's split one between us. I love her sweet icing." I pretended to hold a little cake in my hand as I took an imaginary bite. "So yummy."

"Mother sent us to the village to buy a round of cheese, not Hub Wafers or a cupcake," Hannah said, staring at me with threatening eyes and down-turned lips.

Hannah, my out-of-body conscience.

I raised my eyebrows and placed my hands on my hips.

"Father gave me extra money," I said. "Would you like cake or candy?"

"What did Father give you that money for? I bet it's for something you need. Mother says you should take care of your needs first; wants come second."

"Look here, there is money in my pocket. Think how those sweets will please your tummy. The icing will melt on your tongue."

"Umm, that does sound good." Hannah inhaled through her nose. "I can smell the sweetness. My mouth is watering." She stopped walking. "That's not what Mother sent us to the village to buy. What are you going to give up for these treats? Something you need?"

"I need to make my tongue happy. A delicious cake with icing or candy would work. I'll give you the orange Hub Wafers. Is it a deal?"

"Really? Father says you need food, water, shelter, and clothes. Those are needs. You just *want* a cupcake and Hub Wafers."

As we walked, we continued to discuss what we would buy when we got to the village. I enjoyed the warm sun, but not the conversation, and I made little progress in getting Hannah to agree with me. Her guilt over the purchase of a simple cupcake or some candy seemed to run much deeper than mine. Frustrated, I stopped to confront her straight on. As I started to speak, I realized nothing around us appeared familiar; and, just like that, our walk became an adventure like Hank's, Ben's, and Wes's.

*I am an explorer ready to enter the mysterious unknown.*

"I think we missed a turn," I said. "We've walked too far to go back the way we came. The village should be ahead. Mother doesn't expect us back at a certain time, so let's keep walking in this direction, pretend we are explorers." Hannah grew quiet but followed my lead.

We came to a fork in the road with three possible ways to go. The path on the left wound up a hill and disappeared at the top. On the right, the trail spun down into a gully and vanished at the bottom. The middle way was straight, rutted, and worn from use.

As we stood at the intersection, debating which way to go, a woman appeared, walking up the road from which we came. She wore a long skirt and a short-sleeved shirt, with a shawl draped over her shoulders. She had tied her long, dark hair in a braid and wrapped it around her head.

Which way to the village?

"Do you know which way will take us to the village?" I asked.

"You can choose any of these three paths," the woman said.

"Will they all take us to where we want to go?" Hannah asked with a knitted brow.

"All three will take you to the village," the woman said as she stroked her chin. "I have taken all three, and I can tell you, each is unique. As I walked the high road, vistas made me stop as I took in rocky crags and mountain lakes surrounding me." She looked around and inhaled deeply. "The path narrowed in spots, forcing me to climb over treacherous terrain and cross dangerous bridges. I encountered ways tempting me with even grander views and thrilling dangers." She stared into our eyes. "Be careful, though; the delays may take you away from your mission and distract you from your goal, if you let them."

"Oh, so exciting," I said leaning forward, words rushing from my mouth. "How about the lower path?"

"I took that once." The old woman cleared her throat, folded her arms, and tucked her hands behind her elbows. "As I dropped down onto the lower trail, my chest sank. I wrung my hands and believed I had entered a horrible place." She shook as if a chill overcame her. "Tall trees and dense foliage cut out the light. Darkness affected my vision. The heavy air reeked of mold. The dampness condensed on my skin and mixed with my sweat from the heat. Insects buzzed around my head. I leaned on a tree, for a moment, and fire ants immediately attacked me. Mud oozed over my shoes, slowed me down, and rapidly fatigued me. I decided to turn back."

Hannah's lips trembled, and she appeared pale. "How about the middle way? Did you try that?"

"Ah, the middle way. After I returned from the lower trail, I doubled back to this point and decided to take the middle path. No vistas, distractions, or treacherous climbs, and not as thrilling as the high way. As I walked the broad, flat, middle road, the sunlight flickered through the trees above. The hard-packed, dusty surface did not muddy my shoes. I breathed fresh air. The middle route was moderate, safer, more direct."

Hannah tugged on my arm. Her eyes lit up. "Let's take the middle path," she whispered.

"You don't need to deny yourself the ease of the middle way by suffering the low road, nor do you need to overindulge in the thrills of the high path," the old woman said. "There is no harm in under-indulgence or over-indulgence on occasion. Life is like that." She paused and looked from me to Hannah before continuing. "The key is moderation. Take a walk on the low road or high road, if you like, but don't go too far. In the end, it may be best to choose the middle way. I am about to take my next journey. I came here to decide which path to take. You know, you always have a choice."

I wondered which way she'd choose.

"I don't have much interest in the low road, but the high road calls to me. I should take the middle way," the woman said. "However, as I gaze on the high road, I'm drawn like iron to a magnet. Irresistible and thrilling, I find the temptation hard to defy. You can come with me. I think you will enjoy it."

"But will it lead us to the general store in the village?" Hannah said. "Our mother has sent us to buy a round of cheese." She rubbed the back of her neck, and then crossed her arms.

"These paths all lead you to where you want to go," the

woman said as she tilted her head toward us. "You can always get there from here, though one is more direct than the other two. With the other two, the journey is more difficult, at greater cost, and may take longer, but sometimes that's worth it for what you may learn about yourself along the way."

Hannah and I said goodbye to the woman as she walked to the entrance of the high road.

"Which path should we choose?" I asked Hannah. "The high road is very tempting. I love vistas."

"Do you think the woman will be able to leave the high road and come back to the middle way? Will she avoid all those side paths with their distractions and get to where she is going?" Hannah's eyes darted back and forth from the old woman to me.

"It is all about choices, isn't it? Let's go. Cupcakes and candy are calling me," I said. "Remember, the orange Hub Wafers are yours. I hope Mrs. Johnston baked today."

"Cheese," Hannah replied with conviction.

I considered taking the high path as the woman passed out of view. Then, I thought about the low road. Hannah took me by the hand and started walking. She steered me toward the middle way.

"The Hub Wafers?" I asked.

"Cheese," Hannah repeated, thought for a moment, and added, "Well, maybe only the Hub Wafers. I guess it's not a real need, but just a little want that we can share with Mother and Father."

I prevailed in the end. Mrs. Johnston's cupcakes were fresh out of the oven. We split one, a cake made in a cup with a sweet strawberry frosting. We bought the cheese from Mr. Johnston, and he threw a roll of Hub Wafers into the bag for free. Hannah ate the orange ones. I preferred the licorice-flavored discs. I didn't like the purple ones, not sure what flavor they were. I decided to save those for Father. Mother had her choice of the rest.

When we had to choose a way home, we stuck to the middle way and did not become lost. As I walked, I wondered whether Ben, Wes, and Hank had taken the high road, the low road, or the middle way.

# ELEVEN

# The Cave

BEN

We marched in a line. Hank led, then came me. Wes always followed behind us by a few more steps than I was behind Hank. All things considered, Wes managed to keep up with us better since the mountain lion affair. Rain poured out of the sky in buckets and turned the narrow paths we walked into raging streams. Loosened from the mountainside above, water-propelled stones threatened to knock us off our feet. The wind screamed, and the light of day remained a hazy dusk.

As uncomfortable as the rain made me, at least it wasn't snowing. I had had enough of cold and ice. The temperature during the day had risen high enough that I converted my long pants to knee pants. I unbuttoned the legs and stored them in my pack. The wind at our backs pushed us forward through the heavy rain. Water ran off my oilcloth poncho, flowed down my legs, and into my shoes. Hank wore a constant frown. Wes remained quiet, unusual for him.

"Hank," I shouted over the constant noise created by

the rain and bluster. "I'm tired of fighting the weather. Let's find shelter where we can dry off and wait out this storm."

Hank nodded in agreement, but we walked on well into the afternoon. Beneath a ledge, Wes found a narrow opening, an entrance to a cave. We had to stoop to enter; but once inside, the cavern was easily as large as our town meeting hall.

A hole in the dome above emitted light but let in little rain. The air chilled me, and a musty damp odor hung in my nose. Darkness hid the back of the cave. I strained my eyes, searching the shadows, wondering what might be lurking in a corner. Hank threw a stone into the blackness. A loud crack followed with echoes as the sound bounced from wall to wall.

"Why did you do that?" I shouted and gave him a shove.

"What if you woke up a bear or a wolf? Or worse, what if a saber-toothed tiger is lurking back there?" Wes said, his voice high pitched and jarring.

Hank just laughed. "There are no saber-toothed tigers. Besides, I didn't find any fresh scat as we entered."

Once my eyes adjusted to the dim light, I stumbled over a circle of stones in the middle of the room. "Hank, people have been here before us," I called out, alarmed at first. The ashes were cool to my touch. "I think it's been a while since anyone has been here, though."

Hank and Wes joined me.

"Let's get some light and heat in here," Hank suggested.

We gathered branches scattered around the interior of the cave, fortunate that they were dry enough to start a fire and keep it going. The hole in the dome made for a good chimney.

"We can wait here until the weather improves," Hank said.

"I don't think we have a choice. It is nasty outside," Wes added. "This is the worst spring storm I can recall, ever."

"Look at the positives," I said. "Freshwater isn't a problem. Just hold your pouch up to the sky, it's filled in no time."

After starting the fire and drying off, I took a stick and lit its end to use as a torch to explore the back of the cave. I didn't go far before discovering something.

"Come here. You must see this," I called, and Hank and Wes joined me. The size of the space took my breath away and left me awestruck. I felt small and insignificant.

I led my brother and cousin to a passage that brought us to a second chamber much larger than the first, as big as the inside of a great cathedral, like the ones I saw in pictures from France. A series of natural columns sat on a narrow bridge that spanned the cavern from the passageway to the opposite wall. Each column had the shape of an hourglass, the surface covered by stone guttering like wax on a burning candle. Black abysses lined the bridge on either side. I tossed a stone into the void to measure its depth and counted.

"One and two," I said before we heard the muted splash from below. Wes threw several more rocks and listened for the muffled kerplunk. Crystals like jewels sparkled from the dome of the room, reflecting light from my torch. As my torchlight faded, though, I could still see. The crystals generated light, creating a dim glow with shades of green, red, and blue. Wes and Hank stood still, eyes wide, as we studied the reflections off the rock formations.

A series of natural columns sat on a narrow bridge

"Should we?" I asked, breaking the silence with a challenge.

"Should we what?" Hank responded. He seemed curious but cautious.

"Should we cross the bridge?" I said, taunting Hank and Wes to try it. "I think I can reach the crystals on the other side of the bridge; they are lower on the wall. I must have one."

"Why do you need a crystal?" Wes said. "What if the bridge won't hold us? What if every hayseed who came here took a crystal? Eventually, all would be gone, none left. The cave will curse you and bring us bad luck if you take even one."

"Did you call me a hayseed?" I said. "I'm going across, and nobody will miss just one crystal. The cave's wrath? Really, Wes." I tilted my head back. "The bridge will hold us. It's made of stone."

"What if you fall into the pits on either side?" Wes asked. He stepped back from the edge of the chasm. "You don't know what's down there. How will we get you out? What if we don't have enough rope?"

"Maybe there's treasure on the other side," I said. "I think the bridge is wide enough and appears to be solid. I'm sure it can hold me, and I can see well enough in this light."

I carefully placed one foot on the narrow span, gripped the first column, slid my foot around the base, and reached for the second. My foot slipped. Wes let out a gasp. I held onto the column and got my feet back under me, then looked back at my cousin and gave him a smirk to cover my unease at having nearly fallen before moving on. Once across, I ran to the wall, removed a crystal, and studied its warm glow.

Wes and Hank watched me. The crystal became my torch. Wes shook his head, but I didn't care. *I'll save this gem for Mother.* Without waiting, I entered another passage. The tunnel gently sloped up. Water splashed with each step, and a breeze caressed my face, perhaps signaling another entrance. It was dark here without the crystals embedded in the walls and ceiling. I opened my hand and the crystal's glow provided just enough light to see the walls on either side of me.

"Maybe, we can find another entrance to the cave," I said, thinking Wes and Hank were behind me, but I didn't hear a response.

"Are you guys coming?"

No answer.

*Have they returned to the first chamber?* I considered going back but decided to explore further. The path went up for a short stretch, leveled, and turned, then gradually narrowed. I had to bend at the waist and then crawl to continue. My head scraped the roof of the tunnel. I stopped. Behind me was nothing but darkness.

"Hank, Wes!" I shouted. No answer. "If you are messing with me, you're not funny."

Still, nothing but silence.

"Stay calm," I said aloud. The tight space didn't make maintaining my composure any easier. The passage became so narrow, I crawled, and the wet, rough surface hurt my knees. The tunnel narrowed further, forcing me to lie on the ground in slimy mud that reeked of old pee. My mind raced. *Will the passage become too narrow to slide out? Worse yet, could I get stuck, unable to get back?*

Unaccustomed to reacting to fear, I stopped, listened, then bit my lower lip. A twittering and squeaking ahead of me made my heart skip a beat. Something crawled onto my back. Instinctively, I pushed up with my arms, tried to stand, and smacked my head on the low ceiling. Blood trickled down my face.

"Bats!" I shouted, releasing a storm of flapping and screeching. I covered my face, held my breath, and tried to melt into the stone floor until the tempest passed.

I wiggled backward, as fast as I could, until I had enough space to turn around. I held the crystal in front of me for light and, once able to stand, ran back to the chamber with the columned bridge. I stopped and waited for my heart and breathing to slow. I shouldn't have taken the crystal from the cave. As much as I hated to admit it, Wes was correct: Taking the stone was bad luck. I put it back on the wall where I found it. Calmer, having caught my breath, I spun around until I located another opening to my left. *Did Wes and Hank go that way?* I strained my eyes but didn't see either of them.

"Can you hear me?" I shouted.

No answer.

Any interest in exploring this labyrinth further evaporated, at least for the moment. I put looking for adventure and treasure behind me and realized how rash it was to dive ahead into the cave by myself. *Are Hank and Wes together? I hope they're not lost looking for me.* They couldn't know whether I was safe. I entered the opening to my left and walked a short distance up a passageway. There were no signs of Wes or Hank. I considered going back to the bridge and returning to the original entrance, hoping Wes and Hank would be there. My damp clothes chilled me to the bone, and I started to shake. A scent of pee seemed to be following me.

The short hall I entered led to another room; this one lit by a glistening growth that grew on the surface of a pool of water. Drips as steady as a ticking clock splashed into the pool from above. The ceiling was thick with spires that hung like inverted cones, and ribbons of stone, draping the walls, shone with moisture. Wes and Hank stood next to a wall, examining it. Hank held a torch.

"Guys, didn't you hear me calling?"

Hank turned, his brow was knitted; a frown appeared on his face when he saw me. I walked over to them, curious about what they discovered. Hank didn't say anything to me at first. He and Wes seemed engrossed by their discovery.

"I have read about cave paintings," Hank said. "In the U.S., most are in Tennessee and Alabama. This could be thousands of years old." He scanned the wall slowly, up and down, right to left. "I think this drawing is a map or a story. All kinds of animals must have been here." Hank pointed to the various elements of the picture. I guessed he lost interest in being angry with me.

"I recognize deer, bears, snakes, wolves, and stick figures of men with spears. Spears rain down on the animals. Lines of black may be rivers. Triangles are probably the peaks of mountains, and the yellow ball in the sky represents the sun. If the sun is rising over the mountains, then that means the mountains are east, the Eastern Mountains."

"What if the sun's setting?" Wes asked. "What is the elephant-looking animal with big tusks coming out of its mouth?

"I think that's called a mammoth," Hank answered.

I didn't care. "Let's go," I pleaded as I rubbed the goosebumps on my arms. My teeth chattered. "Actually, I've had enough of this spooky cave."

"What have you been lying in?" Wes said, pinching his nose with one hand and pushing me away with the other.

I looked at myself, covered with muck. Hank stared at me. He lost any appearance of anger and started to laugh.

"You stink like poop, bat poop," he screeched and stepped away from me. "You upset us, disappearing like that. You could have waited for us before you took off. I'm sorry that you're unhappy with us now, but we didn't know which way you went. Don't jump ahead in the future. What if you got lost, or worse, stuck in a place where we couldn't find you?" Hank couldn't keep a straight face as he continued to reprimand me and started laughing again. "You should see yourself."

Wes stood to the side, away from me, still holding his nose. He started to gag.

The three of us made our way to the chamber with the crystals. They asked me to wait until they crossed the bridge first, fearing I'd smear bat poop on the columns.

Hank led me to the cave entrance and pushed me out. "We're glad you are safe. Now, stand there until you are clean," he commanded.

More concerned about the smell than the cold, I danced in the rain to keep warm. By the time I stepped inside, the fire had warmed the chamber and replaced the dankness with the sweet aroma of burning wood. As my clothes hung by the fire to dry, I sat, wrapped in my boiled wool sweater that Mother made me, and absorbed the cozy warmth.

Wes rummaged through our supplies and prepared a soup with dandelions, bittercress, and wild onions. I would have liked a little meat, but we had none left. I didn't complain. The storm continued to rage outside, and I hoped that the weather would break, so we could be on our way in the morning.

As I thought about what happened in the cave, a satisfied smile spread across my face. I was safe. I took a deep breath and thought about what I learned. When meeting the challenge of exploring a new place, I should be more patient, like checking how deep the water is before diving into a pool. I acted without weighing the consequences first. I stopped thinking and lay on the ground, listening to the sound of the wind and the patter of rain outside.

"Hank, you up?" I whispered, not wishing to awaken Wes. "*Patience*, isn't that one of the clues to the keys?"

"You're right," Hank whispered back. "*Have patience* is part of the first line. *Patience* is a key." He paused sat up and gave me an ominous look. "Patience is something for you to work on, little brother." He paused. Although he seemed prepared to reprimand me, he changed the subject. "Do you realize this cave is a huge discovery? The formations, the painting, and the crystals. I hope we can find this place again someday. I want to do more exploring. By the way, do you still have that crystal?"

"No, I put it back."

"Good. Now go to sleep," Hank said.

I heard the box in Hank's pack rattle.

"Remember to make an entry in your journal tomorrow. We've definitely found another key." I said.

"Go to sleep, already," Hank said. "I will."

In the morning, light streamed in through the cave entrance. The fire had died. We gathered our belongings; and once Hank finished writing in his journal, we left.

"Wes, I just recorded another key, *patience*, and added up the days," Hank announced with pride. "Looks like we've been away 340 days."

We stepped out of the cave and into the sunlight and a new day. A clear sky greeted us, and the grand sights previously obscured by clouds stretched to the horizon. In the distance, the jagged peaks gave way to more gentle hills.

We walked on hoping the end of the mountains was in sight.

"Taken with *order*, and *gratitude*," Hank said, "I think we've found three keys."

I turned to Hank. "Do you think we'll find any people when we finally leave these mountains?"

TWELVE

## Enough

───────

HANK

The sun rose ever higher in the sky, and the days grew longer. Warm rays of light pierced the early morning fog, cleared the mist, and chased away the cool night air. At this lower elevation, we waded through more varied vegetation, and each breath filled my head with the sweet aromas of flowering buds. The sparkle of morning dew on petals and leaves made the greens, yellows, and pinks around us glow. We no longer had to contend with the long, cold winter nights or the early spring rain. When we stopped to rest at the end of each day, we slept under the stars in the fresh mountain air.

"I hope we find a place where we can stop for a while and replenish our supplies before we move on," Ben said.

"I want to keep moving. Spring is a good time to travel," Wes countered. "Shouldn't we be looking for more keys? Your mother said there were fifteen. We've found three?"

"My knee pants have turned into shorts, and I'm tired,"

90

Ben groused. "What's left of my shoes pinch my toes. I think everything shrank, or maybe I grew."

"My clothes don't fit either," Wes said. "At least, they are sort of clean from washing them in the streams."

"Stop complaining." I said, although I felt sympathetic. After many months of following narrow mountain paths, we found ourselves high above a broad plain with a slow meandering river running through it much like the valley of our home. The waterway spread out like a giant's hand as it emptied into a vast sea that stretched to the horizon. The surroundings extended for miles under a cloudless, deep blue sky. In the distance, wisps of smoke rose above the trees. I held my head high, shoulders back, and crossed my arms, as I surveyed the scene like the mighty explorer on the verge of a discovery. We had crossed the Eastern Mountains. A broad smile spread across my face. We made it.

"Do you see the smoke in the distance?" I said. "There must be people down there."

"Do you think they will be friendly?" Wes said. "What if they're not?"

"Actually, I would be happier if we could find new clothes and real food," Ben said.

Without a mirror, Ben didn't realize how bedraggled he looked. His shirt was faded, tattered, and at least one size too small. He wore his mop of red hair pulled back into a ponytail. Wes appeared no better, and I was certain, neither did I.

I watched smoke rise at the end of the valley and thought back to our village. The only person we had met so far in our travels was Messyman, so signs of people quickened my step. I hoped another key might be in the offing. As we started to walk, I touched my red bandanna for luck.

The village

The trail sloped gently down at first, then sharply switched back and forth as we navigated the steep grade. Boats laden with bundles coursed the river in the distance. Crops grew in the fields that surrounded a central point from where the smoke rose. I presumed there was a village hidden under the canopy of trees. Walking eased as the track leveled out, and the sharp switchbacks became gentler. Hardwood trees replaced the stubby shrubs and pine of higher elevations. We arrived at a mountain meadow, green with grass and sprinkled with yellow and blue flowers the fragrance of which wafted over us. At the far end of the field, sheep grazed. A dog, aroused by our presence, jumped up and positioned itself between the sheep and us. Triggered by the dog, the sheep picked up their heads in unison. The shepherd looked in the direction of the sheeps' movement, and that led him to Wes, Ben, and me.

"We should wait here until we are invited to approach," I said.

The shepherd, tall and lean, wearing a torn, dirty, white shirt, holey pants, and no shoes, walked to his dog and called to us, "Hello, and welcome."

"Hello," I shouted, grateful to be greeted warmly. The tension in my muscles eased.

"We've come across the mountains," I called back, as we approached the shepherd. "Can you tell us where we are and something about your village?"

"There is a town here, a port by the sea, and many people live in this valley. As you can see, I tend the sheep. My name is Have-Little." He extended his hand in greeting and shook each of ours.

"That is an odd name," Wes blurted, and it appeared to me that Wes had ignored the possibility he may have offended Have-Little. I gave him a stern glance.

"Not so odd," Have-Little quickly responded. Fortunately, he appeared unperturbed. "That's what some call me. Although many live here, I know of two others, special like me, and I suggest you try to meet them while you are here. One answers to the name Enough, and the other to Too-Much. Their names fit, and so they stick."

"How did you and these other people get your names?" Ben asked.

"Simple. I have little, and I tend sheep for Too-Much. He never has enough. That shack by the meadow is where I live, the ground is my bed, and the world is my home."

Ben rubbed his chin. "What if that is not enough?" he asked.

I understood his question, because I too wondered if perhaps Have-Little needed more.

"Sometimes, I think it would be nicer if I had more," Have-Little said, "but, then I think, I have enough. I would like more warmth in the winter, and a little privacy when I bathe and relieve myself. That would be nice. I wonder, maybe having little isn't enough. My life is certainly uncomplicated and efficient, although not very interesting, perhaps. Life would be easier and more stimulating if I had more. Sheep are easy. People can be complicated, as can be love. So, I stay here in the mountain meadows and tend the flock by myself. But, I wonder, would I be happier if I met my needs better and my life was a bit less simple?"

"How do Enough and Too-Much get along?" I asked. Have-Little lowered his eyes as I spoke. When he picked up his head, his gaze was distant.

"You must ask them yourself," Have-little said. "They live in the village by the river in their houses. See what they have made for themselves. Ask them how they feel."

We thanked Have-Little for his time, wished him good fortune, and resumed our journey. We reflected on Have-Little's humble existence.

"I think I would prefer to have more," Ben said, and I had to agree.

"What if that was all I could afford?" Wes said, a valid point. I had to give that more thought.

The trail flattened and straightened until it met the river, where the path took meandering turns as it followed the riverbank. I waved to the boatman on the river and greeted everyone we passed. "We're looking for Too-Much. Have you seen Enough? Do you know where Too-Much can be found? Have-Little sent us to find Too-Much and Enough. Do you know where they live?"

Most people gave us an icy stare. Some acted as if we were invisible and didn't acknowledge us. I began to feel like a pane of glass. *Are we being disrespectful? Did Have-Little play a joke on us?* We eventually reached the village, but still hadn't learned where to find Too-Much or Enough or if they even existed.

"We're wasting time," Ben said. "I don't think this brings us any closer to finding keys."

"Practice patience," I responded, and Wes nodded in agreement.

"I'm tired," Ben said and sat down by the side of the road. "I want real food, new clothes, and new shoes."

I could feel my face redden. My tolerance for Ben's impatience had reached its limit. Just as I was about to explode, I noticed that behind him was a long, majestic flight of steps that led to the top of a hill on which a stately mansion stood. An insignia on the fence that enclosed the grounds surrounding the house contained the letters TM.

"Do you suppose TM could be Too-Much?" I said. "I'm going to find out." I was excited for the potential of finding Too-Much.

I marched up the stairs and knocked on the door. A tall, gaunt man wearing a red-and-blue-striped silk tie and a tailored black suit opened the door. His face was deeply lined, his brow furrowed, his shoulders stooped, his demeanor stern.

"Have you got something for me?" the man said in a short staccato burst of words. "Be quick, I'm busy."

"We are looking for Too-Much," I said.

"I've heard that some of my neighbors refer to me as

Much, Too-Much, to be exact, especially by those who have little, the pitiful wretches."

"Yes, we met Have-Little on the meadow in the hills above town," Wes said. "He said we could ask you why they call you Too-Much."

"My hills, my meadow, my sheep. My life is complicated but look at what I have." Too-Much spread his arms and invited us to look to our left and right. "I have all this and many, many things. I need to work hard to maintain what I have. If I acquire one of something, I want the set, then I need two sets. Never enough; I always want more. I wish I had more time. Too bad you can't buy time, or I'd be able to better enjoy what I have. There is always something more to do, to get, and always a problem to solve. Now, do you have something for me? I have things to do, places to go, people to meet. I'm very busy, too busy. I have wants. Wants are expensive, so I must make money, more and more money."

We shook our heads. Too-Much finished, grunted, looked at us with scrunched-up eyes, and slammed the door shut.

As I descended the steps, I tapped Ben and Wes on their shoulders. "You can't always get what you want," I said.

"And you get what you get, and you don't get upset," Ben added.

"Too-Much has a lot, but he doesn't seem happy."

"Do we bother searching for Enough?" Wes asked as he led us down the steps. "I can't get away from Too-Much fast enough."

"I think so," I said when we got to the street. "I bet Enough is somewhere in the middle, between too much and too little; between too complicated and too simple, but I don't have a clue where we will find him."

"I'm afraid too much simplicity may not be enough," Ben said. "Someday, I may need more. And now, I need real food, clothes, and shoes. I think that is enough and not too much. I think the time has come to satisfy those needs."

"You can want more," I said. "Just remember to live within your means, like the old man said."

Ben stood and beckoned us to explore the town further.

THIRTEEN

# The Almost Endless Summer

JENNY

I tended the sheep alone in the summer once my cousins deserted me. Father and I drove the sheep to the hills where they grazed. He waved goodbye as he left me with the flock before returning home.

"No stray dogs or wolves are going to bother our sheep," I called to Father as I waved back. I stood tall at the ready to chase any intruders away. In truth, we never had to shoo away any wolves, wild dogs, or other wild things. If we had, Father wouldn't have left me all alone.

The sheep, each marked with a spot of indigo dye, bleated as they munched on lush grass while Oscar and I scanned the field, eyes peeled, from the top of our rise. I held a shepherd's crook in my left hand. Oscar lay in the soft grass beside me.

When the sun was high overhead, I took off my backpack, pulled out the lunch sack Mother made for me, and spread out the contents with deliberate care on a cloth napkin. She included a piece of fresh-baked bread, an apple, and a salted, boiled potato. Head tilted, eyeing the selection, deciding which item to eat first, I picked up the potato and took a bite. I relished its saltiness but didn't dare eat it all. Oscar stood in front of me, staring at the morsel with his big, dark eyes full of longing, tail wagging, tongue lolling, wet with drool. He didn't have to worry. I always shared my lunch with him.

Once we finished our meal, I adjusted my hat at an angle, shook the napkin clean, and tied it around Oscar's neck. We became Captain J, the brave, and Lieutenant O, her trusted protector.

"Get sheep, Oscar," I called. Oscar ran in a wide circle to gather our sheep army ready to drive our troops to the nearby watering hole. There, we prepared them to march out of the valley and conquer the world. Leaving home made me think about Hank, Ben, and Wes. We had received no word about where they might be. It was almost a year since they left, and I expected them home soon.

I thought about them a lot, wondered where they were, and whether they were safe. *I bet they're having great adventures.* After they left, I sulked for days, threw things, and sobbed. Now, I just missed them and wished they were here, so I could be with them. I wrote them letters in my diary every day about the great adventures they were missing, but I had nowhere to send them.

If they were here, I'd tell them about fall, my favorite season, when the trees became a mix of yellows, reds, and oranges, and cool air blew out of the mountains. However, it was still summer. Fall was late. I wore Ben's hand-me-down knee pants and a large-brimmed hat to keep the sun off my head. I swore the heat was about to turn me into a prune. I fanned myself for comfort and wondered when the leaves would change and cool, crispy weather would arrive.

As the sun beat down day after day, summer continued,

and autumn failed to return. The rivers ran so low their banks nearly met in the middle. The trickle that remained left the poor sheeps' watering pond with barely enough for the animals to drink. Hot, dusty air filled my lungs as the dry grass rattled in the breeze.

One very-late-summer day that year, as usual, I spotted Father and Hannah far off in the distance. They helped me bring the sheep home for the night. Suddenly, Oscar took off into the hills. I don't know what got into him. *Should I wait here for Hannah and Father or take off after O.?* I tore a page from my notebook.

"Oscar ran away," I said aloud as I wrote. "Looking for him. If not back when you get here, take the flock home without me." I attached the note to my crook, stuck it in the ground, and left to search for my dog.

"Oscar, that'll do," I called as I walked, but he didn't come.

*Where is he?* From the top of a knob, I observed fields of ripening corn spread to the river, where boats made their way to market, but no Oscar.

"Oscar, that'll do!"

I ran up the next rise and then to another. The sun disappeared below the horizon, and the blue hour turned to black. In the dark, I couldn't count my fingers in front of my face. Sweat trickled down my back, my breath came fast, and my neck tightened.

*It was a mistake to walk away from the sheep this close to sunset.*

The ground sloped up as I took small careful steps to avoid tripping over rocks and roots. From another knoll, the faint glow of light from the windows of the homes in the valley greeted me. My heart raced. As I regained my bearings, an urge made me want to run, but I held back. *How can I get through the deep gullies where it is as black as pitch?* I took a breath and started to descend a hill in the direction of the village, taking care not to fall. I shuddered as tears welled up in my eyes. *Mother and Father must wonder where I am. They will not be happy with me.*

I trembled in the cool night air and longed for full-length pants and a sweater. Ground fog formed in the low places, creating a heavy, damp mist with the scent of wet earth that clung to my skin. In this light, bushes became strange animals and monsters blocking my way. I jumped back ready to defend myself. I picked up a stick that I tripped over. It became my weapon, and I used it to help me with balance as my eyes strained against the darkness.

I groped onward, when suddenly the earth disappeared from beneath me. Falling backward, I slid, feet first, down a slope. Using the stick as a brake and digging my heels into the dry, hard-packed soil, I continued to slide.

"Ohooo!" I heard someone yell, only to realize it was me.

The pitch of the hill lessened, and my slide slowed until I finally reached the bottom. I struggled to stand, tried to orient myself, and sat instead. *I'll rest for a minute and catch my breath.*

Deep in a gulley, hills on either side blocking any light from the village, something glowed in the distance, perhaps a campfire. I exhaled slowly, tapped my chest, and moved in that direction. *I hope I find friendly people by a fire.*

As I approached, the bitter smell of smoke choked me. I grabbed my nose to stifle a sneeze and stopped close enough to spy on the people by the fire. Hidden by the dark, smoky haze, I crouched down and listened with care. *Do they sound friendly? If they aren't nice, I'll run and hide.* Four people sat around the campfire, two boys and two girls.

Jenny finds four people around the campfire

"We've been looking for weeks, and I don't think we are any closer to finding it. We can't stay here," one of the boys said. Smoke came out of his mouth, and a chill shook me as he talked. "Remind me why we are still looking under rocks?" Cold air wafted over me, again.

"You're right," one of the girls said. "Seems silly. We fell out of the sky. Maybe the passage back is not under a stone." Heated air drifted by as she spoke.

"Maybe that is where the secret is hidden or some hint giving us a clue," a third member of the party said. His voice rattled as if he were walking in a pile of dry leaves. He sounded guarded and unsure. Another cold blast hit me from the first male speaker, whose nostrils flared as he blew an icy mist at Rattle-voice.

"We've already checked the bushes and combed the grass." This voice was harsh at first, then sweetened as a meek smile appeared on her face. She wore a rainbow tiara on her head and flowers in her hair.

"I guess we can look in the trees. That gets us closer to the heavens," the heated voice said.

"Trees are too tall. I don't like heights. We might as well test the clouds, but I don't know how to reach them." Cool air enveloped me.

The discussion made me curious. *How can I reveal myself without scaring everyone?* I didn't want to rile Ice-breath any further.

"Hello, I'm Jenny," I called out to the group from my place in the shadows. "I'm lost and cold. May I join you?"

"Are you real, or are you a ghost?" Ice-breath said. "We can't see you in this infernal darkness. Please step into the light." A blast of chilly air hit me.

I came out from behind the bush. The four people sitting around the fire didn't appear much older than me. Their clothes were ragged and dirty, and their hair was caked with mud. Each appeared underfed as they sat in the dirt.

"I am real," I said and stepped closer. "I got lost in the darkness and then slid into this ravine. May I ask who you are? You don't look like you are from around here."

"She is real," he said as frost spewed out with his breath. "That's good. I'm not fond of ghosts." He introduced his companions. "These are my sisters, Spring and Summer, and he is our brother, Fall. I'm Winter. Summer is hot. Spring and Fall are our colorful siblings. As Winter, I've been accused of being a little cold and harsh. I apologize in advance."

Even though dirty, Spring's shirt sparkled with pastels of light blue, pink, and purple. An aura of orange, yellow, brown, and red surrounded Fall. Green showed through the mud on Summer's dress, and Winter wore a dreary gray, speckled with white.

"Are you lost like me?" I said. "I overheard you talking. What are you looking for?"

"He is a clumsy oaf," Winter said as he peered at Fall with an icy scowl. "I'm sorry, brother, but it's true." Winter frowned. "He fell through the hole in the clouds. Loyal siblings that we are, we had to retrieve him. I told Spring to keep an eye on the hole's location when we came through, so it would be easy to return the way we came. Unfortunately, she's a bit flighty, got turned around, confused, and can't remember which way we came. Now, we are lost. Can you believe it? I'm sure Mother Nature misses us and doesn't know where we are."

Spring, Fall, and Summer lowered their heads. A tear rolled down Fall's cheek. Spring's chin quivered as they sat in silence.

"Each year as the days grow longer," Winter continued. "Our most beautiful sister, Spring, emerges. She whirls in with lion-like winds, leaps, and spins before the snow melts, and rain begins to fall. Flowers bloom, and the earth is replenished. Spring gives way to our sister Summer, hot and bright. Plants mature and bear fruit, and vegetables ripen.

As the days become shorter, our brother, Fall, appears. He brings his palate of colors, and the green vegetation retreats in a spectacularly colorful display. After Fall, I put everything to sleep under a blanket of snow. Then, the cycle begins again."

Winter pointed his finger at Fall. "It is Fall's fault we're here, and at the time when our sister, Summer, is at her peak. Now, summer has gone on too long."

Fall stood and started to pace; bits of leaves spewed off him as he moved. "I just want to go home, so I can take over," Fall said in his rattle-voice.

"If we stay here, there will be no change in seasons," Winter said. "An endless summer is not good. The world will warm, northern snow caps will disappear, and the oceans will rise. I won't be able to replenish the mountain snowpack whose melt fills the streams through summer."

"We are lost," Summer said. "Logic would suggest the best way home is back the way we came, but the clouds are out of reach from here and are always changing."

Winter turned to me. "I'm not happy with Fall or Spring, for that matter. Perhaps, we'll skip fall this year and go straight into a long, cold winter, if only we could." Winter stared at his siblings with narrowed eyes and a wrinkled brow.

I stood with my head erect, shoulders back, hoping to be helpful. "There are mountains to the east of the valley," I said. "Have you noticed that clouds frequently surround their peaks? They poke right up through them. Perhaps, you can find the hole that way?" I tried to sound cheerful.

"Certainly, we haven't had much luck looking under rocks," Summer said, her upper lip curled in disdain.

The four seasons invited me to stay with them until morning. *What would Hank, Ben, and Wes do?* It made sense to stay since I could not find my way home in the darkness. Fall graciously shared his spot by the fire. I was glad I was far away from Winter, who continued to breathe out frosty air as he slept. Soon, I fell asleep despite the constant rattling as Fall breathed. At least he didn't snore.

In the early morning hours, just before dawn, something tickled me awake. I opened my eyes. Oscar licked my face and alternately nudged my arm with his nose. I gave him a hug and didn't want to let him go. He shook and rubbed against me.

"You found me!" I shouted. "I was looking for you." I gave him another giant squeeze and kissed his nose. His coat was matted and muddy. "Have you been out all night, too? Let's go home."

I turned to say goodbye to my friends. They were gone, without a trace. There was no fire, nor any sign that Spring, Summer, Fall, or Winter had ever been there.

I climbed to the top of a hill and oriented myself in the direction of the village. Oscar ran ahead. Before I turned to follow him, I looked at the Eastern Mountains, where the clouds obscured the mountain tops and flowed down the slopes like white waterfalls. The sun peeked through a break in the clouds, and a rainbow appeared.

Mother and Father had a lot to say to me when Oscar and I arrived home. Many of our neighbors had been out all night looking for me. Hannah gave me a big hug. Mother gave me a lecture and made me promise never to do anything like that again. Father just smiled when I told him about the seasons. Later, while we gave Oscar a bath, Hannah told me my story was very creative, a good one to send to our cousins.

Grammie put me on her bad list. She said that I gave her a terrible fright. It's never good to be on that roster, and

I didn't like it, but I knew she still loved me. I think Ben and Wes were on the bad list as well, but I wasn't sure about Hank.

*Did Winter, Summer, Fall, and Spring get home?* They must have. What had become an endless summer, finally changed to fall, and our seasons have been normal ever since.

# FOURTEEN

# "What if"

HANK

We walked to the southern end of the town where we were told there was an outdoor market. The city ended where the river widened, forming a cove that made an excellent natural harbor. The gentle hills surrounding the inlet provided shelter on three sides. A series of jetties extended into the waterway along a narrow strand, where ships of every size and shape bobbed lazily with the tide.

Stacks of crates, pots, barrels, and bundles lined the wharf. Marching up and down slender planks, men off-loaded goods from some boats, loaded goods onto others, and added to the constant motion that jostled us through the throng. We pushed past people crowding the way, coming, and going, dressed in all manner of clothing, every color of the rainbow. Unfamiliar words floated in the air and people from far-off places scurried past. Merchants swarmed tables and shouted as they bargained.

Tall ship flying the black dog banner

We rubbed elbows with the buyers and sellers, sailors, and laborers and stopped to talk, curious to discover where people were from. Strange aromas, a blend of fish, spices, and unfamiliar foods cooking on grills, aroused our appetites, while we bartered with what little we could spare for food and clothes.

"Look, that ship is flying our flag," Ben shouted. Atop the mizzenmast, rigged to carry giant, square sails, a banner waved with *black dog* written on a green and silver field.

I grabbed Ben's arm and motioned to Wes. "Maybe they have news from home," I said and led them through the busy quay to the pier where the Black Dog ship docked.

"Hello," I shouted to one of the sailors standing on the deck. "We're from a village on the Black Dog River. I'm Hank Falk, Matt's and Beth's boy, and this is Ben, my brother, and our cousin, Wes, Nate's and Cara's boy. We just arrived here. We came across the mountains. We've been walking for almost a year. Do you have news from home?"

"I'm Eli Duff. I was years ahead of you at school. Are you on your journey, the three of you? We haven't been home for many a month. I know your family, though, as I'm sure you know mine. Must be some tale to how you got here. We sail the seas, visit ports, and trade our goods for treasures from all over the world. Once we're loaded, we'll be traveling back to the village to sell our riches. We are always looking for crew. Would you like to join us? It will sure be easier than going back the way you came."

"Yes, I'm on my journey," I called back, reassured to hear a familiar name. "We planned on traveling further; we need to find more keys. But I think we are willing to consider heading home. We've been away a year." I turned to Ben and Wes, leaned in, and raised my eyebrows. The prospect of sailing home interested me. I returned my attention to Eli. "We came over the Eastern Mountains," I said. "Maybe we could find keys on our way home with you."

"Are the three of you together on a journey? That's a little different. I traveled alone by sea. You can see I'm still sailing. Well, if you're coming, don't take too long to decide. We plan to set sail tomorrow. I suggest you pay a visit to Captain Dan. He's at the tavern in the village. He's looking for crew as we speak."

I turned to Ben and Wes. "Let's go see the captain."

We walked back into town via the main road, lined by homes, and stores fronted many of them. We passed places to eat and places to buy supplies but didn't stop. When we arrived at the tavern, we found it full of people. Ben surveyed the room, his head on a swivel. Wes stood at the entrance, eyes straining in the dim light, face pale, like a deer spooked by a hunter. I think the noise and commotion overwhelmed him. Ben and Wes waited for my direction as I made my way to the bar to ask the bartender if he knew Captain Dan from the Black Dog ship.

"Of course," he said. "The fellow at the table by the hearth be he. He's looking for hands to help sail home. Might you be interested?" I nodded and waved to my brother and cousin. I led them to the captain's table, where we waited in line for our turn to speak to him. When we introduced ourselves, he broke into a broad smile.

"I know your parents," he said. "I'm sure they're missing you. Are the three of you on your journeys together? Hmm, hadn't heard of that." He paused and looked at each of us in a measured way. Before I could respond, Captain Dan waved me off. "I don't need to know. Looks like you've been able to clean up some. Your clothes look fresh. So, you are looking to go home, are you? Well, that's where we'll be heading. We should be there in three months with smooth sailing and a prevailing wind."

"We bartered for our new clothes. We have no money or much left to barter with to buy passage on your ship, but we are willing to work," I said as I gestured with my arms and shifted my weight from foot to foot. The prospect of going home warmed me inside, and I took comfort in the captain's familiarity with our family.

"Working on a boat at sea for months sounds hard," I overheard Wes whispering to Ben. "I'm unsure about this." Wes sounded much less enthusiastic than I.

"I'd go right now," Ben whispered back.

I guessed the prospect of sailing home motivated Ben, but perhaps he was too eager for Wes. After all, Ben didn't always think things through. I was sure Wes figured that all Ben thought about was the adventure of going to sea, and that opportunity was at hand. We had crossed the mountains and found some of the keys we were after. I expected to find more no matter which way we went. Why not go home? We'd already spent a whole year away.

"I'm happy to work," Ben whispered to Wes. "Let's just sign on."

"What will they have us do? We ought to think about this," Wes whispered back with urgency. "Can we please think about this?" He wrinkled his forehead. I knew him. I was sure he was considering the risks of months at sea and wanted us to proceed with caution.

The captain looked us over again. After a brief pause, he said, "I'll hold three places for you, but you need to let me know before the sun goes down. We set sail at high tide tomorrow."

We found a seat at a table but, having no money and nothing more we wished to barter, we decided not to order and left. We walked about the town and talked. Without paying attention to where we wandered, we ended up back at the dock by the bay. Wes and I sat, immersed in thought as the ships arrived and departed. Ben paced; he appeared happy with his new shoes.

"We're wasting time," I said. "We crossed the mountains like we said we would. I think it's time to go home, and we have an opportunity here and now. We need to come to a decision."

I had given this enough consideration. I no longer needed to take more time to think about it, but I wanted the decision to be unanimous. Wes, on the other hand, appeared tentative about sailing home. He sat quietly with a down-turned mouth and studied the ground. I wanted to understand why he was so hesitant to go to sea.

"Wes, you're not afraid of work, and you loved being on the river at home. I know being on the ocean is not the same as being on the river, but what are you concerned about?"

"What if I can't do what they want me to do?"

"You're a quick learner," Ben said and rolled his eyes. "They'll teach you."

"What if I can't sleep where we are assigned to sleep?"

"I'm sure they have some type of hammock to sleep on," Ben said. "You haven't had any trouble sleeping under the stars on the ground." He rolled his eyes again and threw up his hands.

"Maybe sleeping won't be a problem. What if I can't eat what they'd be serving?"

"Come on, Wes," Ben said. "These concerns are minor. What are you really afraid of?"

"What if I get seasick? What if I fall overboard? What if I get eaten by a shark or swallowed by a whale? What if we find we are in over our heads?" Wes's voice trembled.

"Why would you fall overboard?" Ben asked as he wrung his hands and rocked back and forth, I could tell he was becoming impatient. He went back to pacing.

"What if . . ." Wes started, but I interrupted.

"What-if is the enemy of enthusiasm, an excuse not to do something, and it sounds like you have a what-if for everything," I said. "You can always find some reason to avoid doing something. Sometimes you need to put away your what-ifs and weigh the risks and benefits of what you want. Ask yourself, do the risks outweigh the benefits?" I turned to Ben. "Your enthusiasm is encouraging but too rash. You need to look before you leap. We need to think this thing through."

I turned back to Wes. "Think about your options and everyone's wish to go home. Are all your concerns real? How likely are you to fall off the ship or get eaten by a shark?"

"I'm sure you can do whatever they ask of you," Ben added. "Sleeping in hammocks could be fun. Not knowing for certain all the what-ifs isn't enough to outweigh the joy of going home."

I paused to let Wes think about what we said, then continued. "So, you miss Uncle Nate and Aunt Cara, your other aunts and uncles, and cousins Jenny and Hannah. It wasn't like you didn't do chores when we were home, and I'm sure you don't relish the long walk back across the mountains, as breathtaking as that journey would be. We all want to get home. Please don't let the fear of the unknown, of something different and less familiar, keep you from what you want."

"I do want to go home," Wes finally said. "Going home

would be a good deed. It would certainly please our parents and make them happy." He picked his head up and our eyes met.

"When you have an opportunity to do something of value, don't hesitate, run to do it," I said. "Approach it with enthusiasm, be committed, don't give up. Don't what-if yourself out of doing it."

"Going home," Wes said his eyes brighter. "Just thinking about being home makes me feel warm all over. Okay, let's go back to the tavern and sign on. I'm still not sure what they would have us do. I guess I can do whatever needs to be done."

We ran back to the tavern well before sunset. I think Wes still had some misgivings but didn't express them on the way. Captain Dan still sat at the same table.

"Well?" he said as we approached him. "Do you want to sign on for the voyage home?"

"Yes," I said as spokesman for all. "I'm afraid we don't have much experience with sailing except for what we did on the river back home."

"We'll teach you, and you will do fine. Now, make your way back to the boat and ask for Rebecca. You'll recognize her, she always has a dog by her side. She manages our voyages from here. She'll find space for each of you and give you your assignments."

We skipped and ran all the way back to the wharf. I touched my red bandanna for luck, anticipating our next adventure. I found it interesting how happy I felt about settling on a decision. On our way to the ship, we stopped to sell things we wouldn't need on the voyage, bought more clothes, and treated ourselves to a hearty meal. We kept some tools, my knife, the fire stones, the fishing hooks and line, and my journal. When we reached the boat with the

Black Dog flag, we asked around until we found Rebecca. She had a big, fluffy dog by her side just like Captain Dan said.

"What experience have you had on ships like this?" Rebecca asked.

"None," we responded together.

"We're strong," I said. "We're good workers. We are quick learners, and we are from the village of the Black Dog."

Rebecca smiled. "Well, that's a good start but have you any skills?"

"I can cook," Wes said.

"I can climb, and I'm not afraid of heights," Ben said.

"I'm willing to do whatever tasks I'm assigned," I said, then added, "I can handle tools. Father taught me how to repair things."

"I will assign each of you a place below deck to sleep and store your things. Ben will go with the men who tend the sails. You will learn how to raise, lower, and maintain them. Wes, go to the galley. Learn about procuring supplies, preparing food, and washing the pots. Hank will follow the ship's carpenter. He will teach you how to keep the ship in repair and doctor the crew."

Rebecca took us on a tour of the boat. As we passed through, Wes studied the galley, mess, and scullery. Ben smiled as Rebecca introduced him to the masts and rigging. I looked over the tools and medical equipment in the carpenter's shop. We settled into our quarters below deck before visiting the toilet facility in the bow. Then, Ben, Wes, and I went our separate ways to report to our assigned crew and pitched in as we readied the ship to sail on the next day's high tide.

The next morning, the ship sat low in the water, fully

laden with goods and supplies. As high tide peaked, the crew cast off lines. We drifted away from the dock and out into the main channel of the river. The boat passed through the delta and made its way out to sea. Once in open water, the crew, Ben among them, raised the sails, and we officially began our journey home.

When our work was done, we met at the ship's bow. The water beat a slow, steady rhythm on the hull as the ship cut through the waves. A cool, salt spray washed our faces, and the sweet smell of the ocean wafted over us. We had taken the opportunity to learn new skills, perfect old skills, and make a new beginning. I thought about how much joy it would bring to be home.

"Wes, are you sorry you are on your way home?" I asked.

"No," he said. "I'm quite pleased with myself. Happy about being here and look forward to working hard. The cook takes the time to teach, and I'm more than happy to learn. Thanks for not letting me what-if my way out of this."

"Actually, I love the ocean," Ben said. "It seems endless and mysterious, in constant motion. I can't wait to gaze up at all the stars tonight. I hope the sky is clear."

I held my red bandanna high and let it wave in the wind as I balanced on my toes.

"We took a risk and committed to this voyage," I said as I reviewed Mother's clues in my head. "Ben and Wes, I believe we found our fifth key, *enthusiasm*. You realize we met a difficult challenge today. Call it change, and I learned that change is best handled with enthusiasm, not fear." I pulled Ben and Wes close and hugged them.

# Tadjar

HANK

The wind-filled sails propelled the ship through the water like a skater on ice. The Eastern Mountains, now to our west, always visible to the starboard, and a vast sea to the east, we followed the coast south to the inland passage. Captain Dan planned to take that channel west to the ocean before heading north to the mouth of the Black Dog River and home. The crew taught us, and we learned as quickly as we could. Each evening, once our work was done, we continued to meet at the bow.

"I've been looking all over the ship for Eli but haven't found him," Ben said. "I wanted to find out more about his journey, the keys he found, and the doors they opened."

"I heard he decided to stay in the port and catch a ship headed east," I said. "Too bad. I guess we're still on our own."

"What if my parents don't know it's me when we return home?" Wes asked Ben and me, his hands clenched.

"You don't look any different to me," Ben answered as if a bit puzzled by the question.

"They'll recognize you," I said. "We've been away from home just over a year, according to my journal, although it seems longer than it's been. I'm glad you are over your seasickness."

"Yes, I didn't enjoy watching you toss your dinner each night," Ben said.

"I didn't enjoy that either," Wes said.

"Did the ginger tea help?" I asked. Ginger was an old Chinese cure for nausea the ship's carpenter taught me.

"It did. Thanks." Wes tried to explain. "Time is funny. With the anticipation of arriving home, I'm certain that the trip will seem longer, just as our journey over the mountain seemed so long."

"If the journey appears to be longer, is it really longer?" Ben asked, with a smirk.

"Did you see the commotion in the hold this morning?" I said, too excited to wait for their answer. "John Jorgenson broke his leg. I helped set it. John gritted his teeth in pain until Paul Arnold and I pulled on the leg and snapped it back into place. Then, we tied on wood laths—a splint, Paul called it—and John relaxed and appeared much better."

"That story makes me shudder," Wes said. His body shook before he continued. "When we went ashore in the rowboat yesterday, we picked berries and greens to add to our hardtack bread and salted meat. We threw nets and caught fish and shrimp."

"Did the skiff take on any water?" I asked. "I helped fix it the other day."

"No water in the boat," Wes responded.

"Actually," Ben began, excitement in his tone, "from the top of the mast, I can see forever. Setting the sails suits me;

I love it. I watch the porpoises pop out of the water into the air as they swim along the ship."

"I don't like heights," Wes said. "What if you fall. Aren't you afraid?"

"I tie myself in," Ben said. "No way I can fall. I face the wind, spread my arms, and fly like a bird."

After dusk, near the bow, we lay on our backs and studied the heavens. I thought back to our time in the mountains where, on a dark, moonless night, I gazed at the Milky Way stretched out across the sky, a haze of stars too numerous to count. On a moonlit night, on the sea, everything had a luminous glow, as light reflected off the waves.

I had stopped looking for keys. Mother's note said they were in plain sight. Therefore, all I had to do was pay attention, and I would find them. During the day, we did our jobs. In the evening, we looked forward to meeting at the bow where we shared new experiences. All three of us attended unless assigned to night watch. Then, we spent the night working in shifts with other crew-members, standing by the captain or his mate, eyes focused on the water, looking for any danger or other ships passing in the night.

The seas were mostly calm this time of the year, the winds steady, and the days governed by routine. Occasionally, a squall appeared on the horizon. The captain judged its distance, direction, and speed, and he either outran it or sought shelter by the coast that was never too far. On the chance we'd be caught in a rough sea, we lashed ourselves to a sturdy spar or stayed below to prevent being washed over the side. No one ever was.

By the second week, we made friends with almost all our shipmates. The crew was made up of men from everywhere, only a few from Black Dog. Questions regarding my journey never seemed to come up. People were too busy. One of the sailors came from a far-off land. Tadjar was his name. Facial scars and tattoos gave him a fearsome look. He was tall. When John Jorgenson broke his leg, trapped under a spar, Tadjar lifted the heavy wood as if it were a toothpick and freed him. He walked with a swagger, shoulders back, with pause and deliberation, always calm, as he made no unnecessary movements. He could do anything the captain required.

I worked with Tadjar some but found trying to engage him in conversation difficult. He labored hard and talked hardly at all. When the work was done, he tended to keep to himself. Everyone respected his solitude and left him alone. Neither Ben nor Wes ever spent time with Tadjar, but they remained curious about him.

"Where do you think Tadjar is from?" Ben asked, eager to learn more about this unusual man.

"I don't know, but Ollie the cook said, that Tadjar comes from a place where they eat their enemies," Wes said, his eyes widened. "Not sure I believe him, but I don't wish to find myself on his bad list, or worse, on his dinner menu."

I smirked at Wes. "That's strange. I have never seen him eat meat. As fierce as he appears, I have never observed him arguing with officers or crew members."

One evening, when we met at the bow, we found Tadjar sitting in the middle of the deck, legs crossed, arms resting on his thighs, palms up, fingers slightly flexed, back straight, eyes closed, facing the wind. He took measured breaths, steady and even. We approached him with caution.

"Is he asleep?" Wes whispered.

"I don't think so," Ben said. "He's sitting up, his eyes are shut. He looks like he is in a trance."

Tadjar in a trance with the three boys watching

"Maybe, he's just resting," I said and held a finger to my lips to silence my cousin and brother. "Don't disturb him or he might become angry," I whispered.

Tadjar moved only his chest as he breathed. Ben walked around him then sat down beside him, crossed his legs, rested his forearms on his thighs, positioned his hands like Tadjar's, and shut his eyes. Wes and I did the same.

I listened to my own breathing and wondered what I was supposed to experience. My mind continued to race, and I thought about the trip, my duties, and my experiences that day. As I sat, I began to realize the silence surrounding me wasn't silent. The sails rippled as gusts of wind filled them, waves lapped against the hull, and wood squeaked as the ship bent with the shifting forces of the sea. These sounds silenced my thoughts, my inner voice, and evoked a mental picture of what was around me, sharp and radiant. I was alone, at one with myself and nature, yet connected to Wes and Ben, and Tadjar, as we sat together, our senses subjected to the same experience.

"Okay," Ben said. "I'm not sure I get it. What are we doing here?"

My eyes popped open, jolted out of my reverie. I looked from Ben to Wes, then to Tadjar.

Tadjar opened his eyes. I expected his body to tense, face to redden, eyes narrowed with rage. Instead, he smiled. His gaze appeared distant and reflective as he turned to Ben. *Does he feel sad for what Ben apparently didn't experience?* He hadn't acknowledged us during the trip except to be polite and always say hello. He apparently didn't object to our curiosity in his behavior. I relaxed.

"Ben, I was visiting silence," Tadjar said in kind, accented tones. "My grandfather taught me this. I find the practice gives me peace of mind. May I teach you?"

"Okay, but is silence something you can actually visit?" Ben asked, scratching his cheek, suggesting to me he was surprised that Tadjar knew his name.

"It has been said, that by listening, you discover an ancient principle: Silence is golden, speech is silver," Tadjar said. "Think about it. While you talk, you cannot listen, so you should only speak when you have something meaningful to say. Otherwise, you should always pay attention. That is a good way to learn. When I visit silence, I attend to the sounds all around me and imagine what I perceive."

Tadjar asked us to sit as he sat, close our eyes, and concentrate on not speaking aloud or to ourselves. He suggested we experience all that was going on around us without interacting or commenting internally.

"Listen carefully in silence," Tadjar said, his voice a whisper. "You must be quiet to hear the spirits. You see, they speak very softly. You may not notice them if you make any noise."

We did as Tadjar suggested. After that night, when we sat with Tadjar at the bow, we practiced listening for the spirits. It took time, but eventually, I experienced the inner peace Tadjar described.

Before going to sleep, I took out the wooden box Mother had given us. It shook as I opened it. I took out the paper and reviewed the clues. "Ben, Wes," I said with urgency. "We found another key, number six! *Practice silence . . .*"

## SIXTEEN

# The Storm

BEN

From the crow's nest at the top of the mainmast, I spotted dark clouds gathering on the horizon and smelled the sweet, pungent odor of ozone carried on the wind. Lightening flashed, followed by rolling thunder, too close for comfort.

"We're heading into a storm," I called to the first mate. "Tell the Captain." I climbed down the rope ladder from my post.

Captain Dan directed the ship sharply away from the fast-approaching storm, but he couldn't outrun it. Instead, he turned the vessel into the wind. I sprinted to the hatch and stairs to go below, but the storm struck, tearing me away from the entrance. Wind, rain, and the rolling ship disoriented me. I fell. Seawater flooded across the deck and carried me with it as my arms flailed, fighting for breath, straining, hands groping for something to hold on to. The crew had no time to reef the sails, and the captain couldn't keep the vessel headed into the wind to gain control. The storm changed direction constantly, spinning us as if we were a top. Massive gusts filled the partially lowered sails, driving the vessel forward with sudden spurts of speed. The wind shifted again, and our ship heeled over and nearly capsized.

Ben in the sea on driftwood

Waves washed over me, filling my mouth with saltwater. Rain fell in heavy sheets, stung my face, and blurred my vision. I reached out again for anything to grab. The sea tossed the ship about like a piece of driftwood as I was swept from starboard to port and back again. I gripped a post, knuckles white, but I was unable to hold on. The raging waters dragged me from the deck and into the angry sea. The wind howled like a wounded wolf. I didn't want to die.

The bow of the ship dipped, then rose out of the water and rolled over on its side. A submerged stony mound appeared in the wake of the wave and crushed the hull below the deck rail. The sea pounded the ship against the rock, and the vessel began to break apart. In minutes, the ship disappeared beneath the waves. The crew escaped in lifeboats and headed away from the spreading wreckage before the ship sank. Nothing but floating debris remained where the ship had been.

I struggled to stay afloat. My heart raced as I fought hard not to drown, beating the water with my arms, kicking fiercely. Panic overcame me. *I'm going to die!* Then I remembered what I had learned about swimming and concentrated on keeping my head up and treading water slowly to conserve energy. I reached some floating debris, held tight, and rode out the storm that moved on as quickly as it had begun. I looked around. The ship was gone.

The sea calmed, and the sky brightened. I saw skiffs already at the horizon, almost out of sight.

"I'm here! Don't leave me!" I shouted, but no one responded, clearly out of view and earshot. I hoped Wes and Hank were safe and bit my upper lip as I realized my situation, left behind, abandoned. My heart sank. I could hardly breathe from the fear. "I can't be the only one here. Please, don't let me be alone."

# SEVENTEEN

# Alone

### BEN

"Wes! Wes! Hank!" I called. "Can anyone hear me? Are you okay? Can you hear me?"

"Ben! I'm here. I'm here!" Wes called back across the water.

"Wes, is that you?"

"Yes, it's me! Help me, I'm scared. What if there are sharks?"

"I'm here too!" Hank shouted. "We refused to climb into the lifeboats until we found you, but then it was too late. They left without us."

"Try to guide your floats to me, and I'll meet you halfway," I said.

It seemed forever before the pieces of wood each of us floated on came together. My arms and legs ached with exhaustion, but once reunited with Hank and Wes, I relaxed a little, although far from being safely out of trouble. At least, we had each other.

A length of rope floated in the debris near us. I swam out to retrieve it. Hank and I joined several pieces of wood to create a platform, and we climbed up on it. The wind blew toward the shore, which was visible on the horizon. We scanned the sea for other crew members but saw no one. The skiffs filled with men were long out of sight. I surveyed the area again, but it held nothing but flotsam and us. We were truly alone.

"We are so lucky," Hank said. "We could have drowned today."

"Luck?" I countered, taken aback by what Hank said. "I didn't drown because I knew how to swim."

"Be grateful you knew how to swim and thank those who had the foresight to teach you." Hank sounded annoyed. "Try to show some humility."

"What do you mean?" I said "How don't I have humility, whatever that is. Someone must have told you; I'd guess it was Father. Now, I suppose, you're going to tell me."

We escaped a very scary trial, but I didn't want to let on just how scared I was. In any event, I was not in the mood for a lecture from my big brother.

"I'll tell you what I learned, and, yes, it is something Father taught me when I acted arrogantly," Hank said. "Humility is knowing who you are, acknowledging your shortcomings, and appreciating others' accomplishments. Think about it."

"Being able to swim was my accomplishment," I shot back. As we floated on the water, my level of anxiety ebbed like the tide, but fatigue overcame me. I noticed that Wes had a tight grip on the rope that held our crude craft together. Wes's face was pale, eyes unfocused; he was half off the raft, his legs submerged. I reached out, grabbed his belt, and pulled him up out of the water.

"Humility is also about space—how much you take up

in the world," Hank continued. "You earn space by who you are and how you live your life. If you take up more than you deserve, you lack humility. Take too little and you have no self-esteem. You give others—"

"So, how am I taking up too much space, big brother?" I interrupted him, annoyed that he had decided to continue to lecture me as we sat in the middle of the sea without food or fresh water, separated from the rest of the crew, isolated. *Maybe he's trying to distract himself from our predicament.* I didn't appreciate the unsolicited advice, but I couldn't make him stop. I turned away from Hank and touched Wes on the shoulder, hoping to comfort him.

"One way you give others space is by listening and showing respect, and not interrupting," Hank said. "Do you remember who taught you how to swim?"

*Is he challenging me?* "Oh," I said. "You did, and I am grateful. Is that enough respect? I still don't think that now is the time to give me a lecture."

"You saved yourself because you could swim. Be gracious and give thanks to those who taught you. Without that gift, you would have died today. I remember how you came to learn to swim. Do you? You were almost eight at the time."

"'Where's Ben?' I asked Wes that day. 'Up there,' Wes said and casually pointed to an old oak tree where you sat on a limb at the top. You peered down at me with a smile on your face like the Cheshire cat."

Wes opened his eyes; some color had returned to his face, as he listened to Hank's tale.

"I shouted, 'Come down and don't fall.' Because, if you fell, Mother and Father would hold me responsible. Instead of coming down, you teased me by swinging from a branch that overhung the river some thirty feet below and laughed at me. 'Stop it! That limb's not strong enough to hold you,' I said. 'Yes, it is,' you called back and began to swing and bounce on it harder. *Snap*, the limb broke. That sound still resonates in my head, and it chills me. You came tumbling through the branches to the water. I held my breath and stood frozen in place as you fell. You hit the water on your belly, bobbed in the river, and flailed your arms. I unfroze, dove into the water to save you, and dragged your limp body to the bank.

"'Ben, Ben!' I yelled. At first, you didn't respond. Water shot out of your mouth. I turned you on your side and pounded firmly on your back. Caught up in the moment, I didn't react emotionally until it was clear you were still alive. Wes ran to fetch Father and Uncle Nate. You coughed and your eyes opened. Then, you turned your head to me and smiled. I wanted to smack you.

"'Stay out of the trees!' I said, then gave you a hug.

"When Father and Uncle Nate arrived, they lectured me about keeping a better eye on you and Wes. They didn't say anything about your climbing trees. I sat and listened respectfully, although I still wanted to pummel you for giving me such a fright. The lecture ended with a plan for me to teach you and Wes how to swim. Father had already taught me."

"Okay, I get it," I said. "You taught me to swim. Thanks. Should I call you Father? You're sounding just like him. Actually, I am truly thankful, Hank. Wonderful story. But now, what do we do?"

"What if we must stay here, on this raft?" Wes moaned. "What if we don't know where we are? What if we must float here forever until we die of thirst and hunger?" Wes tightened his grip on the rope again.

"The current and the wind appear to be taking us to the

shore," Hank said. "I believe the land is not that far off, maybe a mile. I think we should wait it out and we'll get to land soon enough, or we can stand, make like sails, and take advantage of this wind."

We stood for a while, but that proved of little benefit. The raft constantly threatened to break apart or tip over. As each of us grew fatigued, we sat down. The raft, driven by the wind and the current, continued to move us slowly to the shore.

A school of dolphins surrounded the raft. I sat up and smiled as they surfaced, jumped, and swam back and forth. Flying fish took flight racing to flee the dolphins. Wes leaned over the side, reached out, and touched a dolphin as it brushed up against the raft. At once, a large spout of water shot up behind us. A huge gray mass broke the surface, followed by a tail. The water, displaced by the giant, rocked the raft and nearly sent us overboard. The whale resurfaced and moved slowly toward us, nudging our crude craft gently toward the shore. We held onto the raft, smiling ear to ear, as the Goliath propelled us. The dolphins continued to follow, playing all around us. Flying fish landed on the raft briefly and wiggled off. The whale left us in the shallows, turned, and headed back to the depths with the dolphins. I surveyed the sea but saw no other survivors.

"I'll be happy with land under my feet again, but I enjoyed that ride," Hank said. "I'm truly thankful for our sea friends. Now, we better look for fresh water and things to eat."

The three of us jumped off the raft and pulled it the rest of the way to the shore. Wreckage from the ship had washed onto the beach and floated in the water all around us. Hank started gathering whatever he could find and dragged remains of the wreck to dry sand above the tide line. I guessed we would sift through it later for usable gear. Wes and I headed into the forest to find fresh water and food.

Useful items the boys dragged ashore from the
ship wreckage

Wes didn't go far. "Look what I've found," he said, excitement in his voice. "Berries and hazelnuts, grasses, asparagus, cattail, clover, and sunflowers."

"How do you know that?" I asked as I followed Wes gathering the bounty.

"The cook taught me how to gather food along the coast."

Wes and I worked together, grazing as we gathered. We made our shirts into bags by tying knots in the sleeves and neck. I quenched my thirst from a stream and realized I would need a leather pouch or some type of canteen to carry water.

"I think we've gathered enough for now," I called to Wes. "Let's go back to Hank." I was glad to see Wes had color in his face.

"There is plenty to eat here," Wes said. "I'm feeling better about our situation, but what if . . ."

I didn't answer him.

"Hank, Hank," Wes called as soon as he reached the beach. "I found a blackberry bush."

I shouted louder to get Hank's attention, unwilling to be outdone by Wes. "I found two blackberry bushes and blueberries."

Wes gave me a nasty stare. "I found a stream." He smirked.

"I found two streams, strawberries, and dandelions," I said.

"Stop it, you two," Hank said. "Enough. I'm glad you both brought back plenty to eat and we have fresh water to drink, but why are you competing? Both of you are taking up more space than either of you deserve."

I held my breath to regain my composure.

Hank continued. "Now, be happy with what each of you found. I know I am. Try to remember what I said earlier about humility." He paused and his eyes brightened as if a light went on in his head. "Be humble, Mother wrote. That is one of the keys." He frowned. "My backpack must have been lost with the ship. That's where I kept Mother's note and my journal." He sighed. "No worry, I memorized the clues. *Humility* will be key number seven.

"Great, but please don't give us another lecture," I said. "I get it." I didn't want to spar with Wes any longer. Although, I admitted to being happy: We found another key.

"Look what I've pulled out of this mess so far," Hank

said, changing the subject to focus on our next task: returning home. He pointed to an array of litter spread across the sand. "Here's a case marked tools. I'm surprised it didn't sink. These water-tight barrels floated quite well. I recovered plenty of rope tangled in the debris, sacks of clothes including a trunk filled with shoes. Too bad they are mostly saltwater-logged and covered with sand.

"We should consider making a raft bigger and stronger than the one we used to drift to land, fashion a sail, and make a tent to protect us from the sun and rain. The barrels would make it more seaworthy." Hank gestured with his arms as he explained his plan. I listened intently and gave Hank all the space he needed.

When Hank finished, I spoke first. "Actually, I think walking on solid ground is better than going back on the water."

Hank gave me a curious look. "That's not your usual adventuresome self . . ."

Wes spoke up before Hank could say more. "What if we got caught in another storm? I agree with Ben. I don't want to go back to sea."

"Okay, we'll walk," Hank said. "I'm not entirely sure in which direction. We have choices. While we sort this out, may I have some of the food and water you collected? I'm assuming you remembered to bring some back for me."

We showed Hank what we found. Hank always kept his firestone with him and hadn't lost it in the storm. I used a pot pulled from the wreckage to fetch water. Hank started a fire and set the water to boil.

"When we finish eating," Hank said, "let's hunt through this jumble of trash. I'm sure we'll find plenty of things we can use on our journey home."

# EIGHTEEN

# The Cove

WES

I was alone in the ocean, swimming hard against the current. An eddy grew behind me and became a deep whirlpool. The swirling water clawed at my legs, wouldn't let me go, pulling me backward. Choking and sputtering, I fought to raise my head above the water and beat the water with my arms. My heart pounded as I struggled to breathe. Rope entangled me, leaving me unable to overcome the force of the water that sucked me deeper into the hole.

"Hank, Ben, help me!" I shouted with my last breath, but no words came out of my mouth. Above me, Ben appeared, and I reached for him, desperate to grab his outstretched hand. I couldn't reach him. "Help me!" I cried. The current dragged me under as I made one last hard kick to break free.

"Wes, Wes," Ben shouted.

I sat up, drenched in sweat. Ben shook me. "You were dreaming again. It's okay. You kicked and called for Hank and me. We're right here."

I didn't want to admit that I needed more time to

recover from the trauma of the shipwreck. I'm never happy when my what-ifs come true. We came close to death. Ben seemed normal, unfazed, but nothing ever disturbed him. Hank acted calm on the outside, lost in preparations for the next leg of our trip. My faith in our decisions had been badly shaken, but I had to trust Hank would still lead us home.

Wes visiting silence

I sat on the beach and visited silence, the way Tadjar had taught us, hoping he boarded a lifeboat and was safe. We searched up and down the shore for other survivors but found none.

When I rested, I studied the birds nesting in the rocky

cliffs surrounding us and observed the sea stretching to the horizon. The dark blue water turned pale green as it entered our shallow cove. Waves rose and fell, capped in white as they crested, broke, and washed across the beach and the outcroppings of rock protruding from the sand. My mind wandered. *How lucky not to be alone.*

Beyond the sand, a mysterious, dark, dense forest of giant trees grew. We entered the woods to gather food, but none of us ventured far. We built our camp at the edge of the forest, high enough to be safe from the surging tide. We saw no signs of people and assumed there were none. It was peaceful here, and my confidence started to return. The time would soon arrive when we had to be on our way. I knew we couldn't stay much longer, wasting precious time before the cold weather returned. I wanted to go home to our valley.

For days, new debris from the wreck littered the beaches around us. I spent hours with Ben and Hank looking for usable items as we sifted through the remains.

On day four after the shipwreck, Ben found Paul Arnold. His body washed up on the beach a mile from our camp. Ben came running to us. He breathed heavily, so upset he could hardly speak. We followed him back to where he discovered Paul. At first, we stared, unable to act, paralyzed. None of us had seen a dead person before, aside from in a casket once. Buzzards circled above. Hordes of flies few around him. I barely recognized Paul's bloated face, lips contracted, drawn into a painful grimace above his teeth, eyes a milky gray. I pulled my shirt over my nose and mouth to ward off the sickening odor of decay, an odor as rotten as anything I ever encountered. I turned away and vomited.

"We need to bury Paul," Hank said. "Give me a hand."

I held my breath as we dragged Paul's body to higher ground at the edge of the forest, out of reach of the tides. We dug a shallow grave in the sand with our hands and sticks and lowered his body into it.

"Wes and Ben, you didn't know Paul well, but he had mentored me as I learned how to maintain the ship and provide medical care for the crew," Hank said as we stood around the grave, our heads bowed in respect. "We each should say something."

"Paul was always nice to us," Ben said.

"He was from our valley. A good man," I added.

"He was a good patient teacher, always kind. He showed me how to set John Jorgenson's broken leg," Hank said. "Rest in peace, Paul."

My eyes moistened as we covered him with sand. We said a prayer after we finished putting him in the ground. Hank carved his name and "Drowned at Sea" on a stake. To mark the grave, we placed stones on the site, with the marker at the head. I was glad we didn't find anyone else.

# NINETEEN

# Onward

WES

In a crate holding tools, Hank found a knife and strapped it to his hip. Ben opened a box containing pots and pans. Under a board separating the upper portion of the barrel from the lower, I discovered canvas needles, pins of various sizes, and string strong enough for fishing. I bent the pins into hooks. Hank located a barrel of salted beef unharmed by the sea and rolled it back to camp. Saltwater and sand ruined most of what we uncovered, but we cleaned and salvaged enough cloth, leather, clothes, and sheeting from the sails to reoutfit us.

As we selected what we would take with us, I looked to Hank to figure out which way to go. We found a box containing maps, charts, and a small logbook with pencils Hank could use to replace his journal, but most of the contents were destroyed by the sea. At least we had an idea of general directions, although I still couldn't find the exact location where the ship went down. Hank suggested we head north, backtracking for a time before turning west toward home. Ben looked puzzled. Hank drew a map in the sand to try to clarify.

"We are here," Hank said as he drew a cove in the shore line. "The mountains are west of us, here." Hank put stones where he thought the mountains were and stuck a stick where he believed home to be, up and to the left of the mountains. "It might be shorter to go northwest, the most direct route, but we have no idea what we would encounter. I know that's where the mountains are. We could be walking in the high country for months. We also don't know how far south we sailed. I expect we will need to cross the mountains at some point. If we go south to the passage then west before turning north, like the ship was planning to go, we will avoid the mountains." Hank traced a path down the coast to the inland passage then west before turning north to home. "We have no idea how far out of our way or how long that would take."

Hank looked at Ben, then me. When we said nothing, he continued.

"North along the coast here." Hank drew a line in the sand along the right edge of the map. "Then west. It will be easier with fewer mountains to cross than if we go northwest from here.

"If we leave soon, we can take advantage of the weather and the food ripening in the forest," he said. "If we wait, winter will come, and, who knows, what will happen? Probably be cold, wet, and snowy."

"Fine with me," Ben said. "I made sacks for water out of leather, and we could sew bigger bags out of the canvas to make packs to carry our supplies. I think we have enough material to make blankets to keep us dry in the rain and serve as tents at night."

After several days, we gathered and organized what we

needed and cleaned and dried what we wanted to take with us. We agreed to follow the coast north. If the beach continued, the way would be easy, even if walking on sand was tiresome.

In the morning, we left our home by the cove. Luckily, we found lots of footwear in the wreckage. I would have been happier if they fit. Ben's fit no better than mine. Hank didn't complain. I did as well barefoot as I did with my new boots and took mine off. By day two, the beach began to narrow, and the cliffs rose abruptly trapping us by the water. With less sand and more rocks to walk on, I put the boots back on.

We entered a cove surrounded by giant sand dunes. A gap in a dune allowed us to make our way up a steep hill. The climb was slow and hard, but once we reached the top, I looked out at the water that spread out below us for as far as I could see. Low grasses covered the ground. Trees and gnarled shrubs on the bluff, bent away from the sea by the prevailing winds, appeared to be paying homage to the tall pines in the forest behind them. The sun was warm, and fatigue set in. Ben asked Hank and me if we wanted to take a break. I said yes, and rushed to take my boots off, to let my feet air, and to check for blisters. When Ben saw me take my shoes off, he did the same.

We sat in the shade under a scrub oak, surveyed the great expanse of ocean before us, and listened to the crash of the sea against the shore. Ben took a piece of salted beef and popped it into his mouth. He started to chew, gagged, and spit it out. I laughed as he scowled at me.

"You soak that stuff before you boil it. You could eat it raw but you don't have to," I shouted at him.

"I didn't know," Ben said. "I ate it on the ship with no problem."

In the shade of the scrub oak

"That's because we prepared it," I said. "I'll go look for berries and vegetables. We can boil some meat later for supper unless you eat it all before I come back."

I got up and placed some salted beef in a pot to soak. I put my boots back on, took my water pouch, and went into the forest. Ben and Hank decided to rest and, I suspect, quickly fell asleep.

# TWENTY

# The Fairy Ring

WES

I walked along a path made by deer until I came to a small clearing surrounded by a ring of trees, a redwood fairy ring. Uncle Ross told me once how a fairy ring formed. It started with a large, old redwood. When the old tree died, new trees appeared in a circle surrounding the trunk of the fallen tree, forming a ring. I stood in the middle and tilted my head back and looked up. The trees blocked the sun's light, keeping the forest floor in a haze. The dust and mist floating in the damp, musky air didn't help to make things any brighter. Only the occasional bird's call and chatter of insects broke the silence that was all around me. Within the fairy ring, I discovered mushrooms. Once convinced they weren't poisonous, I placed them in my sack. Pleased with my find, I turned to leave. A rustling of leaves startled me.

"Excuse me, kind sir. Excuse me," someone said in a rather unpleasant, nasal voice.

# FIFTEEN KEYS

Within a ring of trees, mushrooms grew

I spun around and stepped back. In my haste, I fell, spilling my bag of mushrooms. When I looked up, I was face-to-face with a little man, round as a ball. He wore tight pants and a vest over his woolen shirt that hung nearly to his knees. A brimless peaked hat, the top of which bent to the side, balanced on his head. His face was old and wrinkled, his mouth turned down and a stern look in his eyes. He thrust his face inches from mine. Although I was surprised by his sudden appearance, his dress evoked laughter, not fear. Out of respect, I strained to stifle a chuckle.

"Excuse me, my friend, and I use that term loosely," he said. "Those mushrooms you picked are my mushrooms."

"I didn't know," I said as I gagged on his breath. "May I keep them?"

"Keep my mushrooms? I think not. Did you raise them and nurture them?"

"No. I found them and picked them. Did you raise them and nurture them?" I struggled not to inhale, moved away from him, and tried to stand.

"No. The mushrooms appear out of the ground, but they appear here, in the fairy ring over which I preside," he said and stepped toward me.

"Really," I said. I waved my hands in front of me to clear the air and moved back to keep some distance between the little man and me. I began to carefully retrieve the mushrooms and placed them back into my sack. "How do I know what you say is true?"

"Truth?" the little man said. "Truth is what is. Truth is reality. Truth is the foundation by which all things interact in our world. Truth has a scientific basis. Truth can be proven. Honestly, though, I must admit, what is true today, may not be true tomorrow."

"Oh," I said. "If truth may change, do you think I should come back tomorrow to pick the mushrooms?"

"Umm, kind sir, perhaps truth is related to time or more likely perception, mine versus yours, or maybe situation and, therefore, changeable by alternative proof. That may be, but you should not tell lies."

"I haven't lied," I said in my defense and took another step back. "I just picked some mushrooms."

"My mushrooms."

"So, you say, but what if the mushrooms aren't yours?"

"Ah, to know is to believe, and I know the mushrooms are mine. I have faith you will agree. My faith comes from my heart and is linked to trust. If you have faith, then I trust you will agree the mushrooms are mine."

"I don't know you. Without knowing you, why should I believe you? My Father taught me faith comes from experience, and trust is earned based on those experiences. I'm not sure, given our limited time together, you've earned my trust."

"I know you have my mushrooms now. That became our truth when you picked them and placed them in your bag," the little man said with a sad kind of look.

"May I keep your mushrooms?" I asked and directed my gaze to the ground.

"How can I refuse? They are no longer mine. They are yours since they are now in your possession. However, I do so very much appreciate your asking."

My head spun. He had come full circle. *Perhaps that is why they call it a fairy "ring."* I thanked the little man for sharing his mushrooms with me, said goodbye, and turned again to leave.

I hesitated. "Would you like some of my mushrooms?" I

said as I turned back to face him, but he had already disappeared.

I walked back to where I left my cousins. I thought about my conversation with the little man. Is truth changeable? If so, how can truth be true? Perhaps the truth is true only for the moment. Faith is related to experience. Faith is not tangible, and can't be held in your hand, nor does faith require proof, but it does allow for trust. I shook my head. "I guess what I need more than truth is faith and trust," I said to myself aloud.

I stepped out of the forest and found Ben and Hank asleep under the tree where I left them. I made a fire and cooked the mushrooms with some nuts, wild cabbage, and Ben's salted beef, now adequately soaked. Ben and Hank awoke to the pleasant aroma of stew. I couldn't wait to tell them about the fairy ring, the strange little man, and what I had learned about truth, faith, and trust.

I had a hunch that *truth, faith,* and *trust* were among the keys we sought. Hank confirmed that I was right, but I still didn't understand how these words would open doors. Hank recited Aunt Beth's note.

*They are in plain sight so always be looking, balance is the · clue. Fifteen in all and nothing new. Have patience, be humble, grateful, and most important true. Have faith, honor all, and be generous too. Show enthusiasm, maintain order, and strive for simplicity. I have trust in you. Practice silence, be happy, show compassion, and maintain equanimity through and through.*

"Good work," Hank said to me. "That makes ten keys, check them off: *gratitude, order, simplicity, patience, enthusiasm, silence, humility, truth, faith,* and *trust.* We need five more. I'll write in the logbook each key, where we found them, and what we learned."

"Did you ask the man if he knew the way to the Valley of the Black Dog?" Ben asked, excited by the knowledge people lived here.

"I would be afraid of being sent in circles based on the path our conversation took," I said. "Besides, the truth he told us today might not be true tomorrow. That's a problem. Although in the end, he did let me keep the mushrooms."

"I think we should go back into the forest to find the little man to see if he can direct us," Hank said. "But, first, let's eat."

After eating, we packed our gear and headed back into the woods to look for the little man, but as hard as I tried, I couldn't lead us to the fairy ring where I'd found the mushrooms. I turned to my cousins and said, "What do you think? Should we go back to the coast and continue north that way or head northwest from here through this forest?"

# TWENTY-ONE

# Too Much Loving Kindness?

## HANNAH

Jenny and I finished our chores and departed for Flo's shop as Mother requested. Jenny carried a package in her backpack that our mother had wrapped with care. I didn't know what it was. Maybe it was something Mother wanted Flo to sell on consignment.

"Promise me you will deliver the package to Flo's shop before she closes for the day," Mother said as we left.

Dust rose around us as we strolled on the dry, clay-covered road. Jenny and I stayed to the right to avoid the oncoming traffic. Most people walked like us, some rode horses, some traveled in horse-drawn carts, and an occasional person pedaled by on a bicycle. Jenny placed a scarf over her mouth and nose to keep the dust out. I did the same. I often followed what my big sister did.

"It's been over a year since Hank, Ben, and Wes left on their journey," Jenny said.

I was eight when they left, and I remembered them as mostly tall and rough. It seemed so long ago.

"The valley's changed a lot. More people here for one,

and our village has grown into a town," Jenny remarked. "The boys might not even recognize it."

As we walked along, questions about our cousins and their journey came to mind. My big sister knew a lot, so I thought about asking her, although she didn't always like when I questioned her about things.

"Why did Hank, Ben, and Wes have to go away?" I asked.

"It's a tradition that began almost a hundred years ago with the first settlers in our village. The way I heard it, the first people thought the younger folks were becoming too soft. Life was too easy. The people here grew crops and raised sheep and cattle. That was hard work, but it wasn't like hunting and gathering. As I understand it, the Elders— old, wise people—feared the children wouldn't appreciate what they were born into. They met and decided that when a boy or girl turned seventeen, they had to go on a journey."

"They *made* them go away?" I said. My mouth fell open.

"Fathers and mothers prepared their sons and daughters to be able to survive in the wilderness without much except what they found, which was pretty much normal living for the original families. The Elders picked seventeen as the age to go away to re-create the experience of the first settlers by living on their own for a year."

"Will they make us go away?"

"Yes. At first, only seventeen-year-old boys went on the journey, but after a few years, girls went too. When they returned, they were eligible to become leaders in the community, and one day, Elders. So, the answer is yes. We will go."

"When we are seventeen?"

"Yes."

"Early on, all seventeen-year-olds went. I don't think there were a lot of them. With time some families elected not to send their children. Not our family; we must go. Father says it's an unbroken chain; everyone has always gone."

"Can we go just like Hank, Ben, and Wes?"

"No, you won't be seventeen when I turn seventeen."

"Ben and Wes went with Hank. They weren't seventeen. I want to go with you."

I waited for a response, but Jenny didn't answer and walked along the road in silence.

"Look at that poor, old woman carrying those buckets," I said, breaking the silence. "Her shoulders are stooped, and her head is down. I bet she is struggling. Can we help her?"

"She's walking in the opposite direction," Jenny said, dismissing me. "We must get to town."

"I know, but we could help her for at least a short distance, and then we could be on our way again. We have time. It would be a good deed."

When the old woman was close to us, we stopped, and I called out to her. "Can we give you a hand?"

"I would be grateful," the old woman said.

Jenny took the bucket filled with ears of corn and bags of flour. I took the other bucket stuffed with sticks for kindling.

"Where are you going?" Jenny asked.

I guessed Jenny was trying to gauge how far out of our way we might be walking. I didn't care so long as we helped her.

"I'm returning to my home not far from here. Aren't you Ross and Annie's girls? Have you heard any news from your cousins?" We shook our heads, no. "You don't have to help me the whole way, although I do appreciate your assistance. I'm sorry I have nothing to give you in return."

"It is our pleasure," I said. Jenny politely smiled and bowed, but I guessed she was annoyed at me for making us go out of our way. We reached the old woman's village. Once there, having rested, the old woman easily picked up the buckets. She thanked us and said goodbye, and we started back toward town.

"You didn't say anything when I said I wanted to go with you on your journey."

"Right," Jenny said. "I'll need to think about that."

It seemed doubtful to me that Jenny wanted me to go on her journey with her.

"You don't want me to go with you?" I asked.

"You can go with me." Jenny hesitated. "Maybe."

"You said you only had to go away for a year. Shouldn't Hank, Ben, and Wes be back already?"

Jenny's mouth quivered; her lips turned down. "I need to believe they are okay. They must find keys, which makes the journey a quest, but the locations of the keys are secret. The Elders added the rule you can't come back without the keys. Perhaps they are having trouble finding them."

We walked a mile past the point where we had met the old woman and approached a steep bridge, at the base of which, I spied a man trying to push a cart up the incline. His face turned red as he struggled to move his wagon.

"Can we help you?" I asked. Jenny gave me a surprised look.

"We must get to Flo's shop," she whispered.

"I'd appreciate that," the man said. "Can't seem to get this wagon over the bridge. These fruits and vegetables need to get to the market just outside the village."

Jenny and Hannah help the man with the cart

Jenny and I got behind the cart with the man and pushed, and the cart began to move slowly up the incline. Once we crested the incline, we eased it down the other side.

"Thank you," the man said, quite pleased. "Would you each like a peach? They are ripe, fresh, and sweet. Perfect peaches."

"Helping was our pleasure," I said. Jenny kicked me and graciously accepted the peaches. The man smiled.

"Thank you," Jenny said and pulled me in the direction of the village.

I took a moment to watch the man push his wagon along the road. "Let's go down to the river beneath the bridge, away from this dusty road, and eat our peaches," I suggested.

Jenny shook her head and threw up her arms. "We don't have all day."

She followed me off the road down a path that led to the edge of a stream. We sat down on a rock and removed the scarves from our faces. I bit into the peach. Its juices dripped down my chin and melted onto my tongue, and its fresh, sweet aroma filled my nose.

I still had questions. "How will being away for a year prepare me to be an elder?"

"I'm not sure," Jenny said. "The journey will teach you how to get along on your own, for one, and give you an appreciation for what you had before you left. You might meet new people and learn new things. The keys you find are supposed to open doors."

As I ate my peach, I watched the water flow past us. The stream was crystal clear, rippled by current and breeze. A fisherman stood in the stream, casting and retrieving his line. Suddenly, the line straightened. He pulled up sharply on the rod and set the hook. His fishing pole bent with the weight of the fish, and the line whipped back and forth as the fish ran in a mad dash to get free. The fish jumped out of the water and shook but couldn't dislodge the hook. The fisherman skillfully moved his rod up and down as he reeled in the fish and maneuvered it to the riverbank. He spotted me watching him.

"Can you help me land this fish?" the fisherman asked. "My net is on the bank by my bucket."

Having watched the fisherman catch the fish, I was more than pleased to help him land it. I fetched the net, slid it under the fish, and lifted it out of the water. The man took the net from me and unhooked the fish. He placed his catch in the bucket, where several other fish were swimming.

"Thank you," the fisherman said.

"My pleasure," I said and strutted back to Jenny quite pleased with myself.

"I think we've wasted enough time," Jenny said. "The day is disappearing. The peach was delicious, but we need to get moving, little sister."

Jenny made it clear she was finished relaxing by the stream, dragged me off the rock on which I sat, and returned us to the road, so we could continue to make our way to Flo. I wanted to see how many loving kindnesses I could do in one day and set a standard for good. It looked like I was up to three, and I was sure I couldn't do too many nice things for people.

I still didn't know whether Jenny would let me come with her on her journey.

"Well, can I join you on your journey?" I asked once I got up the nerve and prepared myself for the answer.

"I think the Elders intended each of us to journey alone, but given that Hank, Ben, and Wes did it together, I guess it would be all right. Let's make this our secret for now."

It was well past the noon hour. We still had quite a way to go. We walked on until I spotted a boy sitting by the side of the road. Tears ran down his face.

"That's Benji from school," Jenny pointed out to me.

I went over to him. "Are you okay?" I asked.

Benji was sitting with his head in his hands. looking at the ground. A dog leash lay on the ground next to him, but there was no dog.

"KC ran away," Benji said between sobs. "I've been waiting for her to come back, but she's gone."

"Perhaps we can find her," I said. "Did you see which way she went?"

"She went that way," he said between sobs and pointed to a stand of trees a short distance down a hill and across a field away from the road.

"Maybe we should start there?" I asked.

"I don't think we have time," Jenny interjected. She pointed at the sun, which was well past its apex. "We need to get to Flo before her shop closes."

"I'm going to help Benji," I said. "Will you come with me?"

"Ugh," Jenny replied but reluctantly came along.

The three of us started in the direction of the trees. As Benji walked, he called for KC. It wasn't long before we reached the trees surrounding a small pond. I noticed a rustling in the grass at the far end of the pond. Then, out of the grass sprang KC. She dove into the water with a large splash and swam toward a small flock of geese. The geese honked loudly and took to the air well out of KC's reach. KC swam until she reached the edge of the pond and pulled herself out. Once on the shore, she shook herself dry.

"KC!" Benji shouted when he saw his dog. "KC, come girl!"

KC's ears popped up, and she looked in Benji's direction. She dove into the pond with another large splash and headed to us. When she emerged from the water, she jumped on Benji, knocking him down. Then she shook off the excess water, wetting him thoroughly. Benji hugged KC. "Thank you," he said to us as he attached the leash to KC's collar.

"Looks like KC had a good time," I said.

"Too good, I suppose. I think we are both going to need a bath when we get home. Her fur reeks like a pond and so do I."

"That's it," Jenny whispered to me. "Enough loving kindnesses for you. We must get to town. I've indulged you enough."

"Thank you for helping me find her," Benji said.

"Our pleasure," I said.

Benji and KC headed home. Jenny and I resumed our walk to the center of the village.

"We better step up our pace," Jenny said. "Flo's shop may have closed, and we won't be able to deliver Mother's package. She won't be happy with us. I'm already not happy with you."

"I think she will be happy with all the good deeds we have done today. Don't you?"

"I'm not so sure, Hannah. We didn't help ourselves, except perhaps to eat a peach. I think she will think that we were too kind. I agree assisting others is good, but would it have been selfish if we helped ourselves a little too? I guess we'll find out what Mother thinks when we get home. After all, the one person we haven't helped yet is Mother."

When we arrived at Flo's shop, the doors were locked just as Jenny had feared, and the sign hanging in the window read, "Closed." There was no way to deliver the package, not today. Before beginning our journey home, we sat on the steps outside the shop for a time without speaking.

"I hope Mother doesn't think the day was completely wasted because we didn't deliver the package," I said. "We made quite a few people happy, didn't we?"

"You didn't make me happy, and I'm worried Mother won't be happy either."

As we walked back along the road to our farm, I tried to prepare myself for what we would tell Mother.

"Maybe if we tell her that we delivered the package, we could sneak into town tomorrow and deliver it then," I suggested. "She'll never know."

"Mother might not know, but I would know, and you would know," Jenny said. "That would make not delivering the package worse by telling a lie. I guess you need to own the results of your choices. Remember the lady we met at the fork in the road. You took the high road today by doing all those good deeds instead of delivering Mother's package. We didn't get done what we were supposed to."

"It wasn't all my fault," I said. "You didn't stop me. Also, I couldn't lie to Mother, anyway."

Jenny stared at me, rolled her eyes, and grunted. "I didn't stop you?"

When we arrived home, I carefully accounted for our whole day. I told Mother about the old woman, the man and his cart, the fisherman, and Benji.

"My," Mother said, "I would think that with all the good deeds you performed, you hardly had time to get my package delivered."

"Oh, about the package," Jenny said. "Perhaps tomorrow we can return to Flo's shop to deliver it?"

"You didn't deliver the package?" Mother sounded stern, then shook her head. I relaxed, glad her eyes didn't look angry. "Yes, you can go back to town tomorrow but promise me that tomorrow you'll get done what you are sent to do. Now, why don't you two run up to the pasture and help your father bring in the sheep?"

I raced Jenny, just like Wes and Ben used to race. Jenny was faster than me, and, unless I got a big head start, she always won. We didn't have to run very far though; Father and Oscar had already brought the sheep halfway home. He knew we'd been to the village and asked if we'd heard any news about our boys.

"Father, when can I start training for my journey?" I asked.

"In time," he replied. "In time."

Jenny glanced in my direction, put her finger to her lips, and shook her head, no, as she mouthed the words, "our secret."

TWENTY-TWO

# A Man Named Happiness

HANK

We walked on, wading through the dense forest undergrowth. Based on the size of everything around us, giants must have lived here at one time. Massive trees reached to the clouds and blocked the light. Moss and lichen wept from branches and covered everything. Ferns grew out of the moss, adorning the tree trunks like bibs of green. Darkness and quiet made this an eerie place.

Deer, elk, squirrels, and chipmunks accompanied us during the day. In the evening, a rabbit might cross our path. We came across scat announcing the presence of bears. Fortunately, none of it looked fresh. Armed with long, sharpened sticks, we kept to the narrow paths left by migrating animals. Pine needles and leaves cushioned the forest floor. The scent of musk and rotting wood filled our noses.

We had been walking for weeks, living off the bounty of the forest. We crossed streams full of fish, easy to spear with our pointed sticks. However, as days grew shorter, the nights became cooler, and rain came more frequently, most often as a heavy mist that soaked us thoroughly.

"How much farther do you think we must go before we reach home?" Ben asked.

"I don't know," I responded with an edge. "I believe if we are walking in the right direction, we will eventually get there." *How many times must he ask the same question?*

"If the sea is behind us, and the mountains are to our right, and we haven't strayed too far east, we should be headed northwest," Wes said. "The sun comes up in the east." He pointed to his right. "Therefore, we are west of the mountains, which are probably what we call the Eastern Mountains when we are home."

"Great," Ben said, his voice harsh with irritation. "I am sure you are correct, but how far do we have to go before we arrive home?"

"I don't know," Wes returned. "Don't be so impatient. Just put one foot in front of the other and you will eventually get to where you are going."

"Patience," Ben sighed wearily. "Patience."

"Yes," I chimed in, "You won't reach home any faster if you become impatient, and you waste energy by agitating about it. It makes you unhappy and annoys those around you. Instead of fussing about the time you waste by being patient, enjoy the time you spend in these strange places with us. We may never be here again. Why don't you focus on the mystery around you? Practice patience; it's one of our keys." I picked up some leaves and dirt and threw them at Ben.

Ben dodged the dirt and leaves. "Not easy," he mumbled. "This place is spooky."

The sky darkened; the air became cooler, and the mist changed to rain. We covered ourselves with our canvas blankets and walked on. Drops grew larger and fell steadily. The long fern fronds bent with the weight of the raindrops as the water ran off them to the ground. The birds abandoned the sky, and the moss glowed an iridescent green in the dim light. Precipitation pattered all around us, a sound soothing to the ear, but the downpour made us wet and uncomfortable. The forest became ever darker and more forbidding.

A tree with a door and two windows

"Ben, Wes!" I called to summon their attention. "Do you see that?" I pointed to an exceptionally large tree, in the middle of which, at ground level, there appeared to be a door and, above it, two windows. The door's smoothness contrasted with the rough bark of the tree, was quite clearly defined, and suggested an opportunity to get out of the rain. "Do you suppose that's someone's home?"

I hoped whoever lived there was home. I walked quickly up to the door and knocked. A round disc in the middle of the door covered a peephole. I heard footsteps behind the door. Then, the disc magically slid aside. Someone was watching us.

"I'm Hank; this is Ben and Wes," I said to the peephole. "We're very wet, and we hope we could come in to escape the rain."

"Welcome!" It sounded like a man, friendly. I relaxed. Someone was home providing the prospect of having found shelter from the rain.

The door opened, and we stepped into a room with polished walls and floor, the air spicy, sweet-smelling, and earthy.

"My name is Happiness," the man said. He appeared old enough to be our father. He wore a gray shirt, sleeves rolled to mid-forearms, and work pants. His boots came up to mid-calf, with his pants tucked inside. He had long, gnarled arms and hands like branches of the tree in which he lived. "You can call me Hap. I am grateful to have your company."

The room was spacious, not a surprise given the circumference of the tree. The entry hall was dark but cozy, warm, and dry. We placed our gear on hooks attached to the wall and took off our shoes so as not to soil the shiny, wooden floor on which we stood. Hap led us up a spiral stair attached to the wall. We climbed to the floor above the foyer, more brightly lit than the entry below. Candles illuminated the second floor, and windows let in additional light. Hap's living room contained a sitting area and a kitchen with a stone hearth. The stairway continued to spiral up to yet another floor, where I presumed Hap slept. Hap took a seat on a stool and invited us to sit.

"Thank you for letting us into your home so we can dry off," I said.

"You're welcome," Hap responded. "Wait here. I'll be right back." Hap disappeared to the third floor. When he returned, he handed each of us a towel. "So, what brings you to this forest?" he said.

"We are on our way to the Valley of the Black Dog River," Ben said. "Do you know the way?"

"I know at the western end of a great lake; a river leads to a valley. I believe the river is called the Black Dog and the valley by the same name. I have never visited that place, and I'm not sure how far it is from here. The lake is like a long narrow inland sea nestled in the mountains."

Ben smiled.

"How did you come to live here?" Wes asked.

"I was on a trek, so long ago I've forgotten my destination. Walking through this forest, I stopped in the shadow of the biggest redwood I ever saw. I stepped back and admired its massive trunk. I walked around it, a full thirty-five strides, 105 feet in circumference, about thirty-four feet in diameter, and maintained its width at least thirty feet off the ground. A portion of the trunk had been cut away. Not sure how or why. I sat at the base of the tree and listened to the birds and insects. Peace and tranquility filled me. I returned to my village and came back to this spot with tools, created a door, and then the foyer, working from the inside out. I carved the living areas with great care to preserve the tree and sustain its life, so my home remains living, as well as lived-in, a symbiotic relationship of sorts. I benefit, and my tree is unharmed. My village is an easy two-day hike from here, so I return whenever I choose. My friends come to visit me when they can. They are always happy to see me, and I am happy to see them." Hap's voice was soft and kind.

"How did you come to be called Hap?" Ben asked.

"My parents originally named me Bill. They started calling me Happiness when they saw how I behaved. If I lost something, made a mistake, or failed to get my way, I didn't pout or cry."

"And none of those things made you unhappy?" Ben asked.

"No, not for long. When I was young, younger than you, I misplaced my favorite toy, a miniature, horse-drawn wagon. I went to my mother and told her I was very sad. She told me if I found happiness only in things, happiness would be too easy to lose. She said real happiness comes from within you. Always knowing from where my happiness comes has been a comfort to me. I know where to find it. It is where I left it and never completely goes away."

"What are the keys to finding happiness?" Ben said. "I mean, what do you do when you lose it?" Happiness was a key we sought, and Ben fidgeted. I was sure he realized it.

Hap gave Ben a knowing look, his soft eyes comforting. "You mean, when I temporarily misplace it. I've never permanently lost it." He paused. "Happiness is in my head and in my heart." He smiled and looked up. "I can bring it out by doing certain things. For instance, I once got upset because I had to meet strangers, people I didn't know from a town other than my own. I asked myself, 'Why am I upset? Am I anxious, sad, or angry?' I paced, jumped at sounds, and my stomach was queasy. I determined I was anxious and that made me sad. I'd given my feelings a name. I didn't ignore these feelings or try to hide them."

"Did that make you happy?" Wes asked.

"Doing that improved my mood, but I needed to do more. I thought about something I could do to reduce my anxiety. I imagined meeting the strangers, shaking their hands, and greeting them warmly. That was my plan and that made me feel even better. Next, I needed to act on my plan, and that is when my anxiety and sadness melted away."

"How about when you are very blue?" Ben said.

"When I'm truly down, I think about how grateful I am for all I have and who I am. I don't dwell on what I don't have. Thinking about the things for which I am grateful raises my spirits. Lastly, being around people puts a smile on my face and warms my heart. For that, I can always go home. All these things make me happy and are the keys to my happiness."

The room brightened as the rain stopped, and sunlight, albeit partially blocked by the tall trees, streamed in through the windows. I was thankful we had gotten out of the rain, and even more thankful we found Happiness. Hap asked if we could stay long enough to share lunch. Happiness, like his tree home, seemed brighter, and I thanked him for sharing his wisdom with us. Once we finished eating, clothes dry, and ready to continue our journey, we said goodbye and started on our way once again.

I looked around as I walked behind Wes and Ben in silence. We headed northwest toward the mountains again, in search of the inland sea, headwaters to the Black Dog River, the gateway to our valley. A blue sky was visible in patches through the mesh of branches and pine needles that glistened from the rain. The air smelled fresh. I thought about how grateful I was for the splendor surrounding me and for my brother and cousin who were with me. We had a plan with clear direction, and we were following it. I broke the silence and said aloud, though mostly to myself, "There's no stopping us now." I touched the red bandanna still tucked into my back pants pocket and hoped I was right. "I'm happy," I said, realizing I'd fulfilled Hap's conditions for *happiness*. "Key number eleven." *Where will we find number twelve?*

# TWENTY-THREE

# Out on a Ledge

HANK

Into the foothills we walked, leaving the dense forest and giant trees behind. We hiked through tall grasses and shrubs, past smaller pines, and scrub oaks, and then the rain returned. On and on we marched, up one hill and down another, all the while gaining elevation.

"I'm hoping we'll be able to see the inland sea once we are up on those heights," I said, pointing to the ridge above us in the distance.

"That would put a smile on my face," Ben said. "Based on Hap's directions, we probably will."

"I wish this rain and wind would let up," Wes said.

At least he had stopped complaining about his shoes, which I guessed he'd finally broken in.

The great trees no longer sheltered us, and we wore our blankets over our heads and draped across our backs and shoulders, but the wind-driven rain still penetrated to our skin. The days continued to shorten, and the air blew cooler. Soggy and cold, we walked slower, humped over, and spoke little to each other.

"Listen, you two, we need to pick up the pace," I said. "We are southwest of the mountains. We must cross them before the snows return. The last thing I want is to spend the winter in those mountains again." Ben and Wes looked at me with soulful eyes; each wore a frown. "Remember, be happy we are together," I added.

As we climbed out of the foothills and into the mountains, the vegetation diminished, trees became scarcer, and the rocky paths steeper and more difficult to climb. I looked back in awe at the forest below. I prepared mentally for the rugged mountains to come. Clouds moved across the mountains west of us and descended their slopes in long, cottony wisps as rain spilled out beneath them.

We found ourselves scrambling over rocks and crossing narrow, fast-moving streams again. The way wound up and up until we reached the narrow plateau I had spotted from below. From that vantage point, I could see a vast body of water that pointed northward. Wes let out a yell that echoed across the valley. Ben jumped and howled like a wolf. I just smiled, bathed in their joy, and reflected on our journey so far.

We started to cross the ridge, looking for a safe way to climb down to the lake. After walking for several hours, we noticed that the broad shelf had become a narrow ledge, two to three feet wide, high above a narrow valley.

We proceeded in a single file. If I dared to look down, dizziness overcame me. I gripped the rock face with one hand. As I proceeded with caution around the next bend, the view took my breath away. I stared into dense stands of trees bordering a deep turquoise lake, and I reveled in it. Finally, the rain had stopped, and a bright sun in a rapidly clearing sky reflected off the dark blue-green water below. I continued to smile. Infused with energy, I had an urge to run but not on this narrow sill.

A narrow ledge high above the narrow valley

The ledge that hugged the side of the mountain weaved in and out as it followed the mountain's contour. Parts of the path appeared chiseled into the rock, suggesting that someone had intended it to be used to cross the mountain, perhaps until the ridge broadened again. I led the way, turning one corner after another. We moved steadily although with great care until our way was blocked. Standing on the ledge, not twenty feet ahead of me, was a man. I stopped. The man's appearance, so unexpected, caused me to stumble, and I almost lost my balance. I threw myself back against the wall and held on with both hands. Gravel rolled from under my feet and headed into the depths below. The man halted, glared at us, frowned, and pursed his lips. Ben and Wes caught up to me and halted.

"Hello," I called to the man. "Nice day."

"Is it?" the man returned. "I'm afraid you are blocking my way."

"Are we?" I responded. "Perhaps, is it possible, you may be blocking ours?"

"It depends on your perspective. From here you are clearly blocking mine. Unless you happen to be walking in the same direction I choose to walk. I believe this ledge is too narrow for us to pass safely."

"Is there a place wide enough for us to pass in the direction you came from?" I said, trying to sound polite.

"I don't remember; and if there was, I would have to be willing to retrace my steps. Is there a place from where you came where we could pass each other safely?"

"We've been walking on this ledge for hours," I said. "We'd have to go back to where we started. I don't think we want to retrace our steps any more than you do."

"So be it," the man said and sat down.

"Is he going to just sit there?" Ben whispered to me. He rubbed the back of his neck and threw his pack down, nearly losing it over the cliff.

"Maybe, I don't know," I whispered back. "What should we do?"

"We could practice patience, and see if that key opens

this door," Wes whispered. His smug look told me he was proud of his clever statement.

Ben stared at Wes with evil intent in his eyes. "We could starve to death on this silly ledge, too," he said. "I think we should force him to go the way we want him to. In the time we wait, being patient, doing nothing, we could have walked back to the entry to the ledge and be done with it. I think we should set a limit on patience. I'm prepared to make him move."

"You're right," said Wes. "Too much patience and we might lose an opportunity to save some time. Act rashly, though, and we might start something we'd regret. What if you just demand he move?"

"I don't think he will comply with our wish if we make it a command," I said.

We opted for patience and waited as the sun rose in the sky and the day wore on. Instead of being annoyed and venting our frustration, we enjoyed the view from our vantage point on top of the world. Then, I decided I had waited long enough.

"Mister!" I called, trying to engage the man in conversation. "Where are you from?"

There was no answer.

"Mister!" I called again.

The man sat with his back against the mountain wall, feet extended over the edge, his hat pulled down, shading his eyes.

"Do you suppose he is asleep?" Ben asked. "Maybe we could sneak over him?"

"What if he startled awake and knocked us off the ledge?" Wes said, shaking his head.

"Mister!" I called again. The man stirred, slid his hat back, looked in our direction, and stretched.

"You woke me up," the man called back, not seeming at all annoyed by the disturbance. "What do you want?"

"My name is Hank, and this is Ben and Wes. We'd like to pass," I responded. "I hope you are feeling better now that you've had a nap."

"I must say, I do feel better," the man answered. "Please call me Igashu."

"We're trying to get to that lake in the distance, and eventually to the Valley of the Black Dog. Have you heard of it?"

"I have," Igashu said. "It's far from here, many days' walk. That way." He pointed in the direction we were trying to go, northwest. "I must say, though, I've never been there."

"Would you like to go?" Wes shouted. "You could join us. We have some supplies with us. We'd be happy to share."

"I was walking south," Igashu said. "You are walking north. I'm not sure I want to walk back the way I came. It took me a long time to decide to go in this direction. I would have preferred to be walking west, but this mountain is in the way. East? Well, that is straight down as you can see. That leaves north or south. It gets very cold in the north—winter will be here soon, you know. So, I finally decided to walk south. Now, you want me to change direction."

"Change is good," I said. "Join us. We make good company, and mountains shelter our valley. The warm ocean currents heat the air so that the winters there are mild."

"Okay," Igashu said. "I wander, without clear direction. Therefore, I can always change the way I'm headed and see where I end up."

The man turned his back to us and began to walk the same way that we were headed. We followed.

I turned to Wes. "That was just enough patience, and a better result than going back or trying to get around Igashu on this ledge. Patience gave us time, and diplomacy led to a solution. I enjoyed the break and the wonderful view from up here."

I called to Igashu. "Where are you from, and where were you going?"

"I'm from nowhere, and, by no coincidence, I'm going nowhere in particular, just wandering, like my name, Igashu, the wanderer."

Once we caught up with Igashu, we walked on together. The ledge widened, making conversation comfortable. I told Igashu about Messyman and Have-Little, and our experience on the ship.

"I can't believe you survived that shipwreck," Igashu said. "That must have been scary. I've enjoyed your stories. Now, I have a tale for you."

# TWENTY-FOUR

# Igashu's Tale

## HANK

Igashu began his tale. "As I walked along a mountain trail last spring, I stopped to rest shortly after sunset to observe the heavens. To the west, the red and yellow sunset dimmed as twilight evolved and a crescent moon appeared. Its morning star hung just above it like a jewel. As darkness descended, other stars began to adorn the heavens. In the cloudless sky, I saw a faint Milky Way and all the constellations. In awe of what stood before me, I saluted the North Star for giving me direction. Although it is hard to imagine, the night was not always bright."

"Weren't stars and the moon always in the sky?" Wes asked. Ben and I turned to Igashu to see how he'd respond.

"No, there was a time when the night sky was black, without celestial bodies, and the earth was very dark long, long ago, well before our time." Igashu paused before continuing. "Three sisters traveled over the mountains, on a journey like yours. They traveled only during the day. At night, without the stars or moon to light their way, they feared they might trip and fall, or worse, lose their way.

"They moved quickly through the mountains along familiar paths until a late summer snow interrupted their journey and trapped them, but they did not become frightened."

"Why weren't they afraid?" Wes asked.

"Because each had a magical power," Igahu said. "The oldest sister, Evie, created delicious food from smoke. The youngest, Rose, drew fire from a stone. The middle sister, Addie, made twigs into warm blankets and clothes. They built a crude shelter out of sticks and stones and prepared to wait out the late summer storm, but that snowfall was followed by another and another. It seemed the sisters would never return home. Though safe and warm with plenty to eat, they were trapped in their hut. Days passed until one night they became restless.

"'I'm bored,' Rose said.

"'So am I,' said Addie.

"'Snowball fight!' Evie shouted. She swung open the door to their shelter and dove into the snow. When she sat up, she only saw the faint glow from the fire in their hut. Nevertheless, she waded through the deep snow, turned, and started throwing snowballs in the direction of the hut, guessing her sisters would be emerging to join her.

"Rose and Addie exited the hut. Evie threw a snowball where she thought Rose should be, but it flew wide and hit Addie in the chest.

"'Who threw that?' Addie shouted as if she didn't know. She waited for Evie to answer revealing her location.

"Evie called out, 'I did,' and continued to throw snowballs. Rose and Addie dove to opposite sides of the hut to avoid being hit. Concealed by the dark, Evie remained unseen by her sisters, but they threw snowballs at the location of her voice. One missile caught Evie in the side of her head. She snickered and started making more snowballs. Addie hit Rose in the arm.

Evie, Rose, and Addie having a snowball fight

"'You're in trouble now,' Rose said.

"Rose and Evie fired one snowball after another at Addie, catching her in the crossfire. Snow flew everywhere. The fight went on, as the sisters laughed and shouted. Balls of snow soared right and left and then up. Evie made a giant snowball and threw it high in the air. The winds carried it above the mountain peaks, higher and higher, until high enough to reflect the sun's light from the other side of the world, and thus became our moon. Rose and Addie watched the creation of the moon and began to throw their snowballs into the air instead of at each other.

"As the balls of snow caught the currents, they drifted up and up, filling the sky and becoming stars, planets, and all the heavenly bodies. Now, with the moon and stars in place, the night sky brightened. An occasional 'star' drifted back to Earth and created a streak of light. If the sisters were lucky enough to catch a glimpse of that light, they made a wish. The three continued to throw snowballs into the air all night; with time, a soft glow began to surround them and gave them the ability to see in night's darkness, a gift for which we are forever grateful."

When Igashu finished his tale, he smiled at us.

"You know," I said. "Gratitude is one of our keys."

"When I gaze up at the stars at night, it makes me wonder and gives me a sense of awe, and for that, I am also grateful," Igashu said.

Ben smiled back at Igashu. "Are you sure you wouldn't like to walk on with us to our village?" he said.

"Have you met these sisters?" Wes asked. "I would like to learn to make food from smoke."

"No, no, they lived a very long time ago. Although I've been told they were the great-great-aunts of all my people."

# TWENTY-FIVE

# Igashu, the Wanderer

HANK

We continued to walk with Igashu along the ledge high above the valley floor. The trail made a long arc that led to a vista from which the great body of water stretched northward to the horizon. However, no matter how many steps we took toward the Inland Sea, it failed to appear any closer. Mist rose from the lake's glacial, blue-green waters, hugging its surface.

The ledge narrowed again, causing us to grow silent, unable to trade more stories while we concentrated on our footing and avoided looking down. Each step became a challenge. My feet slid on the gravel path more than once. I reached for the walls but found little to hold onto. I had a constant fear of slipping into the void below, and I could feel my heartbeat.

Ben, on the other hand, continued to wear a broad smile on his face whenever I dared to turn and look at him. He seemed at home as if he were climbing the masts on the ship. Wes moved slowly, falling far behind, his lips pursed, eyes staring at his feet, his hands groping for places to grip the wall. Igashu led the way, moving easily ahead of us.

When we finally stepped onto a broader patch, I relaxed, sat, and caught my breath. Wes lay on the ground; I think he was trying to hug it.

"Where will you go from here?" I asked Igashu.

"I would like to head west to the ocean. That's where I headed before I followed the path onto this ledge. That took me south. West, south, it hardly matters, but I don't want to walk along that ledge again."

"We're heading northwest until we reach that lake below us," Ben said.

"Then on to the Valley of the Black Dog," Igashu said, "so, you told me. But I have nothing there, except your kind acquaintances. I think I will leave you and head west to the ocean. If you continue northwest, you will find a small village by the lake. The people are generous and fair. Ask for Mica. He'll help you. I stayed with him for a time. This path will lead you there."

"When we met you on the ledge, you were heading south," Wes said. "You chose to walk north with us, so we didn't need to turn around and retrace our steps. For that, we thank you."

"I am a wanderer," said lgashu. "You had direction. I had none, so I put myself in your place, always the first step in finding compassion."

"You put yourself in our place?" Ben asked.

"You seemed to be on a mission. I didn't judge you or examine your motives. Once I understood things your way, I decided to turn around. Why should I, Igashu, hold you up? You had a goal for which you were passionate. I had no clear destination." He paused. "If I helped you to achieve your wishes sooner by changing my plans, that generated a warm feeling inside me. It was an act of loving kindness. Compassion does that for you. I've heard said, what comes from the heart goes to the heart. Put yourself in someone else's shoes, try to experience what they experience, don't be judgmental, then lend a hand."

"Igashu," Ben said, "please consider coming home with us."

"No, thank you. If I want to find you, I know where you will be. You will travel west along the southern border of the Great Inland Sea until you get to the head waters of the Black Dog River. Head north along the river and you will find the Valley of the Black Dog. Should my wandering take me in that direction, we will meet again."

Igashu shook each of our hands, bowed, and started walking west over the crest of the Eastern Mountains, through the valley where great trees grew, toward the western mountains, and the ocean beyond. We turned north and began the descent to the Inland Sea in search of Mica and the village.

"We found our twelfth key, *compassion*," I said. "Now, let's find the village and Mica." I had a lot to record in my logbook when we stopped for the night.

North toward the Inland Sea

# TWENTY-SIX

# The Village by the Great Inland Sea

## HANK

We walked on until dusk. The path led us in a gentle descent toward the valley floor.

"It's getting dark," I called to Wes and Ben. "Time to start looking for shelter."

We found a suitable spot. Ben took off to set some snares, hoping to capture something fresh for supper. Wes and I gathered wood. We had dry grass for kindling, and in no time, flames licked the tinder.

Ben returned and joined us by the fire. "I'll check the traps before it gets too dark," he said. "I hope we'll be able to eat tonight. I'm hungry and tired of eating greens and nuts."

"Do you want any?" Wes said as he reached into his pocket.

Ben frowned and shook his head.

We sat without speaking for several minutes, listening to crickets, birds, and the wind. I breathed in the earthiness around me. Fatigue from our long hike overcame me and generated calm. I leaned back and closed my eyes, grateful that Tadjar taught us how to visit silence. Hap was right, gratitude sent a warm sensation spreading over me.

Poor Ben couldn't sit still. As the sun began to set, he popped up and headed off to check the traps. Fortunately, given his apparent state of mind, he returned with a rabbit. He skinned, cleaned, and roasted it on a spit. We ate and talked about home and our family. Wes put more wood on the fire before we settled down for the night.

The next day, the sun shone brightly. Without rain, the mountain air was fresh, cool, and clean. We spent the day scaling rocks, gradually making our way to the lake that spread out below us.

"I think I see smoke," Ben shouted and began another version of his victory dance, arms waving, legs high-stepping, as he hooted.

"I think you are right," Wes said and joined Ben, mimicking his gyrations.

"That must be the village Igashu told us about," I said. "I hope we can replenish our supplies there. I'm afraid, home is still a long way off. From here, everything looks closer than it is, and travel on the mountain is slow. I think it will take us at least another day to reach the lake."

I was right. It took two more days of walking before we entered the small village. A mixed variety of dwellings lined the way, some with simple thatched roofs, huts made from sticks and mud bricks, and larger buildings constructed with logs.

We attracted curious stares as we passed. Our clothes covered in dirt. We each sported beards, Ben's and Wes's were more sparse than mine. Our hair long and matted. Then, from out of nowhere, a large man appeared and blocked our way. He scrutinized us before speaking.

"Who are you?" the man commanded.

"I'm Hank. This is my brother, Ben, and our cousin, Wes," I answered. "We're headed home to our village in the Valley of the Black Dog River. Igashu told us to ask for Mica when we got here."

"I am Mica," the man said, arms crossed but sounding more kind than he appeared. "You're pretty far from home, and by the look and smell of you, in need of a bath."

Ben pulled up his shirt, held it to his nose, sniffed, and shrugged. He shook his head, and dust rose from his dense crop of red hair.

Mica narrowed his eyes and stared at Ben before continuing. "If you were thinking of completing your journey now, you better consider that winter will be here soon. The weather can suddenly change in these mountains. You may want to wait until spring to continue."

"Should we stay here?" Wes whispered to Ben. "If we do, where would we stay? What if there isn't enough food? What if the people here won't accept us?"

Mica's eyes immediately shifted to Wes, apparently having overheard what he said to Ben. Wes stepped behind me. The big man frowned before his face softened.

"I suppose we could make room for you here," Mica said. "We're still bringing in the last of the harvest, and there is still time to catch fish from the lake. Game remains plentiful. If you are willing to help us prepare for winter, I believe you'd be welcome to stay with us. I think you might want to clean up a bit first."

"That's very kind of you," I said and turned to Ben and Wes to see what they thought.

"We've been walking for months," Wes said. "Our supplies are almost gone. What if we're caught in a winter storm? We might not survive. Starved. Frozen. Remember how the first winter in the mountains went. If we wait until spring, we can travel in safety."

"Actually, I don't want to wait another minute," Ben said. "I want to get home, but staying here does sound like the better plan."

I thought I detected a hint of patience in his reply.

I had my own concerns. How would we sustain ourselves in this place? Should we trust Mica? Would there be enough provisions for everyone including us? Did I harbor reservations about doing our share of the work? I suggested we step aside to discuss this.

Our decision came quickly and was unanimous. We agreed to halt our journey and wait out winter here.

"I will call a meeting of the villagers," Mica said. "They have the final say on whether to invite you to stay. In the meantime, I will show you to a hut where we heat water to make steam, and you can bathe."

When we were done cleaning ourselves, our dirty clothes were gone. In their place, we found clean ones. There was a renewed bounce to my step. I hardly recognized Ben and Wes with hair pulled back and tied into long, single braids.

"Winter is a scary time for us," Mica said in parting. "The cold is bitter, and food becomes scarce. It is important for each villager to contribute to the welfare of all. This applies to food, shelter, and fuel for heat."

"We are not afraid of work and would be happy to help out as much as we can," I said. "We would be grateful if you allowed us to stay with you." Ben and Wes nodded in agreement.

That evening, the villagers held a meeting in a log structure at the center of the village. Everyone attended.

Ben counted 144 men, women, and children. They sat in concentric arcs with the Elders of each family in front.

Mica introduced us to the gathering. We told the group our plan to return home to the Valley of the Black Dog. Mica told them of his advice to postpone the journey until spring. Heads shook, yes. Mica asked if anyone objected to our spending the winter in the village.

"Of course," Mica said, "they would be expected to build a shelter for themselves and find food to sustain them through the cold. We expect them to share their bounty with us just as we share amongst ourselves and with them. They are young and strong and would be of benefit to us all."

"We do not know them," someone called out. "Why should we trust them?"

"On what basis should we question their sincerity and willingness to be generous with us?" Mica asked. "I say, let them show us they are worthy of our generosity, which we give willingly from our hearts. Let them stay."

Others began to call out, "Let them stay."

I smiled broadly and my face felt warm. They decided to give us a place on the outskirts of the village where we would build a shelter in which to spend the winter.

"We will help gather wood for the community woodpile, pitch in with the final harvest, hunt game, catch fish, and gladly share, as you request," I said.

An Elder explained how the villagers managed the food storage kept in a common area accessible to all.

"Mica will assume responsibility for showing you what you must do," one of the Elders said.

After the meeting, Mica led us to his home and introduced us to his wife, Tara, and their daughter, Golden Skye, who was tall like her mother. I caught her glancing in my direction, but when I turned, she looked away.

The sun had long since set, and Mica offered us his barn in which to sleep. We graciously accepted, happy to be inside and out of the cool, night air.

"Tomorrow, Golden Skye will show you where you can build your shelter," Mica said. "Once settled on the spot, return to me, and I will explain how you can help us provision the village for the winter and gather food for yourselves."

One would think that sleeping inside would be a welcome change, even if in a barn. We were used to the sheep and goats. However, Ben lasted only a few short minutes before announcing he preferred to sleep under the stars. Wes immediately joined him. I enjoyed a peaceful night in the straw, which was fresh, though a bit dusty.

The next morning, Mica brought us into his home for breakfast. Tara served us each a bowl of porridge, thick and sweet. Golden Skye helped Tara before sitting with us at the table. She was taller than most girls I had known, only a few inches shorter than me, and about my age. A long braid of thick dark hair hung over each ear. She looked at me and her bright eyes sparkled. She seemed less shy than on our first encounter, and as she spoke, her smile was friendly. Her posture was straight and strong. She wore a buckskin leather jacket that hung below her waist and a long skirt that covered her boots.

After breakfast, Golden Skye led us to the edge of the village where the road turned northeast toward the lake. I tried to think of things to say to her as we walked but couldn't find anything I didn't think would sound foolish or trite, so, I kept quiet. As we approached the lake, the land beside the road banked slightly, then rose into a gently sloping, grass-covered knoll. Beyond the rise, the ground ascended more steeply and was densely forested. Blackberries grew in the underbrush.

"You can set up camp here," Golden Skye said as she pointed to the mound. "Build a shelter. Gather wood for fuel. Rain will turn to snow before the next full moon. You will be busy. You can borrow tools from the village if you need them. I suppose you may want an ax, and perhaps a shovel. Welcome." She tipped her head and started to leave.

You can set up camp here

"Golden Skye," I called as she turned away. "We'll look over this spot, get settled, and then I'll return to your father to find out how we can help prepare for winter. Thank you." She turned toward the village, waved, and smiled back at me. I waved and returned the smile.

"The people of this village are very generous," Wes said.

"We didn't ask for much, and yet they gave us a lot," Ben added.

"The villagers warned us about attempting to travel with bad weather coming," I said. "That was very kind of them. They opened their hearts to us. I think we should open our hearts in the same way to them. Return their generosity freely because we want to. Remember, *generosity* is another key." I thought about Mother's letter. "*Be generous too.*" Perhaps generosity had opened a door.

The air remained clear and crisp, the sky a bright azure blue. I looked over the spot where we would stay for the next several months. Once the snow began to fall, we would be trapped here for the winter. We made camp on the site of our newfound home and started a fire in a hastily constructed hearth. Mica had given us potatoes, onions, and cabbage from which Wes created a tasty soup.

# TWENTY-SEVEN

# The Village

## HANK

I sat on the ground facing the hill, trying to imagine what type of shelter we would construct in the short time we had to build something. We must do better than the lean-to we constructed that first winter in the mountains. A cabin took weeks to erect, and I immediately abandoned that idea. I asked the "twin" cousins their thoughts.

"Something that keeps the cold out and the heat in," Ben said as he studied the site.

Accurate, but not very helpful, I thought.

"The shelter needs to be sturdy," Wes said. "We are close to the lake, and I bet the winds are fierce, and the snow is heavy here. What if the hut gets blown to bits?"

A light went on in my head. "What if we build right into the hill?" I asked. That would take care of three walls, give us support for the roof, and only one side to finish."

"I think they call that a turf house," Ben said. "I remember seeing homes like that in our valley."

We placed stakes in the ground on the grassy knoll, forty yards from the road. Ben laid out ropes connecting the markers on top of the hill to the ones at the bottom indicating the width of the front wall where the entrance would be.

"We'll need spades for digging and an ax to cut poles," I said. "Let's find Mica. He told us we can borrow tools. We also need to see what he would like us to do to help the village prepare for winter."

At the center square, Mica conducted business on the open grassy area in front of the same log building where we met the night before. Homes surrounded the green. A large lean-to sheltered an ample pile of chopped wood, and next to the lean-to stood structures made of logs. I assumed they served as storage areas for community property and a storehouse for food. A freshwater well occupied the center of the square.

"You can share in our bounty by helping with the work to prepare for winter," Mica explained. "Respect everyone's needs. Understand how you meet your own necessities in relationship to everyone else's." He walked us to the next building. "This shed houses gear for hunting, fishing, planting, and harvesting."

"May we borrow an ax and three spades?" Wes asked Mica, who retrieved the tools and handed them to Wes and Ben. They thanked him before heading back to our place on the edge of the village to start work on our shelter.

I walked with Mica to his hut, where Tara and Golden Skye waited.

"Golden Skye," Mica said. "Please show Hank where to gather food, hunt, and fish."

Golden Skye appeared indifferent but willing to comply with her father's request.

"Do you know how to fish with a net?" Golden Skye

asked me on our way to the lake. I detected an element of skepticism in her tone.

"I have never fished with a net, but Wes has. We generally fish with spears or hook them on a string."

"So, perhaps I can teach you something new," Golden Skye said with a small edge to her tone. "Canoes are by the water. The fishing nets are in them. To catch fish, you cast the net, pull it in, and check to see what you've caught. When you become skilled, you can catch quite a lot of fish this way. Try not to fall out of the canoe, though."

I studied the water and struggled to find any fish. Trout fishing in a stream using a spear challenged me. The lake made fishing with a spear that much more difficult. However, confident in my ability with a line and hook, I decided to put aside my ego and learn to use the net like Golden Skye. I reminded myself of what Mother taught me: learning requires humility. Be humble first, then learn. I heard Mother's voice. *One must accept that there is more than one way to do something. Change makes for opportunity.* I still wanted to show Golden Skye how I fished, humility aside. She didn't give me a chance.

We climbed into one of the larger canoes and paddled away from the shore. Golden Skye stood, moving with the grace of a dancer, confident and smooth. The net spun out of her hand in a great arc and hit the water with hardly a splash. She caught a fish on her first try. She sat down, gave me a smug smile, extended her arm, and waved her hand for me to give it a try. I took the challenge and attempted to stand. The canoe rocked back and forth, nearly capsizing us.

"Better sit before you fall into the water or tip us over," Golden Skye said in a taunting tone. "I didn't come here to swim today."

Hank learning to fish with a net

I tried to cast the net from a seated position and almost tipped the canoe again. My net gathered into a knot and splashed into the water next to me. Golden Skye sighed, stood, and demonstrated how to cast once more. The net flew from her hand like a bird taking flight, opened in a wide circle and landed without a ripple. She retrieved the net, extended her arm, and challenged me to try again.

I took greater care standing in the canoe; we still rocked as I took the net and tossed it the same way Golden Skye did. It flew from my hand in a knot, climbed upward, then took a steep dive, and splashed in the water twenty feet from the canoe.

"You forgot to wrap the loop of the hand-line around

your wrist. Nets are valuable. You need to retrieve it. I hope you can swim."

I took off my shoes and dove into the lake. The cold water refreshed me and cooled some of my humiliation. I dove several times before I located the net. Golden Skye laughed until tears ran down her face. Dripping wet, I reentered the canoe in shallow water. I warmed in the sun, and my clothes soon dried. I smelled like the lake.

She wounded my pride, but I was undeterred. I tied the hand-line onto my wrist and practiced casting. We drifted along the shore, and eventually, I began to catch fish. Golden Skye nodded approval once I started to achieve success, but I continued to avert my eyes from her.

"Why do you keep that red bandanna tucked into your pants pocket?" Golden Skye asked.

"It is for luck and comes in handy. Keeps the sun off my head, sweat out of my eyes, and can warm my ears."

"It does all that tucked into your pocket?" She chuckled. "What a special cloth."

We fished for several hours before returning to the village. There, we deposited most of our catch in the communal storehouse. Villagers cleaned and prepared the fish for smoking, salting, and drying.

I wanted to gather some vegetables to bring back to Ben and Wes that would complement the fish that I took with me. Golden Skye took me to the fields on the southern edge of the lake, where we found drying stalks of corn, grains, pumpkins, and squash. Golden Skye suggested I harvest more than I needed to be contributed to the communal food bank, where some would be kept in cold storage and others would be dried. I gladly complied.

"Tomorrow, I would like to teach you how to hunt,"

Golden Skye said. "I will bring my bow and a quiver of arrows. Are you familiar with hunting that way?"

"Not really," I said. "Mostly, we've been trapping game with a snare. Father took me hunting a few times, but he uses a rifle. Do you know how use a snare?"

"I'll show you how to hunt with the bow tomorrow," she said. "You can show me how to hunt with the snare later."

This wasn't a competition with Golden Skye. I would do what I did well, and, for that, I stood tall. I appreciated her willingness to teach me and I wanted to learn. I picked my head up and started to engage her again. Besides, I had to admit, fishing with a net was more productive than using a spear. My fishing line worked, but, again, it seemed less efficient. Tomorrow, I would learn to hunt, and I hoped to be able to show Golden Skye how to use a snare. She started for home, and I watched her until she was out of sight. She walked with grace and confidence.

When I reached the site of our turf house-to-be, I gasped at the number of children from the village who had come to help. Some worked with shovels and picks, and others rolled sod. Ben and Wes dug in the area staked earlier.

"Happy you're back," Ben greeted me as I arrived. "We uncovered a few rocks and need your help to move some of the larger ones. As you can see, we've made some friends. The pile of stones over there is for the hearth. We removed the sod carefully, rolled it, and placed it over there." He pointed to the spots. "We'll put the sod on the roof to keep out the rain."

"I'll use the remaining hours of daylight to look for suitable trees to make poles for the roof and front wall," I said to Ben, picked up an ax, and walked into the woods.

As I chopped, I thought about my conversations with

Golden Skye. I wanted desperately to impress her and gain her respect. I anticipated seeing her again tomorrow for another chance. I wondered how she would hunt with the bow and arrow. Would we be successful? Would she let me show her how to use a snare? I cut as many poles as possible, dragged them back to the hill, deposited them, and returned to the woods to cut more.

# TWENTY-EIGHT

# Hunting with Golden Skye

## HANK

I arose early the following day and headed into the village to meet Golden Skye. The sun just peeked over the Eastern Mountains, shadows had grown long, and everything appeared gray at that hour. The morning air felt crisp on my cheeks as I walked under a nearly cloudless sky. Haze still clung to the surface of the lake. Golden Skye smiled and waved to me as I approached the village. She carried a bow and a quiver of arrows.

"Good morning," I called as she waved, and I felt a smile spontaneously spread over my face as soon as our eyes met.

"Have you eaten?" Golden Skye asked and handed me a piece of flatbread made from ground corn. "Try this. I think you will like it."

I took a bite of the bread.

"That tastes really good. What is it?" I asked.

"Flat cornmeal bread with crushed berries," she said and showed me her bow and quiver of arrows. "Watch me this morning, and I will show you how I hunt. Later, you can practice with the bow."

When we reached the edge of the forest, Golden Skye turned to me. "Walk silently. Be aware of the direction of the wind. If we are upwind from the prey, they will be alerted by our scent. We need to be as close to the animals as we can without disturbing them and take them with a single shot, if possible. If we wound the animal, we must track them. We are obligated to kill them swiftly when we find them to prevent them from suffering. Honor and respect them. It is necessary to kill them so that we can survive, but we will kill no more than we can use or need."

We walked until the sun reached a quarter of the way toward its peak. In the shadows, sheltered from the sun by the trees, we soaked in the cool pine-scented air. The sun burned off the morning mists. As I hastily walked to keep up with Golden Skye, she abruptly halted.

"Please be more careful. Snapping twigs and rustling leaves will scare the game."

Golden Skye seemed to float noiselessly through the forest. I thought l was doing well, but remained unable to make myself as invisible as she. Suddenly, she stopped and pointed ahead to a small group of deer. She held her finger to her lips to warn me not to speak. As I slowed to a stop, I stepped on a stick. The snap seemed to echo through the forest like a great gong. Alerted, the deer looked up in unison, turned, and quickly moved deeper into the forest. Golden Skye whipped her head around toward me with an angry scowl on her face. She shook her head.

"Sorry," I said softly with my head lowered.

"It's obvious you haven't much practice at this," she said.

The snap seemed to echo through the forest
like a great gong, alerting the deer

We circled to the right in the direction the deer retreated and quickly found ourselves behind them again. Golden Skye signaled to me not to move. Not wishing to spook them again, I stood still and held my breath.

Golden Skye moved slowly closer; eyes fixed on her target. She removed an arrow from her quiver and notched it, drew back on the string, and let it fly, all in a single fluid motion. The arrow struck, and a deer dropped where it stood. The others took off and disappeared. I followed Golden Skye to where the deer lay dead. We trussed the legs and cut a pole to carry it back to camp.

"Great shot!" I said in awe of Golden Skye's skill with the bow.

"It was," Golden Skye said with a smile, pleased with herself. "When we return to the village, I will give you a turn with the bow and arrow. I will show you how to practice. Now, let's take this deer back. We'll need to skin and dress it. I'll take some meat for my family, you can have some for you, your brother, and cousin, and we'll donate the rest to the village. Some meat will be salted, smoked, and made into jerky. By sharing, we honor the villagers and show them respect. We receive honor by giving honor. Every person has value. We love our neighbors as we love ourselves. We try to be positive and find goodness in everyone."

*Honor*, I said to myself, is the fourteenth key. I recited Mother's poem in my head, reviewing the clues.

Once back in the village and finished with the deer preparation and distribution, Golden Skye took me to a place to teach me about archery. I wanted to learn to handle a bow like Golden Skye, but it proved harder to master than she made it appear. After I made many attempts to hit a tree just thirty feet away, my left forearm was red and raw from the string, and my shoulders ached.

"Thank you, Golden Skye," I said. "I will practice when I can, but it is time for me to return to Ben and Wes." Golden Skye knit her brow. I wanted her to see me as a better student than I appeared at that moment. I was sure if I kept trying, I'd improve, but it was time to leave.

"Go, if you must," said Golden Skye. "Practice makes perfect, and practice takes time."

As tempted as I was to stay, I needed to help Ben and Wes. I quickly arrived back at the site. Ben and Wes still worked on the turf house. In my absence, they had dug deep into the hill and made considerable progress removing soil.

They told me about their helpers, many of whom planned to return in the morning. We needed to clear enough dirt to have room to stand, lie down to sleep, cook, and store our things, plus a small place for a table and perhaps something on which to sit.

I took a shovel and started to dig. As we worked, I related my hunting experience with Ben and Wes, especially how Golden Skye felled the deer. We worked well into the evening under a full harvest moon and enjoyed venison steaks for supper. I shared what I had learned about *honor*, our fourteenth key.

The next morning, I arose early and took off to a place on the hill behind the knoll where our shelter stood. I picked up the bow and arrows, pointed without barbs, for practice. The target, a broadleaf, hung on a tree twenty paces away. My arms ached as I shot arrows at the target over and over, stopping only after I had rubbed my forearm raw. I finally hit the spot.

IT TOOK the better part of a week to clear the dirt and stones from the site of the turf house. Once done, the excavation measured eighteen feet by twelve feet and stood seven feet from the floor to the top of the knoll.

We placed poles across the top to create the roof and pitched it slightly to allow water drainage. I left a space under the front of the roof to allow smoke out and a little light in. Between two upright poles lashed to the roof, we stacked more poles for the front wall. Ben and Wes filled in gaps between them with mud, turf, and stones.

With skills I learned at home repairing roofs, I fashioned shingles from bark and placed them on the poles of the roof, overlapping them as we worked. We unrolled the squares of sod, placed them over the bark shingles, and left spaces in the front wall for a door, window slit, and hearth chimney. Wes filled in the gaps with more sod, stones, and mud.

Ben and I brought in flat stones we found by the lake for the floor and put strips of bark held by poles against the mud walls to keep out the moisture and dirt. We achieved a lot in a week, grateful the weather remained dry. When we finished, we stood back from the house and smiled at a job well done. Our volunteer crew congratulated us, and we invited them in to look it over.

MY ACCURACY with bow and arrow improved with practice but still not enough to fell a deer. Nevertheless, I enjoyed hunting and fishing with Golden Skye and never minded when she made fun of my clumsiness. I showed her how to snare small game and fish with a line and hook. I taught Ben how to cast a fishing net. Wes had already mastered that. But I kept the bow and arrows to myself.

After we put the finishing touches on the house, we helped with the last of the harvest. Wes built places by our turf house for cold storage and wood, and we stocked up on both. As Golden Skye had predicted, the rains came by the end of the following week; by the end of the month, it snowed. With the turf house surprisingly dry and warm, we prepared to settle in, ready for whatever winter would bring.

# TWENTY-NINE

# Winter

## HANK

I emerged from our shelter to use our makeshift outhouse. Immediately, snowflakes accumulated on my clothes and melted on my face, cold and wet. Almost every day, snow fell by the lake. White covered everything, creating silence all around us with an atmosphere of calm and peace. Everything slowed down.

The fire in the hearth kept our shelter warm. We stored plenty of wood for fuel. The roof leaked in the rain; but once the rain changed to snow, the sod froze, and the leaking stopped. Every several days we carefully cleared the roof of snow to prevent the weight from collapsing it. We took turns maintaining a walkway to the road that led to the village.

Snares didn't catch much, and the lake froze, making net fishing impossible. I made a hole in the ice and dropped in a hook on a line, but even that became difficult as the ice thickened.

The villagers pulled the canoes from the water and laid them high above the lake. They stored the fishing nets in the village for inspection and repair. We contributed food to the communal food bank in the fall, as arranged, and that allowed us to access the stores. Best of all, we were close enough to visit our friends. Each day, Ben, Wes, and I maintained the shelter, cooked meals, and mostly got along.

Ben and Wes took a flat rock and etched boxes on it, eight boxes square. We carved discs from a branch and made them into checkers. The game became part of our routine. The winner of the game kept playing until he lost. Mostly, the loser seemed to be Ben and me. Wes consistently kept control of the board for the longest stretches.

We went into the village at least once per week to help mend and make new fishing nets, construct bows and arrows, and fix tools. People milled about the meetinghouse. I enjoyed the time spent with our new friends, especially Mica, Tara, and Golden Skye.

One day in late winter, we planned to go into the village to see about getting some lamb, salted fish, or deer jerky.

"We need to clear snow before we go," I said. "You two check the roof."

Ben and Wes headed up the hill and began to rake snow from the roof. I dug out the front of the shelter and tamped down a path to the road. As we worked, a loud crack followed by a booming roar startled me. A dead silence followed.

"What do you think that was?" Ben called to me.

"I don't know. Sounded like thunder, but the sky is clear. I think we need to see if something happened."

We moved slowly, as drifting snow covered the narrow road to the village. When we arrived, people shouted and scurried about.

"What's wrong?" Wes called. Tension filled the air.

Winter snow covering the boys' shelter

"An avalanche buried part of the village!" someone shouted back. "Hurry, we need help. People are trapped."

Homes had been swept away; others entombed under feet of snow. Villagers rooted in the snow, looking for survivors. They probed for pockets where people might be trapped. Many moved quickly with purpose; others walked about as if in a daze.

Ben grabbed a pole and joined the rescue. Wes surveyed the scene for a second then joined in the effort. I surveyed the area over and over, trying to locate Mica, Tara, and Golden Skye.

"Here!" Ben shouted. "I found something."

I ran to Ben's side and began to dig, postponing my search for Golden Skye. My heart raced as I pushed snow and ice out of the way. Ben rotated his pole, widening the hole. He uncovered the roof of a cabin. Ben and I expanded the hole until we found an eave. Ben banged on the roof hoping to alert anyone who might be inside and direct them to safety. I continued to remove snow until the couple trapped inside appeared from beneath the roof. Ben guided them to safety.

People worked frantically rescuing others from under the snow. Wes reported that he estimated that only a portion of the village had been struck. Although relatively small, the slide caused significant damage. Fortunately, many of the homes affected were unoccupied at the time the disaster struck. Apparently, people had been out, and some had managed to keep from being swept under the snow. Shadows lengthened as the day wore on. Still, people were missing, and the effort to find them continued.

Once I finished helping Ben extricate one family from the snow, I took a pole and started to probe for others. I looked up frequently as I searched for Golden Skye, but I didn't find her. This made me move faster as I tried to cover a greater area. Sweat ran down my face. I took my red bandanna from my pocket, folded it into a band, and tied it around my head to keep the sweat out of my eyes. I continued to plunge my pole into the snow, ever more fearful that Golden Skye had not escaped the avalanche.

Digging villagers out from the avalanche

"Hank, Hank!"

I turned. It was Golden Skye.

"Come with me," she said. "Our house is gone, and I'm afraid my mother and father are trapped inside."

I sprinted to Golden Skye and hugged her. "I feared you were buried in the snow," I said, grateful she was safe.

We ran to the place where her home once stood and started to plunge our poles into the snow. We moved along the plane of the avalanche. With her pole five feet below the surface, Golden Skye struck something hard. She stopped probing and listened. Faint rapping and voices calling emanated from below. She widened the hole and listened again. The voices sounded clearer.

"We're going to dig you out!" She called into the hole.

"Hurry!" someone called back. Golden Skye's eyes widened when she recognized it was her mother's voice.

I shouted to Ben and Wes. Neither was far from us. "We've located Tara."

The four of us quickly began digging and exposed a window on the side of the home. We entered a partially collapsed room. The avalanche destroyed the rest of the house. Mica was trapped, his leg pinned to the floor by a rafter. Tara tugged on the timber, unable to move it. Golden Skye hugged her mother, grateful she was unhurt. Ben, Wes, and I stood over the joist. "On three, we'll lift it together," I said. It moved just enough so that Golden Skye and her mother could drag Mica free.

"What if the building collapses?" Wes said. "We need to leave, now."

Ben and Wes supported Mica and helped him to the window and the path to the surface. Golden Skye, Tara, and I followed.

Once Mica was above the snow, other villagers assisted us as we carried him to a shelter where we assessed his injuries. I hadn't forgotten what Paul Arnold taught me on the ship about caring for injured sailors. The bones in Mica's leg appeared to be slightly displaced, out of alignment. It was clear it was broken. His foot felt warm, and he felt me poke it, so I knew his nerves and circulation were okay. Ben and Wes held Mica's shoulders as I gently pulled on his foot to set the bone. I took two sticks and tied them to the leg tightly. Once immobilized, Mica relaxed and appeared more comfortable.

Fortunately, no one died that day. There were other injuries, mostly minor. Once peace returned to the village, we headed to our shelter. We returned each day to check on

Mica. It took six weeks before he was able to bear weight on his leg. He mended well, left with only a slight limp to remind him of the ordeal.

Winter finally began to wane, and travel would soon be safe. It was time to plan to head home. Ambivalence filled my heart when I thought about leaving. We had made friends here, and I connected with Mica, Tara, and especially Golden Skye. One evening, back in our turf house, settled in for the night, I decided to speak to Wes and Ben about moving on.

"Tell me, are you ready to leave here once the ice is off the lake and the snow has mostly melted?" I asked.

"Actually, I like it here, but I want to go home," Ben said.

"What if we come back someday?" Wes said. "We can always come back. Can't we?"

"I will miss hunting and fishing with Golden Skye," I said. "I still have a lot to learn from her. I practiced throwing a net and using a bow, but I didn't have enough practice with either skill before the bad weather set in."

"I can use the fishing net, but I'm not so sure how confident I am throwing the net while standing in a canoe," Wes added.

"You know," I continued, "I wasn't always sure Golden Skye wanted me to tag along when she was hunting, but she never turned me down when I asked to join her."

"She probably thought your clumsiness was funny and your incompetence entertaining," Ben chided.

"Are you sweet on her?" Wes asked in a high, sing-song voice as he punched my arm. I felt my face flush. I reached out to grab him, but he slipped away.

ONE EVENING WHILE VISITING MICA, I found Golden Skye sitting by herself and sat down next to her.

"Thank you for sharing your skills with me. I promise to practice using the net and the bow."

"You did very well with the little time you had before the winter snows arrived, but you need to do work on moving in the forest without making so much noise," she said. "You throw the net well." She touched my arm. "I'll always be grateful to you for saving my parents."

My heart skipped a beat, and I averted my eyes. "Thank you," I said. "I expect it won't be long before spring returns."

"Yes, spring follows winter every year." Golden Skye turned to me.

"When it does come, Wes, Ben, and I will be leaving to go home to the Valley of the Black Dog."

"You don't have to go," she said. "You could stay here." She gazed into my eyes. I felt as if I were melting.

"We do like it here, but we miss our families, and we want to go home," I said, but without much conviction.

"I know," Golden Skye said and looked down.

"I will miss the village and especially you and your family. Everyone has been very kind to us."

Golden Skye smiled. She got up and walked across the room, picked up something from a table, returned, and sat down next to me again.

"Perhaps, after you spend time with your family, you will want to return to our village," Golden Skye said. She took my hand, opened my fist, and placed an arrowhead in my palm.

"Perhaps," I answered, and my heart warmed to the possibility, but I needed to make plans to go home.

I looked into Golden Skye's eyes and felt a longing to be closer to her. We hugged for a moment. As we pulled apart, she hesitated, and our lips met.

# THIRTY

# The Raft

HANK

Ben, Wes, and I stood by the water and skipped stones. Green grass and early spring mountain flowers poked up through the last of the retreating blanket of snow. Ice no longer covered the Inland Sea.

"I think we should start preparing to make our way home," I said.

"How?" Ben asked. "It's a long walk."

"I guess we could try to navigate the lake," I said. "Floating would be easier on our feet than walking and probably faster."

"How will we travel on the water?" Wes asked. "We don't have a boat."

We continued to skip stones.

"How about bartering for a canoe with the villagers?" Ben suggested.

"We'd need more than one, and what would we be bargaining with?" I asked. "We don't have much to trade."

"Maybe they'd show us how to make one," Wes said.

"Why not build a raft?" Ben blurted. His eyes sparkled,

encouraging me and Wes to consider his idea seriously. "Like the ones we used to see on the Black Dog River."

"Okay," I said, intrigued, and started devising a plan by drawing a sketch in the dirt. "I envision a platform that provides shelter and is stable on the water. I think eight by twelve feet are the right dimensions. We'll keep it simple."

"Pine trees are straight," Ben said. "If dead, they'll be dry, full of air, and float well. I think, based on the size we talked about, one that is about three to four feet around would work well. From finger to finger with my arms stretched out is about five feet." Ben stood and extended his arms. "If you can easily hug a tree with your hands overlapped, that's about right."

We set off into the forest to look for suitable wood and found one in a marshy area and felled it with an ax. We removed the branches and chopped the log into two twelve-foot lengths.

We maneuvered each section through the marsh to the lake. Ben located the second and third trees closer to the water, and we cut them into similar portions, rolled them to the water, and floated them to the other logs.

"What are you three up to?" Bly, a friend from the village, called as we secured the logs. "The chopping echoes everywhere. I came to check on you."

"We're making a raft," Wes shouted back, excitement in his voice.

"Can I give you a hand?" Bly asked.

The four of us moved the trunks from the water to the shore. As we toiled, curious villagers gathered to see what we were doing.

"They're building some kind of a boat," Bly announced to the spectators as they arrived.

"Oh, are you expecting a flood?" Dani, another village friend, shouted as laughter rippled through the throng.

"I can start gathering the animals," someone else called out, and the crowd reacted with another wave of laughter. Someone started a fire and began boiling presoaked dried corn. Others took a seat and prepared to watch us build our raft. We suddenly became the local entertainment, a festive event. I overheard speculation on how they thought we might proceed and whether the thing would float. Good host that I was, I felt obligated to explain our plan.

"We need to fashion shafts that will lay across the logs, above and below. That way, we can secure the trunks together between the rows of poles and create a platform on which to sit," I said. "I must find material to make rope. Ben and Wes will find trees that will make suitable shafts for the deck."

My brother and cousin took off in one direction, observers in tow, and I headed in another. During the winter, helping to repair fishing nets and tools, I learned how to make rope from milkweed using dead stems that hadn't completely dried. Unfortunately, it was difficult to find suitable milkweed stalks that hadn't been destroyed by the winter cold.

I sent one group of helpers off to salvage milkweed, while others gathered ivy vines and willow bark, also useful for making rope. We braided lengths of cord, combining thinner lengths to make them thicker and stronger, and finished by coating them with pine tar. After hours of work, fingers bloody raw and hands cramped from fatigue, I was grateful for all the help. We gathered the rope and returned to check on my brother and cousin and their helpers.

I found Ben and Wes next to an impressive stack of poles, each three to five inches in diameter and ten feet long. We rebuilt the fire and started boiling pots of water containing potatoes, onions, and dried peas. We combined carrots from the village with vegetables kept in our cold storage. Some of the villagers dug a pit, made a spit, and roasted venison they brought with them. We made enough for all. I welcomed the help, certain we'd be able to finish the task with everyone pitching in. Once we finished eating, we returned to raft building.

"How many poles do we need?" Wes asked.

Ben drew a picture in the dirt of six logs. "The length of my hand is about seven inches. The trunks are a little more than two hands in diameter, about fifteen inches. Together, they will support a platform ten feet wide and twelve feet long. On average, the shafts are three to five inches in diameter and ten feet long and will be placed perpendicular to the length of the logs."

Ben scratched his chin. "So, twelve feet is 144 inches. If each shaft is on average four inches in diameter, that's about . . . 144 divided by four. Thirty-six poles on top. We'll need at least six underneath, for a total of forty-two." Ben took a deep bow, proud of his math acumen. He saw skepticism on the faces around him.

"Okay, you don't believe me? You do the math," he said.

Based on Ben's calculation, the raft required a lot more rope. In fact, if I allowed for five to six feet of rope to cinch each of the six top poles to six evenly placed shafts underneath, I needed at least twelve eight-foot pieces to tie all of them together. With everyone's help, we eventually completed the job.

It took days, fourteen in all, to make and amass all the parts for the raft. We finished by moving everything to the water's edge, where we lashed shafts on the ends first to hold the main logs together. We placed poles on top to create the deck and slid six shafts into place underneath, securing the top ones to the bottom ones. Ben stood a post in the middle front of the raft and attached it to all four corners. That stick supported others over which we draped canvas blankets, creating a tent, to provide some shelter and act as a sail. It wasn't hard to fashion a paddle for each of us, two with which to row and one as a rudder. We cut three long shafts to help move the craft in shallow water.

The raft

IT TOOK several more days of work before we were ready to push off. Everyone helped to slide and drag the raft to the water.

"It actually floats," someone shouted, and cheers and clapping followed.

I climbed on with Ben and Wes. The deck of the raft sat high and dry, precipitating another round of cheers and applause.

Wes and Ben made a low railing on the raft's front and sides and created a place to tie in our belongings.

We still had some jerky, grain, nuts, and dried vegetables. With access to the lake now that the winter thaw was in full swing, we could fish and, in the evenings, trap game after we put in.

We decided to return to the village one more time to say goodbye. I found Golden Skye as she was about to go hunting.

"Golden Skye," I called. She turned toward me. "We leave early tomorrow."

"I know. I hope you have a safe trip."

I took the arrowhead she'd given me and held it up for her to see. "Good hunting," I said.

"I hope to see you again." She ran to me, gave me a hug, and kissed my cheek. I didn't want to let her go.

# THIRTY-ONE

# In the Valley

JENNY

I sat on a hill above the pasture as the sheep grazed below me. Oscar lay in the grass by my side. He dozed, his ears twitching when disturbed by a fly or gnat. From my vantage point, the river spread out below me, a half-mile wide. Rafts, laden with late-spring hay, floated to market. Smaller craft ferried travelers across, and a fisherman cast his line from the bank.

North of town, larger ships docked at the harbor. Our port bustled now, and I frequently visited to marvel at the wondrous things that arrived from far-away lands, especially the spices, pepper, and unusual foods. I stuck my head into the barrels and inhaled, my mouth watering from the distinctive aromas of cinnamon, tea, and nutmeg. Colorful beads, pearls, and cloth of all types of materials, textures, and patterns dazzled me.

"Have your paths crossed with my cousins Hank, Ben, or Wes?" I asked sailors as I strolled the docks. One sailor knew of a shipwreck where most of the crew escaped. His voice echoed in my head. I stood motionless, speechless, stunned into silence by the news.

"Almost everyone made it into the lifeboats before the ship broke up," he said. "When they took account of who was present in the boats, three boys were among the missing. I'm not sure, but it could have been a Hank, Ben, and Wes."

I gasped, unable to continue to talk with him. I finally turned and walked away. Tears ran down my cheeks. I gasped for breath, unable to breathe. I needed to tell my mother and father. They immediately told my aunts and uncles.

"Just because they weren't with the rest of the crew doesn't mean they didn't survive," Uncle Nate said. "I refuse to think the worst."

Uncle Nate prevailed that day in maintaining hope, but I remained concerned I might never see my cousins again. They had been gone so long, and that was the only news I heard. There was no other evidence that anybody had seen them. Joe and Frances, both of whom left on their journeys at the same time as Hank, had returned safe and sound and apparently with keys.

My mind wandered. I thought about the boys and wondered how they would react to me when they did come home. I imagined playing games with them in which I was their teacher, and they were my students, or I'd be the chief, and they'd be my men, and I'd send them off on all kinds of adventures, to fight dragons or search for treasure. We would sit by the fire after dark, listening to tales about their travels, and how they survived the terrible shipwreck.

"They escaped," I suddenly said aloud, lost in my daydreams. With the disturbance of quiet, Oscar's head popped up, and he stared at me, awaiting a command.

Jenny marshaling the sheep

"No, Oscar," I said. "We have time before we start for home. Hannah will be coming to help us, and she isn't here yet. You can put your head back down and rest."

The river flowed north to the ocean. The sun rose high in the sky, and a breeze picked up, washing over me with the fresh spring air. The sheep grazed, feeding on new grass. The ram stood among his flock, horns adorning his head like a crown. I looked around. All was well, and I returned to thinking about my cousins, hoping they might be on their way home.

# THIRTY-TWO

# The Great Inland Sea

## HANK

We awoke before dawn and made our final preparations for the trip. Ben set the sail in place, Wes secured our supplies, and I inspected the raft once more. I made a strap for the pouch that held my logbook and slung it over my shoulder under my shirt to keep it safe.

"Okay," I said. "Before we step on board, we should give the raft a name."

"I think we should call her *Float*, because that is what I hope she does," Wes said.

"I think she should have a real name," Ben said. "How about *Spray*?"

"Now, that does have a ring," Wes said, and I agreed.

"From now on you will be called *Spray*," I said and splashed water on the deck.

We climbed on board. Some villagers, Mica and Golden Skye among them, arrived to wish us well just before we shoved off. We waved to them. My heart raced when I saw Golden Skye again. Our eyes met, I placed my hand over my heart and waved. She did the same in return.

I wanted to jump off the raft, step onto shore, and tell her I changed my mind. But I didn't. We were going home.

I controlled the rope that tied us to the shore, let go of one end, and we floated free. I reeled in the rest of the line as Ben took the long pole and began to push us into deeper water.

Once we were out on the lake, the prevailing wind from the south filled the canvas blanket hanging from the mast. Wes guided us as Ben and I paddled. *Spray* appeared stable, and the deck remained dry. We planned to follow the southern border of the lake as far west as it would take us.

As we floated away, I looked back in the direction of the village and hoped to catch one more glimpse of the place where we had stayed these past months. My last image was occasional wisps of smoke rising above the forest as if they were waving goodbye.

"I think I could live in a village like that," Ben said.

"I think I could live in that village," I added.

"I liked the way the whole community worked together," Ben said.

"Everybody was aware of everyone else's needs," I said. "A study in *compassion* and *generosity* as I see it; both are keys." We'd found fourteen keys by my count. "Now it is time to go home. We can always come back to visit." That thought pleased me.

"Look at the mountain's reflection in the water," Ben said. "I wish I had a way to capture that."

The shore became more distant as the wind pushed us away from it. High clouds seemed to drift with us; mountain peaks remained visible to the south and west, but all I saw to the north was water, though I knew the Eastern Mountains lay beyond.

"Let's sail until the sun starts to disappear behind the

western range," I said. "We can stop paddling. The wind is steady. We'll find a place to put in, do some fishing, set snares, and settle in for the night."

I enjoyed the peace and serenity of the lake as I concentrated on the sounds around me, recalling that in silence, I might be able to hear the angels talking. While Wes steered, Ben and I shut our eyes and listened.

WE SETTLED INTO A ROUTINE. Early morning, after a refreshing swim in the chilly waters, we drifted mostly, paddled when the wind calmed, took turns at the tiller, and camped on the shore in the evening. When it rained, we stayed onshore, especially if there was thunder and lightning or heavy winds. Fortunately, the weather remained mostly fair, and progress was steady, albeit slow. I guided the raft close to the shoreline, to avoid being caught too far from safety if the gusts picked up suddenly or the waves became rough. I remembered the shipwreck all too well. So did Ben and Wes, but they didn't question my judgment here, nor did I.

One lazy late afternoon, we all must have fallen asleep, because when I awoke and looked around, we were beyond sight of any land. I woke Wes and Ben.

"Which way do we go? What if we can't find anywhere to stop?" Wes wrung his hands, his voice stressed.

"It's nearing the end of the day," I responded. "Follow the setting sun. That's west."

Ben stood and surveyed the sea. "I see land over there."

Ben sees land

I stood and looked in the direction Ben pointed. A spit of land floated on the water. A rocky spire capped by a cloud rose from the center. We paddled toward it. Instead of what I hoped would be the eastern shore, we discovered a narrow island covered by a dense forest. As the raft neared the island a dense fog rolled across the water accompanied by an eerie quiet.

I used the long pole to maneuver the raft to a place accessible to the shore. After making camp where we landed, we separated to explore the area. The sun hadn't fully set but the heavy, moist air that enveloped us decreased our visibility to no more than twenty feet. Wes went to forage for berries and greens. Ben set hooks and lines to catch fish. I decided to look for dry wood and planned to start a fire, always seeking another key.

I wandered inland from our camp toward the rocky spire at the center of the island. Once at its base, I climbed it, hoping to get above the fog to see how far we'd drifted away from the southern shore. Forty feet up, fog still obscured any land visible on the horizon. As I climbed down, I discovered a path. It led me through a gap in a stone wall to a circular depression where the fog had thinned. Rocky crags loomed above. Steam rose in places from fractures in the rocks on the depression's floor, and the air reeked of rotten eggs. A run-down log cabin stood in the center, windows emitting light from within. Smoke from the chimney mixed with the haze emanating from the ground shrouded the rim of the stone walls above. As I headed to the shack, somebody grabbed me from behind.

"What are you doing here?" said a deep, gruff voice. I turned to face my captor, prepared to fight, and gasped. He was twice my size. I wrenched my arm from his grip, spun away, and started to run up the path in the direction I came. The huge man plodded after me. I reached the gap in the rock wall with heavy lumbering footsteps thudding behind me.

Think fast. *Dive into the bushes, hide in the brush where you can't be seen, and crawl to safety.* I stopped, ready to jump, and stepped backward. An old woman, nearly my size, wearing a sardonic smile, blocked my way. Her long, gray hair extended from her scalp like snakes, and her teeth were brown and broken. She reached out for me with her knotty, bent fingers. I drew back and stared in horror, unable to move at first, but quickly regained my sense of purpose and ran. Before taking two steps, the ogre caught me and pinned my hands at my sides. I tried to call out to Wes and Ben but found myself mute. I reached for my red bandanna, worked it out of my pocket, and dropped it on the ground as I struggled to get free.

"Well, Sonny," the old hag said in a high-pitched whine. "I think we ought to take this one home." They both cackled. Sonny clamped his dirty, greasy hand over my mouth, picked me up like a sack of potatoes, and carried me kicking back to their hut. He placed me in a chair and tied me to it with my hands behind me and my mouth gagged.

"Don't make any noise," the old crone commanded, "or we'll move our mealtime up. Maybe put you on the menu. Come, Sonny, let's gather some wild garlic, onion, mushrooms, and mint. Find a newt or two, maybe throw in a frog for flavor."

My captors left. I immediately started to work the rope back and forth, trying to loosen it. Across from me, the fireplace held a big cauldron filled with water, set to boil. A pile of bones lay on the floor in a corner next to a cage, large enough to hold a big dog. *Is that cage meant for me?* The pot's sickening odor made me want to gag. *Worse, are they going to boil me in that thing?* A cupboard occupied the wall behind me. *Probably contains knives and such. Try to wiggle the chair there.* I went to work.

There was a window next to the front door and another open window on the back wall opposite the door. I hoped Ben and Wes had started looking for me. I had to believe they would, especially if I were gone too long. *Trust that Ben and Wes will find my bandanna and know to look for me.*

Minutes stretched into what felt like an hour. The ropes that held my hands were loosening, and I continued to work them vigorously as sweat ran down my face. My wrists became raw and painful, but I freed one hand, then the other. I bent over to untie my feet.

They had returned. I listened as the man and woman spoke outside and worked to quickly free myself. *Maintain calm, think about how to get out of here.*

"I heard something in the woods, Ma. I think there are more of them."

They had to be referring to Ben and Wes. *They must be safe for the moment.* I scanned the room and debated whether to jump out the back window and run or pretend I was still securely tied and wait for a better opportunity to escape. I looked over to the window, and Wes was looking back at me. He put his finger to his lips, signaling me to be quiet, opened the window further, and started to enter the room. I raised my hand to stop him, threw off the ropes, tore the gag out of my mouth, and ran to him. I climbed out the window and dropped to the ground just as the hag entered the hut.

"He's getting away!" she screamed, her voice harsh and strained. "He's in the back, Sonny!"

The giant ran around the cabin to the rear, the earth shaking with each of his steps. We headed in the opposite direction. Ben waited in the darkness in the front. The woman stepped onto the threshold of the porch. Ben ran at her, pushed her back inside, and slammed the door behind her. Ben saw us appear as we turned the corner from the side of the cabin and joined us as we dashed down the path that led to the gap in the stone wall.

Moonlight lit our way, the fog having lifted. Fear motivated us to run like the wind and propelled us all the way to the campsite. We hastily tossed our belongings on the raft and pushed off, my logbook securely in place across my shoulder. We were fifty yards from shore before Sonny reached the site. He picked up a rock and threw it at us, but it fell short. He watched us for a moment more, then he stepped back into the woods.

We caught our breath as we paddled in the moonlight. I realized we missed supper, but it wasn't the first meal we missed. I was very grateful I hadn't become someone else's dinner. Ben took my red bandanna from his pocket and returned it to me. I had trusted that he'd find it and know I was in trouble. That *trust*, a key, had allayed my fear.

The night was clear. I found the big dipper and then the North Star to guide us. We arrived at the southern edge of the lake as the sun rose on the eastern horizon. We tied the raft up at a clearing on the shore and rested

*We didn't find a new key, but perhaps old keys had opened doors,* I wrote in the logbook. *I got through this ordeal because I trusted Ben and Wes would rescue me. I relied on trust.* I felt admiration and gratitude.

Still spooked by the events on the island, we took turns sleeping while one of us kept an eye out for Sonny and Ma. I slept fitfully but didn't awaken until late in the day. I pushed Ben and Wes to leave immediately, hoping we would put more distance between that creepy island and us.

THIRTY-THREE

# Ned

HANK

With a constant breeze filling the sail, we took turns guiding *Spray* and enjoyed a much-needed rest from paddling. One of us kept a lookout in front, and one rested or trolled for fish in the rear. We passed other boats on the lake, stopped to talk, and occasionally traded for food or spices. We asked about the island with the rocky spires and steam rising from the ground. Some had heard rumors of such a place but considered it a folk legend; none had seen it. I wondered if it had all been a dream. The bruises on my arms, where the giant held me, and the rope burns on my wrist suggested otherwise.

On an unusually warm afternoon, as we slowly made our way north, far out on the lake, a canoe made its way toward us. Our paths would cross, and I anticipated having someone to talk to and, perhaps, barter with.

"I don't like those clouds gathering to our west," Ben said. "An updraft has flipped the leaves on the trees upside down. We'd better get off the water. Bad weather is on the way."

Bad weather is on the way

We took down our sail and paddled quickly to land. The cool air of the approaching front passed over us. Ben's judgment proved correct. Dark clouds swept across the lake preceded by whipping winds that rattled the trees and tore at their branches. With *Spray* moored safely, we got off the raft and huddled under the canvas sail. Thunder and lightning raged.

Out on the lake, a round, light-colored area of water appeared. The patterns of light and dark intermixed and swirled. From above the center of the light region, spiral bands descended, forming a funnel-shaped column that reached the surface of the water. The waterspout rode the surface of the lake for a long minute before it collapsed. Another funnel started to form but collapsed. Then a third and fourth spout popped up. A drenching rain followed, spreading over us, and just as quickly passed.

*Splat . . . splat, splat.*

"Ouch," Ben shouted with surprise. "Look what hit me." In his hand, he held a fish, suitable for cooking.

"Interesting," Wes said, smiling at Ben's discovery. "It rains fish here."

"Find more. We'll have a meal," I said, pleased at our good fortune.

"Where's the canoe that was out on the lake just before the storm struck?" Ben said, his voice serious with concern.

I scanned the lake and spotted a raised hand waving. Ben threw the sail onto the raft, and I released *Spray* from her mooring. We rowed in the direction of the hand. Ben and Wes paddled furiously. I worked the rudder. We closed on the man who appeared to be calmly treading water.

"Are you okay?" Wes shouted to the man as we approached. The wind had picked up again, roiling the water as the man rode up and down on the waves.

The man took a deep breath and responded:

*A little weary,*
*and grateful for your query.*
*I avoided the waterspout, but for my well-being, I have some*
*doubts.*
*I think you would agree,*
*I lost my canoe, unfortunately.*

"We can help you," Wes shouted.

*I swam enough today.*
*Please remove me from this bay.*
*Thank you three,*
*For coming here to rescue me.*

Ben and I pulled the stranger out of the water and onto the raft. I marveled at his calm. I think I was more concerned than he appeared to be. Once on board, the man introduced himself.

He said:

*I'm Ned,*
*I thought I was dead.*
*No worry, I possess an affinity for maintaining my*
*equanimity.*
*I didn't panic. I knew that you were near,*
*And once safe on land, I'd have no fear.*
*I might have tried to swim to shore,*
*But, oh, that'd be a difficult chore.*
*Would I have made it today?*
*I don't know, the shore seems so far away."*

"Equanimity? An interesting word," Ben said. "It's a

clue to a key we've been looking for." Wes and I nodded. "But what does it mean?"

*A balanced mind.*
*That's my grind.*

"You could say that about life, couldn't you?" I added. "Yes," Ned answered and then continued:

*Life has its ups and downs*
*Like the waves on this great lake.*
*But I didn't frown,*
*Make no mistake; I just rode the wake,*
*Or I might have drowned.*
*Never too high,*
*I won't deny,*
*For the waves may have swept me away,*
*Never to see another day."*

"Well, you seem to have done okay," Wes said and chuckled as he added to Ned's rhyme.

*When I started to become upset, I didn't forget.*
*Maintain an inner calm. Do not fret.*
*A clear head carries me through any threat.*
*Don't become hysterical, energy set too high, or obliviously unconcerned, energy set too low, or you are destined to fail, you know.*

"You're safe, now," said Ben. "I don't recommend a swim in this cold water for any length of time. The sun has returned, and it has become a glorious day."

"We'll take you to shore," Wes said, "build a fire and warm you up."

*You are so kind.*
*I've happened onto a most wonderful find.*

Ned bowed his head.

We wrapped Ned in the sail and headed for land, secured the raft, and disembarked to set up camp. As we worked, I whispered to Ben out of earshot of Ned. "I like the essence of what Ned said about approaching life with an even and balanced mind and maintaining an inner calm in the face of life's challenges. But, what's with all the rhyming."

"I didn't notice," Ben said, and we both laughed.

The fire was warm, and Ned's clothes quickly dried. He said:

*I headed for the village, not to pillage, but to trade my goods,*
*After all, that is my livelihood.*

"I'm sure the villagers will be very sympathetic," I said and shared our experience of the past several months as we ate our grilled fresh fish.

The next day, we bid Ned goodbye, boarded the raft, and set sail again. Ned headed to the village by the lake on foot. We expressed our sadness we couldn't recover his canoe.

"Remember," Ben shouted to Ned as we parted, "Ask for Mica when you reach the town. He's a man of great renown."

Ned laughed and waved before he disappeared up the road.

Once Ned was out of sight, I signaled to Wes and Ben to get their attention.

"We found another key, *equanimity*. I believe it is our fifteenth. We can go home heads held high."

# THIRTY-FOUR

# The Path

BEN

We'd been on the lake for fifteen days. Each morning, I cut another notch on the mast to score how long we'd been sailing. The sun rose higher overhead, and I welcomed its warmth. Summer would soon be here. The trees and foliage along the shore shed their spring flowers, and lush green leaves replaced them.

Hank carefully docked the raft. I had no idea how far we had sailed but remained content with the pace we traveled under sail and paddle. The evening had arrived, and at the current elevation, the night would be chilly. Wes rigged a pole with some fishing string, dug up some worms, baited the hooks, and dropped the lines into the water. Hank and I inspected *Spray*. She had fared well so far and remained in good shape. Hank removed the sail from the mast to use as ground cover. Once the raft was secure, I took off into the forest to set snares.

The road that followed the lake

Just beyond the shore, I found a road that followed the
lake before climbing a hill. I wondered who had made it

and where it went. The road was wide enough for two carts to comfortably pass. Square rocks edged the way and functioned as a curb. Gravel covered the roadbed, with larger stones in the center to give it elevation to promote proper drainage. I walked on for several hundred yards until I came upon a man sitting in the middle of the way. The man couldn't sit still and mumbled to himself. He picked up a stone. His eyes darted back and forth. He put it down, then reached for another one, shook his head, and moaned. I approached carefully, trying to avoid upsetting him further.

"Are you okay?" I asked as I slowly stepped closer.

"Do I look okay?" the man responded. His voice trembled as if he were about to cry.

"No, actually, you don't look okay. Can I help?"

"Are you privy to the secret order in which these stones must be placed?"

"Is there an order to the stones?" I asked, confused by the man's response. I didn't see a specific pattern, except for square rocks on each edge, gravel on the sides, and larger pebbles in the middle.

"All things are ordered. If not maintained, then all you have is chaos. My job is to maintain order and establish harmony. As you walked up this path, I am sure you appreciated how the way is neat and promotes tranquility. But when I arrived at this point, I found that someone, or something, disturbed the stones. I need to put them back into order or—"

"Or what?" I interrupted, patience not being one of my best traits.

"Or other stones will lose their harmony. The whole path will be in discord, and all we are left with is a cacophony of stones."

The man started to wave his arms again before turning back to me.

"You don't seem concerned," he said. "You should be. Disorder threatens to precipitate change. I don't deal well with change. By maintaining order, I can control what should otherwise be constant and predictable. I'm not leaving this spot until I figure out how to reestablish the proper relationship of each stone to its neighbor."

"All right," I said. "What if you put this rock here and move that one there?" I looked at the ground, hundreds of stones lay in front of me. Yet this man worked frantically to establish an order where I didn't perceive any.

"That big rock is not in its correct location," the man said. "I think that pebble should go here." He moved stones, then studied the path.

"The road looks well maintained and makes clear which direction it will take me," I said. "How will the pattern of the stones change which way I walk?"

"The way is important, and order helps us all to arrive at our end."

"Is this the only path to all destinations, or are there many ways to one? Are all roads as ordered as this?"

The man stopped trying to rearrange the stones. He rose from his seated position and stared at me. He scrunched his eyes. His forehead was speckled with sweat.

I hadn't meant to upset him.

"I never considered other paths," he said. "We always walk on this one, which, I might add, *is* the correct one."

"I think that is kind of narrow." I spoke slowly with kindness, so as not to offend him further. "You chose this way, and it may be right for you, but why not acknowledge the possibilities for other ways? I also believe the destination is important, but maybe the journey has even more value?

My mother taught me that when things are in order, it creates harmony and lessens stress." *Maybe that is why she always made me clean my room.* "However, she cautioned that perfection may stymie getting to your goal. If you spend all your time ordering the stones, I don't think you will ever reach your journey's end. By the way, where does this road lead?"

"I don't know," the man replied and looked down. "Do we ever really know?"

I scratched my head. I admit I was curious about where this path led and was tempted to walk on. I decided it would be more prudent to set my snares closer to shore. I turned and headed back the way I came. The man also turned, to see where I was going.

"A wise move," he called to me. "I think it will take me some time to put this path back in correct shape. May you find what you're looking for."

I waved and walked on and quickly found myself by the lake, where I set out several traps. I hoped that Wes was successful fishing, and, that if we were lucky, my snares would produce something for breakfast.

"I met a man while I was in the woods," I related to Hank and Wes when I reached our camp. "He seemed obsessed with order and paths. It made me wonder about our journey. I've been less concerned about the way and more focused on the destination once we decided to return home."

"I can't wait to reach home," Wes said. "Are we still looking for keys? We've found fifteen."

"This is about keys," I said. "*Order* is a key, and order is all around us. Night always follows day, and the seasons of the year follow each other without change. Seems like everything has . . . harmony, a rhythm, and a right way.

Makes things predictable, and that's helpful when you interact with others. But isn't the real challenge in life dealing with what's not predictable?"

Hank interrupted me. "Which is more important, the journey—that is, the way you go—or the destination, where you're going?"

"Actually, I think, if you get to where you're going by fair and honest means, it certainly makes getting there more rewarding," I said. "So, I think it is the way. How important is order? Too much can be bad, even paralyzing."

"Remember Messyman?" Wes said. "Too little order isn't any better."

"Balance is the answer, just enough," Hank reminded us.

We continued to talk well into the night before finally stopping to sleep. Our destination was clear, but the path remained uncertain, and I wondered when we would reach the end of the lake.

# THIRTY-FIVE

# The End of the Great Inland Sea

## HANK

The next day we broke camp, scattered the ashes from the fire that had warmed us through the night, and reset the sail. We boarded *Spray* and pushed off. As we headed west, the northern shore was now clearly visible on our right, and a current I didn't previously appreciate carried us. Increasing numbers of rock outcroppings and small islands of land supporting trees and grass surrounded us.

"We're moving much faster," Wes said and sat up higher. He wore a puzzled frown.

"What's that?" Ben shouted and pointed west. "Do you see that cloud of mist rising from the lake?"

"Sounds like rushing water up ahead," I said. "Probably rapids. We need to pull over before we go any farther. Check what's in front of us before we try to pass through."

Wes attempted to steer *Spray* to the shore. The current interfered by spinning the raft as Ben used the pole to try to direct us. I grabbed a tow pole and coordinated with Ben. We directed the raft closer to an islet. Wes pulled hard with the rudder, I secured one end of a line onto the mast and threw the other end around whatever jutted from the outcroppings. I caught a young sapling and the raft held. No longer fighting the current, we caught our breath.

"Okay," Ben said. "What's the plan?"

"The current isn't as strong by the shore," I said. "We can push the raft from island to island until we reach land or calmer water."

"What if the lake wins," Wes said, "and sweeps us away? I don't think any of us are powerful enough swimmers to fight this current."

"You remember what Father always told us about riding rapids," Hank said. "If you fall out of the boat, roll onto your back, keep your head up out of the water, and feet pointed downstream."

"I think he also said to try not to drown," Ben added.

Wes glared at him, apparently failing to appreciate his humor.

I shouted over the raging water. "Our next stop, that island, fifty yards ahead." I pointed. "Let's go." I pushed the raft back into the current.

We directed *Spray* to the next outcrop and found ourselves behind it in no time. I secured the rope around a rock jutting up as Ben poled and Wes steered. I surveyed the situation ahead and tried to plan our next jump.

"That was fun," Ben said. "I wonder how close we are to the rapids."

"Rapids?" Wes shouted over the turbulent sound of fast-flowing water. He pointed to a place to our right where mist rose hundreds of feet above us as the water disappeared over an edge. "What if the rapids aren't really rapids? What if we've discovered a giant waterfall?"

I studied the lake again. Wes was right; these weren't

just rapids. This was a waterfall, and we were still far enough from the edge of the falls to chance one more attempt at getting us nearer to shore. Unfortunately, each gambit brought us closer to the falls. The current had significantly increased. The water turned white with turbulence as the slope approaching the falls steepened. We had no choice. We had to try for one more leap toward shore.

Rushing toward the waterfall

"Here we go again. Ready?" I released my hold on the rock and pushed *Spray* into the current again. The raft flew with the flow and rocked violently as the once-smooth water of the lake roiled. We came closer to the shore, but twenty-five yards remained between us and safety. The front of the raft dipped, then rose high in the air, flipping all of us off the back. I was underwater, thrown against rocks, and struggled until I found the surface. Wes popped up next, then Ben. We headed toward the precipice, on our backs, feet forward, our heads out of water, in a line, bobbing up and down.

*Spray* floated just ahead of us, caught on a rock, but only for a long moment, swinging from right to left as the water played with it. Rocks jutted out of the water at shorter intervals. Closer to the shore, debris collected between some, including felled trees. Ben grabbed one, held on with one arm, and extended the other. He snagged Wes just before Wes passed him. I slammed into the log seconds later and latched on.

We worked our way down the tree to a stone outcrop and then carefully from rock to rock. We held onto each other until safely ashore. I looked over the edge of the falls, a mile wide and hundreds of feet high. The sound of falling water was deafening. Mist rose into the air, filtering the light into rainbows, one on top of another. I studied the water pouring over the falls and located *Spray* as it spun off a rock and drifted back into the current.

Pointing, I shouted, "There goes *Spray*."

The raft picked up speed and flew over the cascade. It floated in the white haze like a bird gliding on a thermal as it descended into the gorge. I thought I heard it break up, but the dense mist at the bottom hid it from view.

"That could have been us," Wes said, shaking and pale.

"We need to get dry," Ben said, also shaking. "I'm freezing."

"Fortunately, we have most of the day left," I said. "The

air is calm, and the sun is warm. We need to get a fire started to dry our clothes. Put a flat rock behind the fire to reflect heat and cook some dry rocks. That will also help to warm us."

"We lost everything," Wes said, his gaze distant, mouth in a frown. "How will we start a fire?"

"We didn't lose everything. We'll be fine," I assured him, although I was equally distressed. *Will we be okay?* I didn't know but didn't want to upset him further. "I still have the fire stones and my knife. I kept them in my pocket." I put my hand in my front pocket to check that the arrowhead Golden Skye had given me was still there. I checked my back pocket. I still had my striped bandanna. I kept my journal in a leather pouch under my shirt. The pages were wet, but the writing was still legible.

"We can sharpen some sticks to use to spear fish and make some string for setting snares," I added. "Let's stop here and think about what we need. We have access to water and food in the forest. The weather is good. I say, camp here tonight in the open, above the falls, out of the mist. We'll be okay."

I might have reassured Ben and Wes, but I hadn't convinced myself with this rhetoric. I was grateful for what we had and didn't dwell on what we'd lost. I had to trust my skills and have faith that all would be well; after all, we'd made it this far.

That night, as we sat by the fire, Ben broke the silence by asking me if I really believed everything was fine.

"I'm not sure," I said.

Ben considered the answer for a moment. "Do you always tell the truth?" he asked.

"What brings that up?" I responded.

"Just thinking. I asked you earlier if you thought we'd be okay. You said we would, without hesitation. Now, you say you're concerned. I think honesty is important."

"I agree," I said. "No one should lie, but what if the only result of truth would be to hurt someone? Is it okay to lie then?"

"Interesting," Wes said, joining the conversation. "You bump into someone who just bought a new shirt. You think the shirt makes them look silly. They think they look great. Do you tell them they look silly, or do you tell them they look great?"

"I wouldn't tell them what I thought unless they asked me," I said.

"So, what if they asked?" Ben said.

"I might say, nice shirt. It might be a nice shirt, even if the person looked silly in it. Why make them feel bad?"

"But then you'd be lying or telling less than the whole truth," Ben said. "Is the saying 'honesty is the best policy' only correct depending on the situation you are in?"

"I still think the truth is the best way regardless of the consequences," I said, "but don't go out of your way to hurt somebody with the truth. Tell the truth with kindness in mind."

"I'm going to keep thinking about this," Ben said.

"Let us know what you conclude," I said. "Perhaps, the truth is so complicated that it is easier to just make sure you distance yourself from lies. Remember that honesty leads to trust, and trust is often given willingly. However, once trust is lost, it's difficult to regain. Truth wins you another's trust. I hope you still trust me."

"I feel more confident about our situation now, and I'm glad you didn't share your anxiety with me right after the raft went over the falls," Ben said. "I'm calmer now and can better handle you sharing your concerns. So, what do we do next?"

# The Black Dog River

HANK

Above the falls, we rested in camp to let our wounds heal. Wes had a gash on his scalp, and Ben had bruises across his back. I had twisted my knee. We welcomed the period of rest. As the days passed, Ben started to fidget and complain. Wes mumbled aloud over what we had lost, and that amounted to just about everything. My knife, the fire stones, and the arrowhead from Golden Sky survived. I still had my red bandanna for luck and my logbook.

From our camp, the gorge's tall trees and dense foliage stretched out below us. The roar of falling water filled the air. Mist rose from the falls so dense that it obscured our view and made everything damp.

After a few days, we searched for a path to the river and discovered a way that led us into the hills surrounding us, away from an abrupt descent with moss-covered, mist-drenched, slippery rocks, which would have been a more difficult path with my banged-up knee.

The waterfall

This river flowed north. It had to be our river, and the valley it flowed into, our valley, the Valley of the Black Dog. Although the waterfall was broad, the basin was narrow and steep, and the river, too swift and rocky for transportation. We found ourselves walking once again. I started with a limp, but that faded quickly as my knee recovered. Wes's scalp healed, and Ben's bruised back appeared minor.

We took all day to make our way to the river away from the mist. I looked back and marveled at the sheer might and volume of water cascading over the cliff. I felt small and insignificant in the presence of something so immense and powerful. As far as I could recall, no one had ever spoken of this waterfall. Why not claim it as our own discovery? When we arrived home, we would check if that was true.

"Hank's Great Falls," I declared as I watched the falling water. "I am the oldest and therefore entitled to the honor of naming it."

"A little humility, please," Wes reminded me.

"Really," Ben added. "Hank's Falls? I don't think that is fair."

"What's not fair? I saw them first," I said.

"I don't think so," Ben responded.

"We all discovered them at the same time and almost too late, if you remember," Wes said. "How about, the WBH Falls, for each of us?"

"Really, sometimes you both take up too much space," I said. "This is the headwaters for the Black Dog River. How about we name it the Black Dog Falls?"

"Okay," Ben said. Wes nodded.

I frowned, unhappy with the compromise, still unwilling to give up a chance at fame and immortality by naming the waterfall after ourselves. The Black Dog Falls suggestion was a humbler choice.

We broke camp the next day and headed to higher ground away from the river. The foliage was less dense and travel easier at this height. We still had a long way to go. As we climbed to the top of an elevation, we left the lake and waterfall behind.

We walked on for several hours before taking a break to find a suitable place to camp. It was a bit early to stop for the day, but it afforded us an opportunity to scavenge for food. The weather favored us: warm, with little humidity. The sound of rushing water still rose from the valley. Dry, grassy fragrances filled my nose as I sat in the shade of an old oak tree.

Wes headed to the river a hundred feet below our camp to fish. Ben entered the woods to trap game. I walked ahead along a trail until it forked. One way led to the water; the other rose in a gentle ascent. Never liking to lose altitude on a hike, I decided to walk up.

The path ended in a meadow, where I moved through tall grasses until I reached a place where a basin far below opened before me like welcoming arms. A stream meandered through its center. This must be our valley. Even without signs of people, I knew we were close. Before rushing back to Wes and Ben to tell them the news, I collected a bunch of blackberries and greens.

Wes started a fire and prepared to cook the fish he caught. Ben sat across from him resting when I entered the camp.

"I think we are almost home," I said. "From the top of a hill, the valley widens, and the river wanders back and forth. It must be our valley."

"Did you see the village?" Wes asked.

"No, but I think we are close. I do."

"I can't wait to eat Father's special chicken and roasted mushrooms," Ben said.

"What's that noise?" I interrupted. We all turned in the direction of what sounded like voices. Two people argued.

"Listen, Mac, when you meet someone for the first time each day, you start with hello. When someone says hello to you, you say hello back." Spoken with an edge suggesting frustration.

"No. You listen, Stan." The words were spoken loudly and pointed in return. "I'll say hello or not. That's up to me. I just didn't feel like saying it to you."

"Mac, that's not right," Stan said with forced but measured calm. "By not returning my hello, you dishonor me, and I don't like that. Makes me frown, like I've been told to get lost."

"Okay, why should I honor you?" Mac asked, his ire still evident.

"Because everyone deserves to be honored," Stan responded, sounding less irritated.

Oblivious to their surroundings, the two men continued, at times in a most uncivilized manner. Ben, Wes, and I glanced back and forth at one another. Our brows wrinkled. The voices got louder as the two men came closer.

"Well, what have we here?" Mac said as he entered our camp.

"Hello," Stan immediately interrupted Mac, staring at him with pursed lips and narrowed eyes. "How are all of you this fine evening? My name is Stan, and this is Mac."

Before any of us answered, they began to argue again.

"What do you mean everyone deserves honor?" Mac said.

"Pardon my friend's rudeness," Stan said to us, then glared at Mac again. "Yes, Mac, everyone deserves to be respected and honored, and a wonderful way to honor someone is to greet them properly. A simple hello is sufficient."

"I don't like most people," Mac shot back at Stan. "Why should I respect and honor them? They scrutinize me with untrusting eyes, dress different than me, act funny, and part their hair on the wrong side. Why should I honor them?"

"Why are you so judgmental?" Stan said. "Do you really know what people are thinking?" A spark lit up his eyes, "Tell me, do you like to be honored?"

"Of course," Mac said. "Everyone likes to be honored. I deserve honor."

"Simply say hello when you meet someone," Stan said. "That way, you show honor, and by honoring someone, you honor yourself. If you are too critical of a person and neglect to say hello, you miss the opportunity to demonstrate your regard for that person."

Stan turned to us; I think he was looking for some sign of support. Not finding any, he turned away and faced Mac again.

"Guess what, Mac? Don't say hello. You won't be honored," Stan went on. "You see, all people have a spark of worthiness in them." Stan pointed his finger at Mac. "Show respect for that, regardless of any other feelings you may have."

I looked at Wes and Ben and spoke softly. "Do we invite them to stay?"

"Actually, the argument is interesting," Ben whispered back.

"Reminds me of how angry Father gets when I don't greet him properly first thing," I said. "Maybe Stan's points explain Father's reaction to me when I fail to say good morning to him when we meet at breakfast."

"What if they argue like this all night?" Wes added. "Nobody will get any sleep. I think Stan has made his point, though. Not that we should take sides."

"Of course, I made my point," Stan said, having overheard Wes. "I've been arguing my point with Mac for days."

"Where do I find a spark of goodness in you?" Mac continued, still with an edge. "I'm not sure that I do."

"I find a spark of it in you," Stan said, his voice soft and kind. "Albeit, a small spark," he added and smiled.

Mac stopped and gazed at Stan.

"That's nice," Mac said and his face relaxed.

"Yes," Stan followed. "Rebuke with kindness, be less judgmental, honor with a friendly smile and kind hello."

"Then, hello," I said interrupting them. "Would you

like to join us? We haven't much, but we would be happy to share."

Stan and Mac sat down by the fire. They explained that they had come from the Village of the Black Dog. "We arrived by ship in the village and passed through it on our way south."

Ben jumped up. "You just came from Black Dog," he shouted. Wes and I leaned in interested to hear more.

"How far are we from Black Dog?" Ben asked. He like me seemed anxious for the answer.

"Two days' walk," Mac said.

"We have some salted, dried lamb and beans that we picked up in the village," Stan said. "We're happy to share.," Stan turned to Mac, who nodded in agreement.

With the knowledge we were so close to home, we hardly slept that night and hastily got going in the morning. *Honor* was a key, and I saw its potential for opening doors by helping to forge relationships.

# THIRTY-SEVEN

# Road to the Village of the Black Dog

HANK

With just a two-day walk away from home, we quickly broke camp in anticipation of reaching our destination. Stan and Mac awoke with us. When Stan greeted Mac with a cheerful hello that went unanswered, they started arguing again.

Stan and Mac wandered off to the south, voices raised and urgent, each trying to make their point understood by the other. We headed north. As we walked, we began to pass houses and fields of wheat, corn, and vegetables. The river widened and slowed. We left the hills and worked our way down to the water, where we found a trail that followed the river.

As the day progressed, we encountered people to whom we nodded and gave a friendly hello, followed by "Nice day," or "How are you doing?" We always got a "Hello to you," and "It is a nice day," or "Just fine" right back. Occasionally, we stopped and asked a question or tried to strike up a conversation. "Are we heading in the correct direction?" we asked, although we knew we were on the right path. I asked one woman, "By any chance have you heard any news about the Falk family, my parents, Matt, Beth, or my Uncle Nate and Aunt Cara, and Uncle Ross and Aunt Annie, or our cousins Jenny and Hannah?"

"Yes, I believe I have," the woman said as she walked along with her sister, daughter, and son. The family stopped and lowered the bundles that dangled between them from poles. "Sad to say, that family had three boys one seventeen years old on his journey-rite, and the other two followed. They never returned. I heard said they may have been lost in a shipwreck, and that according to a survivor of the terrible accident. Poor boys."

Wes and Ben looked at each other. "We were never lost," Ben said, puzzled by the question. "Were we?"

"I don't think we've ever been lost," Wes said. "We may not have known exactly where we were at all times, but we've always been together. So, I always knew where you both were, and you always knew where I was."

"Oh, my, it's you?" the woman shouted, and all three gasped and smiled. "Your parents will be very happy to see you. It's been years, as I understand it, much too long a time to go without seeing your relations. I know you must be anxious to get home, but it's time to eat, and you must be hungry." She paused and stared at us with a measured gaze. "Please come and share our midday meal with us."

She singled me out as the oldest and our leader. "You know, everyone was quite upset when you left and took the younger boys with you. If you'd been my boys, I may have been quite stern with you, but now you're home and safe. So, that'd bring me joy."

As anxious as I was to continue home, I was famished, and I figured that Ben and Wes must be hungry as well.

Ben and I took the poles with the bundles and hoisted them onto our shoulders.

"Thank you for the invitation," I said. Ben and Wes nodded in agreement.

"LAURI," her husband said when we arrived, "who have we here?"

"We found guests," Lauri said as she entered the cabin, a simple structure made of logs and stone with one large room. We helped set the table as pots of soup warmed by the hearth. The aroma of fresh bread filled the room. "You know Matt, Ross, and Nate from the Black Dog Village. These are their lost boys."

Ben shook his head. "Not lost," he whispered to me.

"Go with it, Ben," I urged and smiled as I greeted Lauri's husband.

We accepted the food graciously. We hadn't eaten a meal like this since bidding goodbye to Mica. The people in the village by the Inland Sea were so generous to us. I thought about Mica, and how warm and kind he had been. I missed my friend, Golden Skye. I thought about her every day.

"Boys," Lauri said, causing me to refocus on my current company, "tell us about your adventures. Were you really shipwrecked? How did you survive?"

"Yes, the ship was wrecked in a storm," I responded, and we told them the tale, shamelessly embellishing it.

We would have told many more stories, but we were

anxious to get on with our journey. Ben, Wes, and I thanked our hosts. We offered to help them in any way we could in return for their hospitality, but I sensed that our hosts realized our urgency and pushed us to be on our way. Energized by our visit with Lauri and her family, and with plenty of light left in the day, we decided to travel well into the night.

The Black Dog Inn

We started out walking briskly, almost at a trot. Within an hour, our pace slowed to a comfortable stride. As the sun set, a coolness descended on the valley. With darkness, our progress slowed further. By late evening Ben, we began thinking about stopping. Homes along the road appeared at more frequent intervals as the population density increased. I spotted what appeared to be an inn. A sign hanging above the front door contained a picture of a black dog above and the words "Room and a Meal" below.

Wes stopped. "A room, perhaps with a bed?" he said. "That'd be a change."

"Do you suppose they'd let us stay for free?" I said. I rolled my eyes and shook my head.

"I guess we can ask," Ben said, shrugging his shoulders.

I marched up to the door, opened it, and entered an ample room that contained tables and chairs. The soft din of voices and someone singing gave the place a cheery atmosphere. A large fireplace heated one end of the room. The ceiling was low with exposed rafters, giving it a cozy, warm, den-like ambiance. The scent of smoke from the hearth mixed with the mouthwatering fragrances of food cooking in the kitchen filled the air.

People occupied half the tables, some eating and some drinking and talking. Waiters and waitresses scurried about filling glasses and serving supper. We looked around for the inn's proprietor. As we scanned the room, Ben spied a man sitting alone at a table. His back was to the room. He appeared to be gazing at the hearth, watching the flames dance above the logs they consumed.

"Hank, Wes. Is that who I think it is?" Ben pointed to the man.

The man was powerfully built and wore a leather vest, his shoulders bare. As we approached, I noted that his eyes were closed as if in a trance, palms on his knees, and the only thing moving was his chest as he breathed slowly in and out.

It was Tadjar.

"He must be visiting silence," Ben said, recalling how Tadjar taught them to meditate. "He still looks a little scary, but we know better. Let's go sit at his table. He will be surprised to see us when he finishes listening to what the spirits have to say."

Tadjar finished his meditation and opened his eyes. When he found us sitting at his table, he let out a shriek that caused every head in the room to turn toward him. He leaped from his seat. With one hand he drew his knife; with the other, he grabbed the long stick he always had with him. He assumed a defensive posture, eyes bulging, mouth open, his tongue protruding, ready to do battle.

"Tadjar!" I shouted. "It's just us, Ben, Hank, and Wes. We came to say hello, not to fight."

"Are you ghosts?" Tadjar said as he sheathed his knife and lowered his stick. "I thought you drowned in the shipwreck."

"We survived, and it really is us," I said.

"Then come, eat with me," Tadjar said, with a broad smile on his face.

"We have no money," Wes said.

"Then I will pay. You can sleep in my room on the bed; I prefer the floor. I'm leaving in the morning for the docks at Black Dog Harbor. I hope to find a ship in need of crew. I'll go anywhere. Would you like to join me?"

"We've had our fill of the sea, the lake, and possibly the river," Wes said. "We'll stick to land."

We told Tadjar how we survived the shipwreck and how the dolphins and a whale saved us. He became quiet and sullen when we told him about Paul Arnold. Tadjar knew of several others who were unaccounted for after the storm and presumed lost. We talked well into the night.

Tadjar had shared many stories during the summer evenings when we met at the bow of the ship. He had enticed us with those tales of far-off places, myths, and folk tales of exotic lands we longed to visit.

"Come with me, then," Tadjar would say.

"Temping," I always responded.

Despite the hour, too excited to sleep with the prospect of reaching home the next day, I asked Tadjar to tell us a story. "Make it a legend from your home," I implored.

He paused for a moment. Most of the tavern clientele had retired to their rooms, but the fire in the hearth still glowed. Several patrons overheard us and asked us to join our table. As we all gathered around, Tadjar began his story.

"When I was young," Tadjar said, "each year my father took me to a special place where a large stone jutted out of the ground and pointed to the sky. He would build a fire, and as the sun set, we sat together as he told me this tale. Listen with care and, maybe, someday you may have the good fortune to travel there."

Tadjar made a sweeping gesture with his hands, light from the hearth illuminating his face. Shadows danced behind him as he stared into each of our eyes before he began to speak.

"A long time ago, people lived in the clouds. The earth below was a forbidding place, barren and devoid of life. It didn't matter to the people in the clouds because they were happy and content, a proud people, prosperous, with plenty of food, water, and strong warm homes.

"The leader of their community, Arjun, had many sons but no daughters. He longed for a daughter. His wife finally gave birth to a girl, and they named her Bala. All the people rejoiced. Bala grew to be a fine young woman. But, unlike the other young women of their village, she became spoiled without shame from the indulgences she received as Arjun's only daughter.

Bala learned to crave attention. When she turned fourteen years old, she refused to eat. The result provided her desired effect. Everyone encouraged her to take sustenance and lavished attention on her. They offered her all kinds of good things: berries, fish, and corn, but she would not open her mouth to take a single bite. The people worried that Bala would starve, and they began to cry. Tears fell from the clouds as rain onto the barren earth below, forming the lakes, great seas, rivers, and streams.

"Bala became weary of all the crying and started to feed herself. Once she started eating, however, she would not stop. She ate the fish, bear, and deer meat. She ate the berries and corn. At first, the people celebrated their leader's daughter, but Bala ate and ate without regard to others's needs. It became clear to the people that Bala endangered their provisions, and they might starve. They pleaded with Arjun to make his daughter behave. Arjun spoke to Bala, but she would not listen.

"Arjun loved Bala, but he also had an obligation to protect his extended family, the community, the people in his village. After much thought and consultation with his wife, he convened his counsel of men and women.

"'Scour the land. Gather salmon, trout, and all kinds of fish roe, pinecones, berries, vegetable seeds, grains, birds, and young animals, and put them in a sack.'

"When they returned with what Arjun requested, he took the sack to his daughter.

"'Bala,' Arjun said, 'you must leave the clouds. You threaten the existence of our people if you continue to consume all our provisions. Pass through the hole in the clouds. Go down to the earth, scatter the salmon and trout roe in the sea and lakes, streams, and rivers. Cast seeds about the land, release the birds, and let the young animals roam. You will live in that place, find happiness, and hopefully learn that you are a small part of something much larger than yourself.'

"Bala took the sack, descended through the hole in the clouds to the earth, and did as her father asked. She placed a great rock on the site where she landed and pressed it firmly into the ground so that it would not move, and she would always be able to find the hole in the clouds from where she came.

"Many years passed, and the earth grew green and rich with the bounty that Bala had brought with her. The waters ran thick with salmon and trout and all the other species of fish. All kinds of vegetation grew in the forests, and deer and bears roamed free. Even the coyote, wolf, and mountain lion flourished. Each year, Bala, now a full-grown woman, would return to where she first alit, looked skyward, and call to her father.

"'Father, Father, this world is beautiful. I have not known hunger; I have shelter. I am in awe of what I have, but I am lonely. I need a companion. Please lower a rope so that I might climb back through the hole in the clouds and rejoin my people. I am so lonely.'

"Arjun heard his daughter, and, like any father, he longed to be with her, but the people feared Bala and begged the leader not to let her return.

"Arjun secretly decided to help Bala. He found a man named Tal, who, as a young boy, loved Bala. His heart was broken after Arjun made her leave the clouds. When asked if he would like to join her on earth, Tal gladly consented.

"Arjun transformed Tal into an eagle and sent him

through the hole in the clouds to join his daughter. The eagle descended onto the rock that marked the spot where Bala had landed years before and turned back into a man. Tal became Bala's husband, and their children became the earth's first people from whom all people stem.

"When Bala left the clouds, the people were forever saddened because happiness escaped with her. From time to time, the people cried, as people do, and thereby replenished the seas with their tears. In winter, the cloud people swept the dust from their homes and thus produced the snow.

"My father always ended the story with the same words, 'This is the rock where Bala landed, and this is where we come each year to tell our tale.'"

"Tadjar, where is that rock?" Ben asked. "I want to go there."

"Far, far from here. It has been many years since I returned." Tadjar smiled. "Across many seas."

The bed in Tadjar's room was small, so we drew lots. The winner would get to sleep on it. In the end, Tadjar, Ben, and Wes slept on the floor. I enjoyed the soft straw mattress, sheets, pillow, and blanket.

Before I fell asleep, I thought about Tadjar's story. Awe, a thing that Bala felt, required experience but was a hard concept to grasp. Perhaps awe was an emotion precipitated by something so grand that it took her breath away, and made her step back, as she pondered all that was around her. She realized she was only a small piece of something much larger, like the mountains, the waterfall, the ocean, the moon, and the stars. Such awe made me feel humble. *Awe* should be the sixteenth key.

In the morning, Tadjar treated us to breakfast, a thick porridge with butter and brown sugar. We left the Black

Dog Inn just as the sun fully appeared over the Eastern Mountains.

"Come join me," Tadjar repeated.

"Tempting," I responded. But I made up my mind: I was going home.

# THIRTY-EIGHT

# Home

HANK

Tadjar, Ben, Wes, and I strolled along the path and continued to greet everyone we passed, honoring the people of Black Dog. The scenery became more familiar, the road and the river beside it, but the village still lay farther to the north. We walked up the west bank and located the ferryman, Mr. Sam, who transported us across the river. He didn't recognize us, and we needed to introduce ourselves.

"Welcome back," Mr. Sam said. "I must admit, rumor had it you drowned in a shipwreck. This ride is on me. Our village has grown into a town. There are many new people, more homes, and our dock has grown into a port."

As we approached the outskirts of the village, tears began to form in my eyes, happy tears. We invited Tadjar to meet our family. He declined, needing to go to the dock to discover what opportunities awaited him. Once that was done, he promised to visit before he departed.

On the hillside, sheep grazed. We headed there first. Someone must be tending them, I hoped with Oscar. I imagined his big black tail wagging expectantly and wondered if Jenny would be the one guarding the sheep with him.

As we approached the pasture from below, I recognized our flock, each sheep marked with indigo dye. We froze for a moment as we surveyed the scene. Suddenly, Oscar's head popped up from the tall grass. He leaped in the air and started running toward us. A tall, thin girl jumped up close to where Oscar lounged.

"Oscar! That'll do!" she shouted. Oscar stopped, looked back, turned, and bounded toward us.

*That must be our cousin Jenny.*

She grimaced, no doubt annoyed at Oscar's uncharacteristic behavior.

I figured that she didn't recognize us and wondered what piqued Oscar's interest to cause him to disobey her. Oscar reached Ben first, wagging his tail and moaning with pure delight. He ran to Wes next, then to me, and back to Ben. He shook, panting, as he rubbed against each of us.

"Oscar!" Jenny shouted, a sharp edge to her voice. "That'll do!"

Oscar glanced back at Jenny and took off in her direction with equal exuberance. Jenny watched us approach. Oscar reached her, leaped in the air, and headed back to us, where he spun in place and continued to rub against each of us in turn. Jenny approached us slowly, carrying her crook. She appeared quite annoyed, ready to reprimand us for disturbing her peace.

"Easy boy, you'll make yourself dizzy," I said as I scratched Oscar's neck. "Who's this you're with?"

"I'm Jenny, daughter of Ross and Annie Falk," Jenny fired back.

We stopped fussing over Oscar and stared. I had

already surmised it must be Jenny, but she looked so different. She was twice as tall as I remembered her. Her long, dark hair, tied in a single braid, fell halfway down her back. Her fierce eyes pierced us as she stood erect and bold, not ready to stand down to three strapping boys with their long, unruly mops and facial hair. She appeared on the verge of striking us with her crook if necessary to defend her flock.

"And who said you could take over our job, with our dog?" Ben said, feigning annoyance as he stepped into her space.

"He's not your dog," Jenny said, defiance permeating every word, standing her ground, toe-to-toe with Ben. "He's mine and Hannah's, my mother's, and father's dog."

*Couldn't she see that we had a certain amount of familiarity with her dog?*

"How does Oscar know you?" she demanded.

"We're your cousins," I said and laughed. "I'm Hank." I put my arm on my brother's shoulder. "This is Ben." I pointed to Wes. "That's Wes."

Jenny's eyes widened as she stared at us, then she burst into tears. "I didn't recognize you with the beards and long hair," she said. "You're so tall. We thought you drowned in a shipwreck. I thought I'd never see you again. I think about you every day."

She hugged each of us in turn, then hugged us again, too excited to talk. She grabbed Ben's red beard, scrawny as it was, and gave it a tug.

"Let's get these sheep home," Wes suggested. "We'll help put them in their pens, say hello to your parents, and then head to our homes."

We recounted stories about our adventures all the way home. Jenny had a thousand questions.

"How did you cross the mountains? Did you find the keys? Did you have to deal with bears? Did you almost drown in the shipwreck?" Jenny stopped talking and turned her attention to Wes. "Oh, Wes, your parents have a surprise for you." A broad smile spread across her face.

When we got to Jenny's house, she ran to Uncle Ross and Aunt Annie.

"Look what I found," Jenny shouted.

Uncle Ross and Aunt Annie appeared puzzled at first, then ran to us with hugs and kisses.

"I'm so grateful you're alive and well," Aunt Annie kept repeating. Hannah stood by Uncle Ross. She wore a wary grimace, unable to speak as she devoured us with her eyes.

"Wes almost got eaten by a mountain lion," Jenny blurted. "And Hank got stuck on a cliff in the snow." We wanted to share the details of our journey, but Aunt Annie stopped us before we got started.

"You better head on home. Your parents need to see you. Now that we know you're alive, Grammie will probably put you all back on the bad list," Aunt Annie said and laughed.

"Grammie put me on the bad list for a time," Jenny said with pride. "I've been off for a while though."

We found Wes's mother and father in their cabin. They met us with the same outpouring of love. Aunt Cara and Uncle Nate grabbed Wes and wouldn't let him go.

"You shouldn't have snuck off the way you did," Aunt Cara scolded.

"What if I promise never to do anything like that again? Can you forgive me?" Wes asked.

"Really," Uncle Nate responded. He looked deep into Wes's eyes. I thought he was angry, but, instead, a tear formed at the corner of his eye, and he hugged Wes again. "We're just very happy you are home in one piece."

"That must be the surprise Jenny warned me about," Wes said as he looked past his mother into the bedroom.

"Yes, you have a new little brother. We call him Stu," Uncle Nate said.

BEN and I found Father and Mother in the vegetable patch, their backs to us when we arrived. We approached quietly, hoping to surprise them.

"Hey," I called as we neared, "need a hand with that?"

They stood simultaneously and turned in our direction. With their mouths wide open, they hesitated for a long second without saying anything, then ran toward us with tears streaming down their faces. We grinned with pride for what we had accomplished, able to leave home and return safely. I was happy to be back where love was unconditional and freely given, even if we caused so much anxiety.

"Do you realize how selfish it was to take Ben and Wes with you?" Mother said and hugged me. "Is Wes all right?" she asked.

"We left him with Aunt Cara and Uncle Nate," Ben said.

Mother gave me a squeeze and whispered in my ear. "Was my letter helpful?"

"Very," I whispered back. Father pulled Ben and me together and wrapped his arms around us. Mother finally stepped back to survey me and Ben.

"You're so tall," she said as she squinted at us. "Way too

skinny and in desperate need of baths. My nose detected your presence before I saw you. The beards must go, and you both need a haircut."

I asked Father to forgive my behavior before we left. He just smiled and continued to beam with pride. "You need to meet with the Elders. Did you return with the keys?" he asked.

"Yes, sir," I said. I wasn't sure if Mother told him about the wooden box and her poem containing clues. I left that discussion for another time.

Ben ran to his room to change into knee pants, but nothing fit. I still had my red bandanna. I took it out of my back pocket; it was tattered, dirty, and worn. I found a small square basket and placed it inside with my firestone and the arrowhead Golden Skye gave me. I carefully set the container underneath my bed. I was happy to be home, but, as I lay on my bed, I thought about the Village by the Great Inland Sea and Golden Sky and wondered if I would ever return.

The red bandanna, firestone, and arrowhead

ONE WEEK after we arrived home, we stood in the meeting hall in front of eight Elders, who represented the original families, and their leader, Elder Jaq, who sat at the center.

"Well, we are pleased you three made it back," Elder Jaq began. "Although Hank was to travel alone, we found no harm in the three of you sharing the experience. It did, however, generate a bit of debate. You've shared stories around the village. I am impressed by what I've heard, but we have some questions about some of them. Amazing how lucky you were." Elder Jaq rolled her eyes. "Now, tell us, did you find the keys?"

I took out my logbook, and for the next several hours, we told the Elders about each of the fifteen keys we found, where, and how we discovered them. I told them about Messyman and his lack of order; Tadjar and silence; Igwasu, patience and compassion; Have-little, Too-much, and Enough, and simplicity. Wes told them about the little man's mushrooms and truth, faith, and trust, and his struggle with enthusiasm before we traveled on the ship. Ben talked about his experience in the shipwreck and humility and getting lost in the cave because he wasn't patient. I told them about Mac and Stan and honor, Ned and equanimity, and about Mica and generosity. Ben spoke to them about Ma and Sonny and how trust saved the day. We all discussed Happiness and his tree home, but we talked mostly about how grateful we were to be back in the Valley of the Black Dog.

Ben whispered to Wes, "Hank tried to explain it, but I still don't understand how these keys open doors?"

Elder Jaq overheard Ben and immediately addressed him.

"Ben," she said. "Each key is a virtue. Live by them, apply them. You will be a better person. I promise you, doors will open."

Elder Jaq looked at the four Elders to her right, and then she looked at the four Elders to her left. They all nodded.

"Welcome home," the Elders said in unison, stood together, and clapped.

# Author's Note

When I started studying Mussar, "Jewish mindfulness," I was immediately struck by two elements that made the process very appealing. First, the values I explored were universal, and second, the application was practical. I've asked myself, is religion relevant in our modern society? Aren't religions based on collections of myths created by our ancestors to explain unanswerable questions about why and how? Science has done well with how, but I don't think we will ever get at why.

The lessons passed from generation to generation in the form of religion, I believe, are meant to teach us how to survive in harmony with our fellow beings and give purpose to our own existence. I reject the idea that the most important aspect of religion is ritual, that is, how to pray, to whom to pray, who can intercede between people and God, or that praying should bring one material benefit. Common rituals help to identify the group to which one belongs, and that is good for the community, but it isn't the real essence of religion. I believe the essential core of religion is to teach people how to best get along, how to lead an ethical life, how to find happiness and contentment.

Mussar is about ethics. It is about teaching one how to be a better person. Although Mussar may teach ethics from a Jewish perspective, the values studied are not unique to Judaism. They are broadly espoused by all religions, Judaism, Buddhism, Christianity, Islam, and Hinduism, to name a few. Ignore the gods and prophets, look at what religions teach. Love your neighbor as you would love yourself; do unto others as you would have done unto you. Show humility, be patient, practice generosity, value simplicity, maintain order, express gratitude and compassion, find peace. Strive to be a better person.

Mussar is an ancient Jewish practice that evolved from traditional thinking, but in the past, was a personal and private study. Mussar literally means moral conduct instruction or discipline. In the mid-1800s in Lithuania, to bring greater relevance into religion, *Rabbi Israel Lipkin Salanter* (1819-1883) reconstructed the study of Mussar.

Mussar subsequently changed from a personal endeavor to become a popular social and spiritual practice. Schools sprang up, and the study flourished until the Holocaust, when many Mussar masters were murdered; however, those who survived founded schools in Israel and elsewhere.

As a result, Mussar has become a popular practice in the United States, not just among Orthodox Jews, from whom Mussar sprang, but across the spectrum of Jewish practice, and subsequently throughout the country.

Pre-pandemic, schools instituted Character Days, time set aside to study the ethical virtues of mindfulness/Mussar.

The practice of Mussar involves study, discussion, implementation, and reflection. The study of individual values is well defined from the Jewish perspective; resources include Alan Morinis's book *Everyday Holiness*, and Greg Marcus's book *The Spiritual Practice of Good Actions*, from which I derived much of what I used to structure what I have presented in this story.

Before I retired from my regular job, I accepted an invitation to head up the adult education committee at my Temple. It was there that I was introduced to Mussar by one of the committee members. We brought in an outside speaker to introduce the concept to the congregation, then got together a group interested in participating in the process. At our monthly meetings, we discuss a virtue, its significance, and the consequences of practicing too much or too little of it. We feel it's very important to explore how we personally apply the virtue to our everyday experience. This is how we bring the study into mindfulness. We ask ourselves: How will we use what we have learned? How will we make ourselves mindful, so we opt for the best behavior in the appropriate context?

Initially, study is carried out individually, followed by a group discussion at our monthly meetings. Implementation involves being mindful of one's own strengths and deficiencies. To gain that knowledge, we encourage self-assessment. Sit back at the end of each day and ask, "How did I do?" One is encouraged to keep a diary in which one records these observations. For me, a way to gain a more meaningful understanding of the virtues involves creating stories that illustrate them.

I further thought it would be fun to make the stories fantastical with my grandchildren as characters. I hoped that this might easily engage them in the intended instruction. My hope was for them to listen, learn, and talk about the ethical lessons presented in a simple, straightforward format to which they might relate. They dubbed these stories life lessons.

I have presented these stories in *Fifteen Keys*. Please enjoy and share.

*~Pete*

The following chapters were adapted from previously published short stories, the rights and permissions all of which belong to Peter J Barbour:

9: Barbour, P.J, "Messyman," short-story.me, 2016
10: Barbour, P.J, "Simplicity," short-story.me, 2016
13: Barbour, P.J, "The Almost Endless Summer," storystar.com, 2017
14: Barbour, P.J, "Enthusiasm," short-story.me, 2016
15: Barbour, P.J, "Silence," short-story.me, 2016
16: Barbour, P.J, "Shipwrecked at Sea," short-story.me, 2017
20: Barbour, P.J, "The Fairy Ring," short-story.me, 2017
22: Barbour, P.J, "A Man Called Happiness," short-story.me, 2017
23: Barbour, P.J, "Out on a Ledge," short-story,me, 2017
24: Barbour, P.J, "How to Brighten the Night," short-Story.me, 2015
37: Barbour, P.J, "Big Rock," Raconteur 1: 9-13, 11/93.

# Bibliography


1. Marcus, Greg, Ph.D., *The Spiritual Practice of Good Actions: Finding Balance Through the Soul Traits of Mussar*, Llewellyn Publications, Woodbury, MN (2016).
2. Morinis, Alan, *Climbing Jacob's Ladder: One Man's Rediscovery of a Jewish Spiritual Tradition*, Broadway Books, (2002).
3. Morinis, Alan, *Everyday Holiness: The Jewish Spiritual Path of Mussar*, Trumpeter, Boston and London, (2008).
4. Thompson, Stith, *Tales of the North American Indians*, Selected and annotated by Stith Thompson, Indiana University Press, Bloomington, IN, (1966).

# Acknowledgements

I'd like to acknowledge Barbara Barbour, my wife, without whom I would not have been able to complete this project, for her support and encouragement, for tirelessly reading and discussing each chapter as I worked through them. Her photographs provided inspiration for many of the illustrations that appear in the book.

I'd also like to give a thank you to my sister, Nancy Barbour, who provided feedback to the stories depicted here. Thank you to the core of my young test audience, my grandchildren, Justin, Jake, Elan, Etta and Quynh, A.K.A. Hank, Ben, Wes, Jenny, and Hannah, who endured listening to the chapters as I produced them, and who gave me valuable feedback.

I'm indebted to the members of Bethlehem Writers Group whose critiques of each chapter were invaluable, including Carol L. Wright, Marianne H. Donley, Dianna Sinovic, Dan Krippene, Christopher D. Ochs, A. E. Decker, Janet Robertson, Ralph Hieb, Debra H. Goldstein, Paula

Gail Benson, Jeff Baird, Jerome W. McFadden, Russ Uhler, and Diane Sismour.

I'd especially, like to recognize Carol L. Wright and Marianne H. Donley for providing their skills for design of the book and its cover, and to Dianna Sinovic who edited the book.

A special thanks to members of Synagogue Keneseth Israel, Allentown, PA, including Rob Cohen who introduced me to Mussar and the core participants in our monthly discussions: Rob and Jane Cohen, Art and Barbara Hoffman, Barry Cohen, Bob and Laura Black, Sam Bub, Lynda Pollack, and Barbara Barbour.

Finally, I'd like to express gratitude to Alan Morinis, author of *Everyday Holiness*, and Greg Marcus, author of *The Spiritual Practice of Good Intentions*, for providing me, through their wonderful books, a road map and inspiring me with their discussions of Mussar.

# About the Author

Photograph by
Barbara Barbour

Neurologist **Peter J Barbour,** M.D., retired his reflex hammer to become a full-time writer and illustrator. His works include a memoir, *Loose Ends*, three illustrated children's books: *Gus at Work, Oscar and Gus,* and *Tanya and the Baby Elephant*, and over forty short stories that have appeared in e-journals and magazines. One of them, "The Fate of Dicky Paponovitch," earned him Raconteur of the Month from Susan Carol Publishing Company. He belongs to the Bethlehem Writers Group, LLC, and the Society of Children's Book Writers and Illustrators.

He lives in Oregon with his photographer wife. They enjoy traveling and the outdoors. He is actively involved in Mussar, an ancient study of Jewish ethics, virtues, and mindfulness leading to character development. He participates in the process as a group facilitator and brings Mussar's timeless wisdom to the writing of Fifteen Keys.

For more information:
https://www.petebarbour.com/

# Also by Peter J Barbour

Loose Ends

Heartbreak can bring families together or tear
them apart.

Oscar and Gus

**Oscar and Gus**

Gus was a good host until Oscar decided to sleep
in Gus's bed.

Gus at Work

Gus is a soft coated wheaten terrier who would
rather play than work. Never-the-less, he always
tries his best even though he wasn't the best.

Tayna and the Baby Elephant

Tanya and the
Baby Elephant

written and illustrated by

Peter J Barbour

Wouldn't it be great to have a baby elephant as a
pet, but baby elephants may miss their mothers
and don't stay babies forever.